According to The Daily Mail

According to The Daily Mail

Laurence Simpson

Cover design by Andy Dymock

Matador
9 Priory Business Park,
Wistow Road, Kibworth Beauchamp,
Leicestershire. LE8 0RX
Tel: 0116 279 2299
Email: books@troubador.co.uk
Web: www.troubador.co.uk/matador
Twitter: @matadorbooks

ISBN   978 1784625 412   Paperback
ISBN   978 1784625 429   Hardback

British Library Cataloguing in Publication Data.
A catalogue record for this book is available from the British Library.

Printed and bound in the UK by TJ International, Padstow, Cornwall
Typeset in Aldine401 BT Roman by Troubador Publishing Ltd, Leicester, UK

Matador is an imprint of Troubador Publishing Ltd

MIX
Paper from
responsible sources
FSC® C013056

For Ruckle, who turned darkness into light.

Acknowledgements

For reasons many and varied, the author would like to thank Alan, Andrew D, Andrew W, Barney, Brian, Elena, Fergus, Gabby, Gerard, Greg, Karen, Leslie, Nick, Phillida, Rob, Simon, Smirnov and Tony.

Thanks also to Ed, without whose input this would be a lesser work, and to Dai, without whose forbearance it might never have been written at all.

Thanks are also extended to Dr Sofia Johansson and to Professor Bob Franklin, for allowing reference to their respective studies of the tabloid media.

The author would also like to thank his Father, whose words still resonate long after he passed away.

Contents

1 | The bloody media

Jonathon swore at the radio for the second time that morning. This outburst was in reaction to an economist prattling on about the ups and downs of a car manufacturer's fortunes, in which he referred to people as 'consumers' and maintained that the car manufacturer was 'suffering'.

Jonathon disliked the way the media habitually called people consumers, for he felt it debased the human condition, reducing people to just the wheels and cogs in companies' profit and loss mechanisms. And anyway, it implied that some people were not consumers, which was nonsense, because everyone consumes stuff to a greater or lesser degree. And they're all people, so why not just call them 'people'?

As for 'suffering', he reasoned, it was tortured political prisoners, war refugees, starving children in Africa and the pitiful, helpless homeless who were suffering, not large corporations who were experiencing a momentary downturn in their profits, the poor lambs.

Crossing to his desk he sought distraction at his computer, where his inbox contained several offers of cheap Viagra and Cialis that had not been automatically marked as junk. Many of them were written in a strange kind of code, using variants as transparent as 'vagria' or 'cialees', in fact anything to get past his spam filter. In the body of these emails there was often a weird series of words designed to further obfuscate the matter, like 'triangular raccoons seldom order wisely in restaurants'. If

Jonathon succumbed to even just a fraction of these offers of erectile jubilation, he would be permanently priapic.

There were also several kind offers from people in Nigeria, promising transfers of several million US dollars in exchange for all his personal details. Occasionally he would entertain himself by stringing one of them along.

'Wow!' he would reply. 'You mean you're really going to give me $8m dollars just because I have the same surname as your deceased client? That's the best news I've had since last week, when someone promised me $10.5m!'

Missing the wind-up, these scammers would assume Jonathon had taken the bait and he would then derive great pleasure from receiving a string of increasingly hysterical messages pointing out that first he must transfer to them some of his own funds before his account could be credited with the millions that were waiting for him. First he would suggest that they could simply deduct the amount they required from the millions available and transfer the balance. This suggestion never went down very well with his kindly benefactors, who each had some sort of procedural reason why first he needed to send them some of his own money in order for them to release the funds. Obligingly, Jonathon would promise to do so very soon and would then happily picture them, mopping their sweaty brows as they checked their bank accounts every five minutes.

Marking as junk all these promises of untold riches, he was left with just a few bona fide messages that were more or less welcome in his inbox. One was from David Strange, his oldest and dearest friend, who wanted to meet up for a drink sometime soon as he had some exciting news to share. Irritatingly, it was signed off 'sent from my iPhone', as so many were. As much as Jonathon would have loved to have an iPhone, he couldn't afford one and as consolation had created an automatic email signature of his own: 'sent from my eight year-old, dusty, clapped out laptop – sorry about the virus'. This always amused him, especially when he sent it to someone for the first time, and when he suspected they might be of a nervous disposition.

Next was a message from his ex-wife, Wendy, who was keen to learn when he might next send her some money. He replied that he was keen to learn when she might give him a good reason, given that she had run off with their marriage guidance counselor, an outcome which had confirmed Jonathon's suspicion that their visits were a waste of time.

Working as a jobbing gardener, Jonathon was not exactly in poverty, but then neither was he rich, or even a bit rich, or even comfortably off. Instead, he just about managed to keep the wolf from the door. Financially, his life was now a far cry from his days as a commissioning editor for a TV station, earning well into six figures before the corporate axe fell and nobody else would touch him. He considered it grossly unfair because all he had been trying to do was improve artistic standards. In so doing, he had rejected an idea for an abysmal reality TV show which then went on to be a phenomenal success for another station. Now aged 46, a part of him wished that he hadn't stuck to his principles, but most of him was glad that he had.

His emails dealt with, he turned to the online news, first from the websites of newspapers which could still justify that description and then to the tawdry offerings of some of the tabloids. Jonathon couldn't help taking a peek at their daily contribution to the world of journalism. It was like passing a car crash. He knew he shouldn't look, but he *had* to look. He couldn't resist suspending disbelief and seeing what drivel they were peddling to the nation.

First was The Sun, which at least was open and honest in its prurient, lascivious take on what mattered to its readers, but whose interminable, excruciating puns could make a grown man groan.

Then came The Daily Star, another red-top, whose masthead once claimed it was 'simply the best, 7 days a week'. 'Simply the worst, any day of the week,' thought Jonathon.

Next was The Daily Express, which modestly asserted that it was 'The world's greatest newspaper.' This always made Jonathon titter, for he considered the Express to mostly contain endless nonsense about the weather, the fate of house prices, things that cause cancer, things that don't cause cancer, and things that used to cause cancer but which scientists have now discovered do not cause cancer. Or vice-versa.

Jonathon was as averse to the idea of contracting cancer as the next man, but he was fortunate to have learned to dismiss the poppycock attributed to red wine; that it either caused it, or helped to ward it off. Otherwise, he would be drinking it only every other day, in accordance with the latest update on the matter.

In the Express, 'longest, hottest summer on record' was as likely to run before the summer had even started as when it was over and there was some kind of proof, and 'icy storms to lash Britain' had a habit of appearing the day after they announced 'time to dust off the barbecue'.

In truth, all the tabloids tended to exaggerate what they obtained from the Met Office, but it was the Express which had truly mastered the art of terrifying people with their estimates of the wind speeds to be expected in forthcoming storms.

'Winds of up to 130mph to batter Britain!!' would scream a headline.

People were usually much safer sticking to one of the quality papers, whose readers would only have to endure winds of 'up to 60mph'.

Having found nothing of import from the world's greatest newspaper, Jonathon turned to the Daily Mail, which was also obsessed with cancer, the weather and house prices, but which Jonathon felt was also the epitome of hypocrisy.

Here was a paper which piously protested against certain types of behaviour yet was itself regularly guilty of the exact same transgressions. Here was a website that proudly claimed to be anti-porn and anti-paedophilia, yet which thought nothing of describing a fourteen year-old girl as 'flaunting her curves', or an eight year-old as a 'leggy blonde'.

Pot. Kettle. Black.

There was always a mountain of mindless trivia about the D-list celebrities who happened to be its current focus of attention. Occasionally one would fall from favour, only to be replaced by another reality TV bimbo who had been snapped by the feral paparazzi 'displaying her curves' as she stumbled out of a nightclub. That phrase, along with 'ample cleavage', 'taut tummy', 'showed off her bikini body' and countless others, could be found not nearly every day, but *every* day.

The fact that some of the Mail's fodder had appeared only in some crass reality TV show, on one or other side of the Atlantic, did not dissuade the writers from fawningly describing them as 'stars'.

Jonathon considered that the word had lost its meaning since the golden days of Hollywood, when it usually carried veracity and when people often had genuine claim to be called a star, be they outstanding actors, musicians, singers, writers, or people who had excelled in other fields.

These days, although there were some notable exceptions, the word had been bandied about so much that a single appearance on Big Brother could guarantee that some talentless nobody would daily receive the epithet 'star', until they crashed and burned a few months later, remembered only for 'a very revealing top'.

So important did the Daily Mail regard the day-to-day activities of these wannabes that they would regularly buy whatever the paparazzi offered up to the news desk and then attempt to construct a story around the images. Such stories could often be summarized as 'woman eats a salad' or 'woman goes shopping' or 'woman wears clothes'.

Jonathon noticed how obvious it was that there was often no actual reporting to speak of, the writers having been nowhere near their subjects, let alone spoken to them. Instead, the hapless hacks, presented with just a bunch of long-lens snaps, were reduced to describing what was already quite evident from the photographs. 'The actress, 25, wore a bright red bandage dress.' 'The stunning blonde model, 22, carried a simple white leather clutch.' 'The star, 28, completed her look with a pair of sunglasses.' And they would constantly have to rely on surmise. 'So-and-so seemed to'; 'so-and-so appeared to'; 'so-and-so looked as if...'

The frequency with which the Mail featured certain women was often directly proportional to the amount of lewdness they had become famous for. If, for example, there had been a homemade video of an American fat-arsed reality show 'actress', in flagrante, leaked onto the internet, then that would guarantee almost constant reporting, including that she had been to a restaurant, or that she had had her nails done, or had talked on her mobile, or had gone to the gym, or had left the gym. Or that she had been seen drinking a skinny latte.

Nothing was too trivial. Nothing was too banal.

Jonathon would sometimes ponder the private lives of the sad hacks who wrote such dross.

'What did you do today mummy?' a young daughter might enquire.

'I wrote an article about a famous actress darling!' replies Jenny Carntwrite.

'Wow' says the daughter, impressed, 'who was it?'

'Oh you won't have heard of her dear.'

'But you said she was famous!'

'Well, she's a little bit famous, but not for anything you would know about.'

'Ok, what did you write about?' asks the daughter.

'She had a wardrobe malfunction,' explains the hack, 'I saw a picture of her which showed her bra-strap poking out from under her blouse.'

'Er, anything else?'

'That was it, really. Oh, and she was seen eating an ice cream.'

Woman with visible bra-strap eats an ice cream. Hold the front page.

Of course, it was easy to write for the Daily Mail, especially for the MailOnline.

First, you typed the name of the model or actress or singer or footballer's wife of whom the paps had provided you with pictures. Then you put 'stuns', 'sizzles', 'wows', 'dazzles', or 'smoulders'. Then you put 'as she', followed by 'flaunts her', 'shows off her', 'flashes her', 'reveals her', 'showcases her', or 'displays her', followed by 'cleavage', 'ample cleavage', 'toned pins', 'bikini body', 'svelte bikini body', 'svelte bikini beach body', 'long legs', 'taut tummy', 'curves', 'pert derriere', or 'incredible post-baby body'.

And wherever possible, you put 'sideboob', or 'underboob'.

MailOnline was also obsessed with baby bumps. So-and-so 'parades her baby bump', 'shows off her baby bump', 'covers up her baby bump', 'conceals her baby bump' or 'proudly displays her baby bump', etc, depending on what the hack decided was going on in the pictures. Of course, it was never any of those things; the women were just pregnant, that's all.

It was no wonder the Mail was the most reviled and ridiculed publication in the country, finding itself the regular target of columnists, the intelligentsia and comic performers, many of whom regularly mocked both its values and the quality of its journalism.

Obligingly, the MailOnline made it possible for readers to post comments on its articles. Jonathon often contributed, posting things like 'Does anyone know where the DM keeps its internet servers? A powerful electro-magnetic pulse would put a welcome end to this mind-numbing drivel'.

In practise, Jonathon would shortly be responsible for using a rather more subtle method of bringing down the website, but not before meddling with its content and humiliating them.

Given the frequency with which they trotted out the same old snippets of titillation, he also wrote 'It's time to play MailOnline Bingo! – it's like ordinary bingo but instead of numbers you cross off these: 'pert derriere', 'bikini body', 'tiny skirt', 'sideboob', 'toned pins', 'wardrobe malfunction', 'proudly displays', 'ample cleavage', 'reveals her curves', 'incredible post-baby body', etc, etc. Fun for all the family and it never takes long to get a full card!'

Encouragingly, other Mail bashers often complimented him on his posts, or 'liked' them, and they posted thousands of belittling comments of their own.

Of course, the use of 'pert derriere', which was one of the Mail's feeble attempts to maintain a middle-class stance, was laughable. The aristocracy say 'arse'. They don't say 'dessert'; they say 'pudding'. And they dab their mouths with a napkin, not a serviette. And they don't say 'cleavage'. They say 'tits'.

Nothing seemed to escape the Mail's preoccupation with ribaldry and sensationalism, and they appeared desperate to inject even the most mundane activities with an air of something from la-la land. When reporting on the air travel of whoever they were infatuated with, these folk had seldom flown anywhere.

Instead, they had 'jetted'.

Simultaneously, their devotion to hum-drum trivia was

staggering, and surely no other publication could ever outshine the startling revelation that once appeared about a former reality show 'actress': 'so-and-so narrowly avoids walking into a puddle during day out in Essex.'

Woman does not step in puddle. Hold the front page.

Jonathon thought much of the media was dangerous. It was harmful to feeble-minded individuals and in turn, it was harmful to society. And it was getting worse. In the fight for peoples' attention, the media had stooped to hacking into the mobile telephones of celebrities, politicians, the royal family, even a murdered child, in the hope of unearthing something they could exclusively 'reveal'.

And it was to reveal what, exactly? It was to reveal the latest kiss-and-tell, that one Big Brother contestant had 'hit out' at another Big Brother contestant and that a premiership footballer had been scoring more off the pitch than on it.

Jonathon felt it was the constant *diet* of drivel that did the harm, which cauterized the emotional health of much of the population and reduced their brains to a misguided mush. A few snippets of sensationalist tosh were unlikely to matter, but there was a daily torrent of abject rubbish served up to the public, for the public had been taught that that is what they desired and, sheep-like, they lapped up the fatuous observations and gorged themselves on the gormless, never-ending tripe.

Jonathon discovered an interesting game he could play with the MailOnline's on-site search engine. If he typed in 'cleavage' or 'derriere' or 'flaunts', the system would find dozens, scores, *hundreds* of stories which had included that word. Once, on typing in 'Kardashian', he was rewarded with 262 pages, each displaying links to 50 'articles'. The 263rd page contained 29 articles. That was 13,129 separate pieces about, or mentioning, a family who first found significant fame through a leaked sex-tape featuring one of its self-obsessed members. Had the search engine gone back further in time, it would have found thousands more.

So poor were some of the pieces, so lacking in depth, so pathetic the subject matter that often there was no byline naming the writer. Instead, they were credited to 'MailOnline Reporter'.

But Jonathon knew that the mental and spiritual health of society was being undermined not by just the Daily Mail, and indeed not by just the tabloids. Weekly and monthly magazines were also playing their part in a never ending dumbing-down process and the constant worshipping of tin-pot celebs who had been snapped by the paps 'nearly falling over' or 'looking worse for wear' as they exited a nightclub, or 'emerged', as they were so often prone to do.

He would sometimes gaze in horrified awe at the sight of the newsstands, heaving as they did with dozens of trite titles, their mastheads mainly in shades of red and lurid pink and at least three of which were devoted to reporting the goings-on in soap operas. And people actually bought and read these magazines to find out about people who were just the products of scriptwriters' imaginations. Whole magazines were reporting on fiction, not fact.

Indeed, now and then, one or other of the tabloids would run as its front page splash headline the news that, in a forthcoming episode of a soap, 'Gary to die in fire' or 'Tom and Madge to split', such was the attention given to people who didn't even exist.

The broadcast media, too, were complicit in compromising much of the nation's ability to appreciate what was truly worthwhile, for although there were many excellent dramas and documentaries; their number was far outweighed by what Jonathon regarded as facile garbage. There were soaps whose 'stars' did little but shout at each other, their faces contorted into ugliness. There were talent shows in which the judges were afforded by the cameras far more screen-time than their contribution could possibly justify, and for which they were paid hundreds of thousands of pounds. There were cookery shows in which the judges were plain nasty to the contestants, occasionally mocking their efforts with an air of 'is that the best you can do?' And there were game shows centred on trivia; shows which often served to illustrate how the superficial media had infiltrated peoples' minds. He could scarcely believe one example he came across.

Host: 'I'm going to give you one of the names in some famous pairs of names; all you have to do is name the other. Ready?'

Contestant: 'Yes.'

Host: 'Anthony and…?'

Contestant: 'Dec.'

Jonathon thought it was bad mind-food and wished it would all go away.

Think.
Think of your eyes.
What they've seen.
What they've taken in.
And think.
Think of your ears.
What they've heard.
What they've taken in.
And now,
Think of your mind.
Why it believes.
What it believes.
Whether it is all yours.

Jonathon was infuriated by much of the media and how he believed it addled people's minds, and he wished he could do something about it.

That morning, he had no idea that he really was going to do something about it, and that he was going to start doing so within the next few days.

Meanwhile, he had promised Mrs. Wilson at number 37 that he would come and mow her lawn and prune her hydrangeas.

After all, bills were bills.

2 | Poor man, rich man

Having assured Mrs. Wilson that he would come back in a couple of weeks, Jonathon returned home to find a man knocking on his front door. Next to him on the ground was a wooden crate.

"Can I help you?"

"Delivery for Mr. Taylor."

"Well, that's me, but I'm not expecting anything," replied Jonathon.

"You didn't order any wine, sir?" asked the man, who Jonathon now noticed was rather smartly dressed for a bloke who was delivering things. He was even wearing a tie.

"No."

"But your name and address is on both the crate and the delivery note, sir."

"I'm sorry but there's obviously been some kind of cock-up," insisted Jonathon.

"Twelve bottles of Chateau La Lagune 1982?" the man further enquired.

Jonathon caught his breath. This was a wine of the kind of quality he could only dream about, settling as he had to for some dodgy offerings from the local supermarket. He couldn't afford one bottle of such a wine, let alone a case. He had to think quickly. Obviously there had been some kind of clerical error, but maybe he could open a bottle of this glorious nectar and enjoy it before the vintner cottoned on.

"And, er, is there anything to pay?" he asked.

The man looked at his notes. "No, the account has been settled."

"Ah yes, now I remember," said Jonathon, barely able to believe what was happening, "silly old me, eh?"

The man gave him a look. He was unaccustomed to delivering such fine wine to such a ghastly little street.

"May I ask for some kind of identification sir?" he said, in an accusatory tone.

"Yes, yes, of course," said Jonathon, fumbling for his wallet and taking out his driving licence, "here you are." He fidgeted, like a schoolboy petrified of being found out about that business in the chemistry lab.

The man examined it and, satisfied, returned it to Jonathon.

"Thank you sir," he said. "I hope you understand, but of course we have to be very careful with such high-value wines."

"Hah! Yes I understand perfectly," said Jonathon, beginning to recover his composure. "And, um, I forgot, how much was it exactly?"

The man looked at his notes again.

"Three thousand six hundred pounds sir," he replied, "for twelve bottles."

Jonathon gulped, twitched, and tried to look nonchalant. "Ah yes, that sounds about right," he said, "honestly, me and my memory eh?"

"Shall I carry it in for you sir?" asked the man.

"Good heavens no," replied Jonathon, who was now keen for this man, who he thought was one of the kindest people he had ever met, to nevertheless leave as soon as possible, "I'm sure you must be very busy."

"As you wish sir," said the man, and he bade farewell.

Jonathon watched him return to his van and watched him drive off. He then watched the van drive all the way to the end of the street and turn off out of sight before he let out a whoop of joy.

"YE-ES!"

Gingerly he picked up the precious wooden crate and then just as gingerly put it down again, having in his excitement to have forgotten to first open the door.

Once inside, he placed it on the kitchen table and gazed at it lovingly, hopelessly smitten like a young boy falling in love at primary school.

But Jonathon was now in a quandary. There he was, with a case of mistakenly and recently delivered very fine wine, and he had a difficult decision to make. Should he address the situation directly and call the vintner? They would know what to do, surely? The question Jonathon was wrestling with was this; given that the wine had been bumping around in the back of a van that day, roughly how long should he wait before opening a bottle?

But of course calling the vintner would be too risky.

Jonathon decided that thirty days would probably be about right, but taking a stout kitchen knife, he prized open the case and opened a bottle after just thirty minutes.

Looking at the clock, he then wondered how he would busy himself while he let it breathe for an hour, but five minutes later he poured himself a glass and took his first sip.

If there is a Heaven, thought Jonathon, then there would surely be an endless supply of this sublime, silken liquid.

But his mobile interrupted his reverie.

Doo-de-doo-doo, doo-de-doo-doo, doo-de-doo-doo-dooooooo trilled his steam-driven Nokia.

"Hello?"

"Hi it's David," said his oldest chum. "Fancy a drink this evening? I've got something rather important to tell you and I think you'll be very interested."

"Er, well," replied Jonathon, "I er…"

"Don't tell me you've got something on?" demanded David, who knew that, these days, Jonathon's pocket precluded him from having much of a social life.

Jonathon looked fondly at the bottle of La Lagune. "Well, I um," he faltered, "I suppose I could pop out for…."

"Excellent, meet me in the pub in ten minutes."

"Ten minutes!!??"

"Yes," said David, "it won't keep." And with that he hung up.

As Jonathon looked at his wine, 'it won't keep' was exactly what he was afraid of but, even though it was a close call, he knew that David, on balance, was probably more important than a bottle of La Lagune '82.

He took one more sip and reached for his jacket.

Then he took one final sip.

And then, just to be on the safe side, he took one final sip.

Jonathon and David had known each other forever, having met at school when they were both aged 13, and when each had found in the other a kind of mental jousting partner and had been trying to determine the winner ever since. But as with all great friendships, there never would be a winner, for the moment one of them saw that he was gaining too much of the upper hand, he would deliberately expose a metaphorical weakness of his own underbelly and allow the other, if not to deliver a coup de grace, at least to get back on level terms. After all, where was the fun in being the victor and bringing the contest to an end? No, the fun was in the banter, the constant mickey-taking and the delicious feeling of turning on its head a statement the other had made, the latter unaware that he had exposed himself to a thrust to which there was no parry.

In Kent, twinned with their Grammar School for Boys there had been a Grammar School for Girls, and David and

Jonathon had frequently found themselves the twin subjects of some lusty girls' affections, or had themselves been the twin admirers of other, different lusty girls. And inevitably, these girls had sometimes been one and the same. Happily, there came to pass no serious challenge to their respective egos and they had escaped their teens with a friendship that grew stronger every year. This was despite David being consistently better at playing pool and Jonathon being consistently better at table football. And it was despite David one day introducing Jonathon to the woman who was later to become his wife and the mother of his children. She was also the woman who, one day, was to become his downfall.

★ ★ ★

It was twenty-five years earlier and Wendy was all Jonathon had ever dreamed of in a girl.

They had met when he was just about to leave university and when she was just starting, which prompted Jonathon to stay on and study for his Master's degree immediately after finishing his Bachelor's, instead of taking time out to goof around for a while.

With raven hair, Wendy had pale, sensitive skin which prevented her from staying in the sun for longer than fifteen minutes but which, to Jonathon, gave her an aura of delicate, vulnerable, infinite feminine appeal. And she had a little-girl voice; a voice which served to disguise her impressive intellect and make a man feel like he was protecting her, when in fact it was usually the men who needed the protection.

"Oh hello," she said when they first met, raising her eyelids to get a better look at him, "I believe you're Jonathon." And then, "what a shame."

"Excuse me?" said Jonathon.

"I was hoping you might have a more interesting name," she continued, mischievously aware of how she was coming across and the effect it was having.

"Well I think that's something you need to take up with my parents," said Jonathon, who was more than a match for that kind of thing, "sadly they didn't consult me before the Christening."

"So what would you have chosen?" Wendy said.

"I think I would have chosen something that was to reflect one of my favourite pastimes in later years," said Jonathon, who was beginning to enjoy himself after being wrong-footed.

"And that would be…?"

"Roger," said Jonathon.

Wendy was preparing a cutting retort when David returned from the bar, drinks in hand.

"Ah, jolly good," he said, "you're getting to know each other."

"Your friend seems to think he's some kind of wit," said Wendy, who still felt she was on the defensive, "do you have any others?"

David chuckled. "Wendy does like a bit of mischief."

"Me too," observed Jonathon.

The university bar was mercifully cheap and the three of them drank themselves silly, their circle expanding and contracting as other students joined them and later left. Wendy eventually mellowed and forgave Jonathon for being called Jonathon and their conversation was lively and far-reaching, each allowing the other the space and the freedom to develop their thoughts and points of view. What had started so awkwardly had become intense fun and they respected each other's minds and political views. David sensed their growing intimacy and ended up disappearing into the night with a feisty callipygian girl who perhaps would have declined his invitation had she been aware of his reputation on the campus.

Jonathon and Wendy were now alone.

"So, what now?" he asked.

Wendy looked at him. Jonathon was no Adonis but his mind more than made up for his unsuitability as arm-candy. And anyway, he certainly wasn't bad looking and he seemed very firm to the touch. Jonathon took the trouble to go to the university gym, not fanatically but enough to keep himself in reasonable shape and to prevent all the beer taking its toll. And at school, he and David had taken a few karate classes and they continued to train occasionally at university, which kept them supple and sinewy. Neither ever tried for a belt but they had each learned enough to get themselves out of trouble a few times in later years. They never actually started a fight, for to do so would be against the ethos of martial arts training, but separately they had to defend themselves on occasion, each time leaving their aggressors wishing they hadn't started anything.

"Well, I suppose we could go somewhere for coffee," said Wendy.

They both knew this was a euphemism and before long they were fumbling at each other's clothes in Jonathon's room, some soft jazz providing harmony with their breathing.

"I want you to lick me," she said, her beautiful soft hair tumbling over the pillow.

"Eh?"

"Down there," sighed Wendy, rolling her eyes.

"Ah yes, yes of course," he said.

'It's dark and lonely work but someone has to do it', thought Jonathon, and he applied himself to his task with enthusiasm and not a little skill, much to Wendy's surprise, for he had been feigning his apparent naivety.

Unfortunately, it was at this moment that she broke wind.

★ ★ ★

Twenty-five years later, wondering what David wanted to talk about, Jonathon rounded the corner at the end of his road and saw the welcoming glow of The Ferret's Knees in the distance. The pub had been named by a playful entrepreneur who had given each of his premises a bizarre name. Jonathon was particularly taken by The Frog's Elbows and The Koala's Armpits, the latter being in Earl's Court, that favourite outpost of the descendants of the supposed criminal classes. The chain further distinguished itself by serving only real hand-drawn ales and having bare floorboards instead of unspeakable swirly carpets. Each also eschewed music and had a separate games room for darts, pool, table football and shove 'apenny.

Nearing The Ferret's Knees, Jonathon noticed a group of youths gathered around a car, each peering through the windows with what he assumed was malicious intent. This kind of thing always made him feel uncomfortable, for although he could handle himself up to a point, he would be no match for a gang of six or so fit youngsters. He paused and considered crossing the road to avoid them but decided to brazen it out and carry on past.

"Oi, who are you looking at?" demanded one of them.

"Yeah, got a problem?" sneered another. He was wearing an innocent looking fluffy bobble-hat, which was an item of headgear that did nothing to detract from his menacing demeanour.

Jonathon decided to employ a diversionary tactic he had used with good effect in the past and he affected a pronounced limp as he continued on his way.

"Silly bastard's crippled," said a third, "let him go."

Jonathon reached the entrance to the pub and couldn't resist winding-up the youths, on the assumption they wouldn't dare follow him in. "Heh, guess what?" he said, "I'm about as crippled as you are intelligent," and he executed a nimble heel-click in mid-air.

After a pause, Bobble Hat realised what he meant.

"You bastard," he said, "we'll be waiting for you."

Slightly unnerved by this, Jonathon turned his back on them and entered the pub, where he found David sitting at a table tucking into a pint, with another ready for his chum. There were also two large whiskies.

"Hi," said Jonathon.

"Glad you could come," said David.

"Well, I wasn't really up to much," replied Jonathon, "cheers, thanks for getting them in."

David looked at his friend as he took a gulp of his pint, followed by a healthy mouthful of his whisky.

"Blimey, what's this?" asked Jonathon, who was used to drinking cooking, blended Scotch.

"The Dalwhinnie," replied David, "I thought we might treat ourselves a bit."

"Well I hope the drinks are on you mate," said Jonathon.

"Actually, yes they are," beamed David, "all of them."

"Crikey, had a spot of luck on the gee-gees?"

The two of them had long observed two unwritten agreements. First, they had decided to never feel obliged to remember the other's birthday, still less to actually buy him a present. Secondly, if either of them ever came into a bit of luck, he would look after the other.

"Sort of," said David, "I've won the bloody lottery! Three days ago. The big one."

Jonathon was mid-sip and he spluttered. "Bloody hell; congratulations."

"Do you know what the chances are?" asked David.

"Many millions to one," replied Jonathon, "perhaps you did something special in a former life."

"I don't recall," said David, "anyway, how was your day; anything unusual from the postman?"

"Well actua…," began Jonathon, and then, "you mischievous sod."

"Yes I thought you'd be pleased," said David, "you do like a nice drop of red."

He reached into his jacket pocket, took out an envelope, placed it on the table and pushed it towards Jonathon, who stared at it.

"What is it?" he asked.

"It's a cheque," said David, "a big one!"

"A big cheque?"

"It's a normal sized cheque but with a lot of zeros," said David, "and it's in my handwriting, and it's payable to you."

Jonathon didn't dare open the envelope.

"Look," said David, "I know how strange this must feel but it's the least I can do; you haven't remembered my birthday for years."

Jonathon chuckled and knew he would be doing exactly the same for David if their situations were reversed. "This is all a bit of a shock," he said, and he drained both his pint and his whiskey.

"I'll get them in again," offered David.

Jonathon remained at the table, his mind free-wheeling as he stared into the middle distance. How much could it be? Five thousand? Ten thousand? A hundred thousand? More? Surely he'd at least be able to treat himself to an iPhone. And maybe he'd be able to replace his old van with a new one. No, hang on, maybe he could give up doing gardening jobs; maybe he could retire and travel the world. Maybe he could visit all the major cities, staying in the best hotels and eating the finest food and drinking the finest wines. Maybe he could…

"Here you go," said David, returning with another round, "has it sunk in yet?" And then he noticed that the envelope remained unopened.

"I didn't dare look," said Jonathon.

"Don't be so silly."

As Jonathon finally reached for the envelope, the calm of the pub was disturbed by a piercing alarm coming from outside. But it was no ordinary alarm; this had an air of something sophisticated; something serious.

"Bugger," said David, "I did wonder if it was wise to drive here this evening."

"So it's yours?" asked Jonathon, who now remembered about the youths who were gathered around a car; a car which he also remembered as being something sleek and exotic.

David jumped up and made for the door.

"No!" said Jonathon. "It could be dangerous," and he recounted his unpleasant experience outside the pub, after which he remarked, "it's only a car."

"Only a car?" David said. "It's a bloody Bentley!"

"Good grief, you didn't waste any time."

"Well, I've always wanted a Bentley," said David, "and when I popped along to the showroom they had just the right colour and everything."

Jonathon lifted the bottom of the curtain and peered out into the street. He could see David's car, its indicator lights flashing brightly as it continued its cacophony, but there was no sign of the gang of youths.

"I think your new toy may have done me a favour," said Jonathon, lowering the curtain, "they've run off."

David pointed his key fob towards the window, pressed a button and deactivated the alarm. "Good," he said, "well done Bertie."

"Bertie?"

"Bertie the Bentley," said David with a wink.

"Good grief," said Jonathon, who was familiar with the kinds of things David had always hankered after, "and what will you call the helicopter?"

"Harry," said David, who had always wanted to fly a helicopter and had in fact already booked his first lesson, "Harry the helicopter. Or maybe Charlie. Charlie the chopper."

"Please," said Jonathon, "enough."

They returned to their drinks, each deep in his own thoughts, with Jonathon's being rather more tangled than those of David, who was now simply picturing the water lapping around his yacht at an exclusive berth in Antibes.

"The yacht will be tricky though," continued David. "Yehudi, Johann…"

"Oh bloody hell; Yogi," offered Jonathon.

"Perfect," said David. "Yogi the yacht," and he pushed the envelope closer towards his friend.

Jonathon drank off the rest of his pint, replaced the glass on the table, took up his whiskey and downed it in one. He had been doing some rough guesswork and had figured that David's cheque might well be for as much as a million pounds. He couldn't contain himself any longer. Picking up the envelope, he tore it open, removed the cheque and stared in disbelief.

"Ten million!"

"It's the least I could do," said David, who was rather enjoying himself, "don't spend it all at once, there's a good chap."

Jonathon's first thought was Mrs. Wilson at number 37. She was expecting him in a fortnight and he couldn't let her down. Well, he wouldn't let her down. And of course he'd do the work for free.

David saw that Jonathon was miles away and at first he gave him the space to think. His friend had just been given a cheque for ten million pounds and he was obviously going through a gamut of emotions. He remembered how he himself had felt a few days earlier when he learned that he had won several times that amount. There was elation, disbelief, the fleeting notion that maybe there *is* a God, and his mind had raced with thoughts of all the possibilities that had suddenly become, well, possible. His own thoughts had turned rapidly to a Bentley, a helicopter and a yacht, but right now he was wondering what Jonathon was dreaming of.

"Well?" he asked eventually. "What are your thoughts?"

"Mrs. Wilson at number 37," replied Jonathon, "she's expecting me in a couple of weeks to mow her lawn and to trim her bush."

"Yeah, yeah, yeah," said David. "I meant how are you going to treat yourself; what are you going to get?"

"I'm going to get the Daily Mail," said Jonathon, deadpan.

"Eh?"

"Never mind."

David suspected that suddenly becoming a multi-millionaire was a shock that Jonathon was finding hard to handle and that his mind was no doubt a jumble of disconnected thoughts, dreams, and wild ideas. "I'll go to the bar," he said, "you obviously need another drink."

"Look, David, you're driving, remember?"

"Just one more round," David told him, "I'll be fine."

While David returned to the bar, Jonathon was quietly planning. He had no doubt that he was going to attack the Daily Mail, but he would have to be scrupulously careful. He would need to find experts in different fields, namely explosives, computers, and internet servers, and the people he hired must never learn his true identity. He would have to pay them in cash, because not only would they insist on it but also he couldn't risk any investigation of his bank account unearthing any large payments to individuals. It was exciting. And it was scary. And it was naughty. But above all, it was funny, and he was smiling inside.

David returned from the bar with another two pints and a further two large whiskeys.

"I thought we'd have The Lagavulin for a change," he said, grinning.

The Lagavulin was a peaty single malt from the island of Islay and was very much an acquired taste. Jonathon presumed David was grinning at the memory of his stag do the week before he married Wendy. There had been a lot of Lagavulin drunk that night, most of it by Jonathon, who had woken up naked on an overnight sleeper to Edinburgh. What larks. David had very nearly been relieved of his best-man duties.

"David," said Jonathon, "I'm a bit short of cash."

"Sure, how much do you need?"

"I think a million should cover it."

"What?!"

"I mean," Jonathon continued, "could I possibly have a million of it in cash instead. Just rip up this cheque and write another for nine million?"

"I can't be bothered," said David, "keep the ten and I'll drop round tomorrow with a million in cash."

"Bloody hell, how much did you win for Christ sake?"

"Never you mind," said David, "what do you need a million in cash for?"

"Never you mind," said Jonathon.

They sat in silence once more, with David picturing himself driving the Bentley to the airport and then piloting his own helicopter to the harbour where he would board his yacht. Meanwhile Jonathon was picturing himself carrying out audacious attacks on those he considered to be the worst offenders in the British media.

"Fancy a curry?" said Jonathon at last.

"Excellent," said David, "let's drive over to the Taj."

Jonathon did some sums involving units of alcohol. "No, you'll have had three pints and three large whiskies," he said. "I'm not letting you drive. Besides, you'd feel pretty bloody stupid if you got caught and banned for a year."

David considered this and thought also of somehow being prevented from getting his pilot's licence. "So what do you suggest?"

"Let's finish these, then walk back to my place and order a takeaway," said Jonathon, "besides, I happen to have rather a nice red waiting for us."

It was like the old days. They drained their glasses and got up to leave. Jonathon, who had earlier also drunk half a bottle of wine, weaved slightly as he negotiated his way out of the pub.

Once in the street, he couldn't resist having a peek at David's new Bentley and he peered through the window at its immaculate leather upholstery and walnut dash. He wasn't much of a car enthusiast but nonetheless he was looking forward to having a go in it, if only in the passenger seat.

"There he is!" shouted an aggressive voice from earlier.

David and Jonathon turned to see four youths walking rapidly towards them and there was no doubting their intentions; they weren't about to share a box of chocolates.

"Fight or flight?" said David.

"Fight," said Jonathon, full of Dutch courage. "I don't want them finding out where I live."

Suddenly Bobble Hat, the largest of the gang, was upon them and he snarled at Jonathon. "I'll fucking teach you to say I'm stupid." He rushed at him but Jonathon sidestepped and hammered him square in the throat with the heel of his hand, leaving him choking and gasping for air as he clutched at Bertie's wing mirror for support. Meanwhile David had left another writhing on the ground clutching his groin and was busy fist-pumping the cheek of another who he held firmly in a headlock. The fourth came up behind Jonathon and grasped him, pinning his arms to his sides. Jonathon rapidly snapped his head back onto the bridge of his nose and whirled round as he loosened his grip, whereupon he delivered a vicious straight-fingered jab to the solar plexus. As the thug doubled-up in pain, Jonathon brought his knee up sharply under his chin and left him needing a visit to the dentist.

David paused his assault on his captive. "Have you had enough yet?"

"Fnnarrghh," came the reply.

David let him go and patted him on the cheek he had previously been punching. "Then run along, there's a good little prat."

The little prat didn't need telling twice and followed the others into the night, all of them clutching their respective injuries and with Bobble Hat still finding it hard to breathe.

Although David and Jonathon had dealt with them without too much trouble, they were not natural or habitual street fighters. Their pulses raced and their nerves buzzed from the adrenalin rush that comes automatically to cornered animals. There was only one thing for it; they decided to return to the pub for another whiskey before going back to Jonathon's place for a takeaway.

This time they each had a large Laphroaig, a cousin of The Lagavulin in that it too was distilled on the island of Islay and in fact was even peatier.

Later, pushing open his front door, Jonathon turned to David. "I wonder; may I offer you a glass of Chateau La Lagune 1982?"

"I thought you'd never ask," said David, nursing the knuckles of his right hand.

"Can I get you something for that?" asked Jonathon.

"Yes," said David, "a glass of Chateau La Lagune 1982."

Jonathon poured the wine and rummaged in a drawer for one of the many leaflets that had dropped through his letterbox. Forty-five minutes later they were tucking into the finest that

The Star of India had to offer, together with a very palatable chilled Auslese, for they agreed one should never drink red wine with Indian food, the taste of each doing nothing to compliment the other. A crisp, slightly sweet white wine, however, was perfect with spicy foods; the flavour of each allowing the other to cut though and be properly appreciated.

After their meal they couldn't resist trying another bottle of La Lagune, just to make sure it was as delicious as the first one. They agreed that it was; all of it. They also agreed that David should kip in the spare room and, drunk as skunks, they retired and passed out.

3 | Military personnel

In the morning, Jonathon's hangover was every bit as bad as hangovers have every right to be and he made a mental note that if he were to be successful in his quest, he must stay sharp. The previous night had been highly enjoyable, despite having to fight off some hoodlums, so it was only to be expected that he had overdone the alcohol. But from now on he was going to have to focus. 'Bloody hell', he thought, as he stumbled out of bed, 'I'm a multi-millionaire.'

He did the decent thing and took a cup of tea up to David, who just growled at him.

"Fancy a full English?" asked Jonathon, making no attempt to lower his voice.

"Are you out of your mind?"

"You'll feel differently in an hour or so," continued Jonathon. "I'll go and get the necessary."

On his way he stopped at the bank and deposited the cheque. The pretty young cashier looked at him wide-eyed through the glass. She had always liked the look of Jonathon, who often came in to deposit his modest earnings as a gardener, and now she wondered whether she dare flout the bank's rule about fraternizing with the customers. Furtively she scribbled something on a piece of paper and passed it to Jonathon, who looked at it, winked at her and put it in in his pocket. "You deserve a spanked bottom," he told her.

"Promises, promises," she winked back.

As he left, the pretty young cashier wondered what the community had done to suddenly become awash with so much money, for it was only the other day she had dealt with a deposit of well over £80m.

At the supermarket, Jonathon picked up eggs, bacon, sausages, black pudding, mushrooms, tomatoes and orange juice. He also selected a freshly baked crusty loaf, made his way to the self-service checkout and scanned the orange juice.

'Do you have your own bag?' asked the machine.

"No," said Jonathon, and he wrestled one of the plastic bags from its holder.

'Please place the item in the bag,' said the machine.

"Really?" he said. "I'd never have thought of that."

He continued scanning the items and placing them in the bag, but the tomatoes failed to register and Jonathon didn't notice the lack of a 'beep'.

'Unexpected item in the bagging area,' said the machine.

"It's not fucking unexpected at all," said Jonathon in a loud voice and to the great surprise of the woman at the adjacent machine, "I distinctly remember choosing them. I was there when it happened you automated idiot!"

Of course, he knew that what the machine was really saying was 'Listen, you light-fingered sod, don't you go thinking, even for a second, that you're going to get away with stealing anything from this fortress of a supermarket.'

'Wrong weight,' continued the machine, at which point an assistant arrived.

Up and down the land, supermarkets had seen an opportunity to increase their profits by installing self-service checkout machines and thus do away with some cashiers' jobs. It hadn't completely backfired, yet, but the inherent complexities of humans interacting with machines and macaroni and milk at the same time meant that the self-service areas had to be constantly watched over by a member of staff; a member of staff who could otherwise be, perhaps, working as a cashier at one of the several unmanned checkouts.

Jonathon's loathing of much of the media was almost matched by his dislike of the power and guile of the supermarkets. They were grinding farmers, especially dairy farmers, into the ground, by forcing them to accept cruelly low prices for their produce. And they were adept at cheating their customers with various 'special offers'. Many of these, on closer examination, proved to be cunningly disguised methods of duping people into spending way more than they needed to.

"Can I help you sir?" asked the assistant.

"Yes," said Jonathon, "you can fetch me an axe."

"I know how you feel," confided the assistant, "we hate them, too," and he proceeded to satisfy the machine's expectation of the correlation between the items scanned and the weight of Jonathon's bag.

He paid and was finally advised 'please take your receipt, change and bag. Thank you for shopping with us.'

As he left, he glanced at the magazine stand. And there they were: 'Soaplife', 'Inside Soap' and 'All about Soap.' He winced and muttered under his breath, "good grief."

Back home, he found David on all fours in the kitchen, dustpan and brush in hand, surrounded by several dozen coffee beans.

"Having fun?" asked Jonathon.

"The bag burst," said David. "I don't think I'm ready to tackle anything domestic just yet."

David was in fact rarely capable of tackling anything domestic. After the death of his parents when he was just six years old he had been raised by his doting grandmother, who did absolutely everything for him. This was perhaps why he remained single, with a succession of girlfriends horrified at how helpless he was. He could scarcely boil an egg with any degree of confidence and most mornings he breakfasted at a workman's café.

Jonathon relieved David of the dustpan and finished sweeping up the rest of the beans, which he briefly rinsed and placed in in the oven for a few minutes to dry.

"How do you want your eggs?"

"Tomorrow morning," said David, who was still in two minds about being confronted by a large fry-up.

"Ok I'll delay it for a while."

"Thanks."

"I er, I banked your cheque on the way to the shops," said Jonathon, trying to sound matter of fact, "you should've seen the girl's face."

"Take my advice," said David, "don't let anyone know you've suddenly become rich."

"Don't worry, I won't."

Jonathon considered this to be good advice, especially since it came from someone who was now probably richer than Croesus' richer brother.

"Go on, tell me how much you won."

"No. Tell me why you need a million in cash."

"No," and then, "maybe one day I will."

Jonathon prepared a cafetierre and after they had benefitted from an invigorating hit of caffeine he turned his attention to cooking up the full Monty, which he served on warm plates. Time and again in cafes and restaurants he had had to complain about being served hot food on a cold plate. What was the *matter* with those people?

David did very well for a man who had been near death and he left just half a slice of toast. "Thanks," he said, putting down his cutlery, "tell me, when do you want that million?"

Jonathon thought for a moment. He wanted to start

executing his plans as soon as possible and there was no telling how soon it might be before he had to start paying people. It surely wouldn't be today, but then, one can never be sure…

"Would today be ok?"

"Sure," said David, slipping on his coat, "I'll be back in an hour or so."

"Give my regards to Bertie," said Jonathon, closing the door behind him. Returning to the kitchen, he grabbed the toast that David had discarded and wolfed it down. Jonathon was passionate about not wasting food, on the grounds that it was offensive to starving children in Africa and elsewhere. How could one explain to people who were desperate for food the disgraceful waste of that which they so craved? In much of the Western world, every year, tens of millions of tons of perfectly good nutrients were either thrown away or simply left to rot in the kitchens of people whose main problems were of the first world kind, like worrying about their online presence or the battery life of their various devices. He determined to himself that, once he had been successful in his immediate ambitions, he would put to philanthropic use a handsome chunk of the wealth that even now was being processed into his bank account.

But first to business.

He went to his computer and reminded himself why he was about to risk going to prison, or worse. Scanning the MailOnline's sidebar of shame, he found no fewer than five headlines which were overtly breast-centric. That day's snippets included 'bares her cleavage', 'shows cleavage', 'displays her cleavage', 'puts her enhanced cleavage on display' and 'flashes her cleavage', each appropriated to a member of the usual collection of models and actresses and singers and WAGs with whom the publication was currently infatuated. There was, of course, absolutely nothing wrong with a nice pair of breasts, of which Jonathon was a keen fan, but for a self-declared 'family newspaper' to steadfastly maintain its pious stance and yet at the same time publish an endless stream of soft-porn was the kind of hypocrisy that made his blood boil.

He was also saddened that people took interest in and actually posted earnest comments about the 'articles' that featured the plethora of sickening, simpering, symbiotic relationships that existed between the tabloids and the collection of talentless totty who would routinely alert the paps to their whereabouts, be they in Dubai, Essex, Chelsea, or 'jetting' into LAX.

'I don't like what she's done to her hair.'

'That dress!'

'I hope they'll be very happy.'

David, meanwhile, had been relieved to find that Bertie the Bentley was unscathed, save for a wonky wing-mirror, and had hopped in and driven off to his bank, where a pretty young cashier fluttered her eyelids and told him that he would have to wait until later that afternoon if he wanted to withdraw a million in cash. "That's a lot of money sir," she said, "we'll have to have it sent over by secure courier."

"That's fine," said David, "I'll come back later," and he went home to study the websites of various yacht-builders on the south coast.

Jonathon sat back in his chair. Deep in thought, he touched his pursed lips with the tips of his forefingers as he wrestled with the magnitude of his undertaking. Importantly, he would have to maintain absolute anonymity and he started to make a mental list of the many things he would need to do. First he would obtain a set of false number plates from a breaker's yard. It made sense to continue to use his old van, but although it wouldn't attract any attention, he couldn't risk it being traced back to him. Also he needed a disguise; something simple and unremarkable that he could both adopt and discard quickly and easily. A moustache and a wig should do it, both of which would be easily obtainable from any good theatrical costumier. He could also wear a pair of glasses with non-corrective lenses. And of course, he could put on one or more of his many accents. A natural mimic, Jonathon could convincingly have been born and raised in any one of several parts of the country.

And then there was all that money. It would be madness to keep it all in one place so he decided to parcel it up into twenty batches of fifty thousand and keep them in different locations. He would keep a few at home, hidden in separate places, a few in left luggage lockers at Heathrow, maybe hand in a couple as lost property and, yes, he could bury a couple in Mrs. Wilson's garden at number 37. Perfect! Jonathon felt he was on a roll. And then it hit him. Who the hell was actually going to carry out the attacks?

His mind dragged itself from one fuzzy idea to another, but feeling dozy now, he decided to go and have a lie down. His breakfast had well and truly landed and his blood was far more interested in extracting fuel than in feeding his brain.

Closing his eyes as he lay on the sofa, he was soon at the limen between wakefulness and sleep and he slowly drifted off to a distant time and place.

The doorbell rang and he went to see who was there. It was Wendy, dressed in rags and pleading for bread and water, a nice sandstone cottage in the Cotswolds and a brand new Range Rover. He promised her he'd have one of his secretaries send them round straightaway. The street behind her was now a deep river along which David sailed, drinking Dom Perignon on the deck of a 100ft yacht which bore the name 'Paddington'. "No," Jonathon shouted after him, "it was Yogi!" Mrs. Wilson followed in a punt, smiling sweetly and pointing at the freshly mown grass which constituted her cardigan and slippers. Propelling her was a pretty young bank cashier wearing a skimpy bikini made of fifty-pound notes which couldn't quite hide her bright pink bottom. And then the paperboy arrived. He was wearing a bobble-hat and he threw a rolled-up copy of The Daily Mail straight at his face. Three other paper boys threw at him other tabloids and several dreadful pink-topped magazines, at which a smug, hairy chested talent show judge gave the thumbs up and said 'that's four yesses!' Arriving by parachute came dozens of soldiers, each blazing away with automatic weapons until all the paper boys were dead and the tabloids and magazines were obliterated and reduced to tiny fragments of paper, on each of which could be seen the words 'poured her assets'.

Again the doorbell rang, but this time Jonathon got up to answer it, basking in the warm glow of his epiphany. Of course, soldiers! Every area of expertise he needed was right there in the forces, albeit he would need to find disaffected and abandoned men; men who had given their all to Queen and Country only to find themselves cast aside in the recent rounds of defence cuts.

He opened the door to find David holding out a plastic bag.

"You mentioned something about a million pounds, sir?"

"Come in you fool."

The two of them sat at his kitchen table for the second time that day and drank more coffee. Jonathon donned a pair of gloves and began preparing wads of fifty thousand pounds.

"Why the gloves?"

"It gives a better grip on the notes," said Jonathon, unconvincingly, "that's why people in banks used to use a rubber thimble."

"Hmm. You're not actually going to count it are you?" asked David, nonplussed.

"God no," said Jonathon, "I'd just like you to keep some of it safe for me."

"Safe from what? Safe from who?"

"From whom," said Jonathon.

"Pedant."

"Listen David, please, just keep fifty grand in the back of Bertie and another fifty somewhere at your place, just in case."

"In case of what?"

"That's just it," said Jonathon, "I have no idea."

"You're scaring me," said David, who was now beginning to question the wisdom of letting his friend have access to so much money, "what are you up to?"

"You'll read about it, but you won't be able to read about it everywhere."

"You're not about to do anything silly are you?"

"Oh yes, yes I am," chuckled Jonathon. "I'm about to do something very silly indeed."

4 | Aldershot

A couple of days later, Jonathon drove down to Aldershot, where he had booked himself into a cheap but apparently comfortable B&B. Half way there he had donned his disguise and fixed false number plates to his van. Then, giving a false name and address at reception, and paying cash in advance, he went up to his room and rested on the bed while he turned over in his mind how he was going to play his hand.

Aldershot was arguably the home of the British army and would be full of pubs in which he might be able, if he was careful, to start to secure the services of the kinds of men he needed; men from the services.

Refreshed from a light nap he crossed to the bathroom and regarded himself in the mirror. His mop of light brown hair was concealed by a long dark curly wig, complimented by a thin moustache of roughly the same colour and a pair of glasses that he didn't need to wear. He didn't much care for how he looked, but it was effective. He certainly didn't look anything like Jonathon Taylor, and he considered himself indebted to Kenneth, who he had thought was a bit overly attentive at the theatrical costumier from where he had bought his disguise.

"And is sir desirous of anything else?" Kenneth had asked with a wink. "Are you sure you don't need one of our rather dashing frockcoats?"

"No thanks, the theatre is supplying all the costumes so all

I need are the wig and the moustache. I think I'll be able to pull it off rather well."

"And which of the Three Musketeers are you playing, sir?"

Jonathon fought hard to remember anything about the story. "Ah yes, d'Artagnan."

"Oh no sir," corrected Kenneth, "d'Artagnan was the young man who went and joined the other three; thus becoming the *fourth* musketeer.

"Silly me," Jonathon said, "I really must get around to reading the script."

"I can read it through with you if you like; I'm not busy this evening," said Kenneth with a twinkle in his eye.

"Thank you but no; perhaps in a couple of months when I'm playing Oscar Wilde," teased Jonathon.

"Oh that would be heaven sir; meanwhile I hope you'll knock 'em dead."

'Well, perhaps not quite that far,' thought Jonathon.

He had researched the pubs in the immediate vicinity of the central barracks in Aldershot and had decided to start at the Crimea Inn. His plan was simply to get chatting with the regulars and see where it led. He tucked two wads of ten thousand pounds into his inside jacket pockets, taking great care to hold them only by the edges, and punched the postcode into his new black iPhone which, so far, was one of the only two things he had bought and into which he had placed a sim card that could not be traced back to him. The other purchase was a white iPhone, to which he had transferred his existing mobile number.

It was only a five minute walk to the pub and when he arrived, the chill of the early evening air had left him feeling relaxed and alert.

He settled into a seat which gave him a view of the entire saloon bar and nursed his pint, which he sipped rather than gulped. The place slowly began to fill up, with the majority of the customers having a military bearing; straight backs, substantial chests, and haircuts which were strictly of the short-back-and-sides-and-plenty-off-the-top variety. And some of the men were still in uniform, which was also a bit of a giveaway.

Before long he was idly chatting with a couple of paratroopers who had joined him at his table and to whom he eventually told one of his favourite stories; the bees joke.

"So these two guys," began Jonathon, "get chatting in the pub and one of them asks 'so what do you do for a living?' 'I'm a beekeeper' says the second one. 'Well stone me, 'I'm a beekeeper too!' Then the first one says 'how many bees have you got?' 'About fifteen thousand,' says the other, 'how many bees have you got?' 'About twenty-five thousand,' says the first. Then the one with twenty-five thousand bees says 'so how do you keep your bees?' The other one says 'well, it's funny you should ask because only the other week I was leafing through The Beekeepers' Gazette when I came across this amazing new hive system. It's all brushed-aluminium casing, computer controlled, and it's got a live read-out of how much honey is being produced at any given moment. Cost me a lot of money but I'm sure it'll be a sound investment. How do you keep your bees?' 'I keep them in a shoebox,' says the first one.

'What? You keep twenty-five thousand bees in a shoebox?'
'Yeah, fuck 'em'."

The soldiers roared and Jonathon sat back, satisfied.

"So what brings you to Aldershot," asked one of them, "you're obviously not from around here."

Jonathon had been using his Birmingham accent; one of the easiest to slip into.

"I'm a freelance journalist and I'm looking for ex-soldiers to interview about the Ministry of Defence laying them off, especially after them returning from a tour of duty. It seems to me a pretty rough deal to risk your life for your country only to be turfed out onto the scrapheap."

"Frank," said one of the men, extending his hand, "and this is Eddie."

"James," said Jonathon, and he shook their hands firmly.

"Yeah you're right," said Eddie, "we know a couple of guys like that and they're seriously pissed off about it."

This was exactly what Jonathon wanted to hear. He needed to find men who had some anger inside them and who could also use some money. "I don't suppose you've got their phone numbers have you?"

"Yeah," said Frank, "we do, but it wouldn't be right just to hand them over to you like that."

"No it wouldn't," said Eddie, "tell you what, give us your number and we'll tell them what you're after and then they can get in touch if they're interested."

Jonathon liked this. It was correct behavior and he admired the principles behind their refusal to mindlessly give out their mates' numbers. He took out his pen and then realised he had no idea what the number was for the black phone, which he'd had only for a day. He had to take it out of his pocket, go to 'settings' and find it.

Frank noticed it was the very latest model. "So they pay you pretty well then James?"

Nothing.

"James?" he repeated. "You do ok then?"

"Eh?" said Jonathon, as he wrote down his number on a beermat. "Oh, yes, I suppose I do ok – here you go."

Eddie took the beermat and tucked it into his shirt pocket. "Cheers, we'll call them later."

"Then the least I can do is get them in," said Jonathon, "what will you have?"

"We're both on the Ringwood," said Frank.

42

While Jonathon was at the bar Frank observed to Eddie that James didn't seem to know his own phone number and didn't even respond to his own name. Eddie thought nothing of it but Frank was sceptical. There was something about James that didn't quite add up.

Jonathon returned with two pints of Ringwood and set them down.

"You're not joining us?" asked Frank.

"I've still got a half left," he said, indicating his glass, "and I want to go easy this evening."

"Why's that?"

"I'm working," said Jonathon, "at least I'm hoping to be."

"Fair enough," said Eddie.

"Tell me," said Jonathon, "what are the names of your two chums?"

"Why do you want to know?" demanded Frank.

"Just so I'll know who they are if either of them calls me."

Eddie thought this was reasonable enough. "One is Brian and the other is Graham. They were both in Afghanistan, twice, and the army got rid of them a few months ago."

"Tell them I'll pay them," said Jonathon, "handsomely," and with that he downed the rest of his pint and rose to leave. "I'm staying at a little B&B not far from here; it would be great to speak to them tonight; maybe even meet up."

"Only Brian is local," said Eddie, "Graham lives in Exeter."

"Cool," said Jonathon, "I don't mind driving down there; nice to meet you."

"You too," said Eddie.

"Yeah," said Frank, unconvinced.

Jonathon stepped outside to find that it was now raining heavily. He half walked and half ran back to his B&B, where he kicked off his shoes and hung up his clothes above a radiator, which was barely warm. It was a typical B&B, equipped with a small television, a bedside radio and a tray with a small white kettle, teabags, and sachets of disgusting instant coffee supplied by a manufacturer which didn't give a damn what they did to the planet in their relentless pursuit of profit. He filled the kettle, flicked the switch, then lay down on the bed and interlaced his fingers across his chest. His mind cast back to the Crimea Inn, and Frank and Eddie. Eddie had seemed okay, but he felt that Frank's attitude towards him had changed during the course of their time together. 'Don't be daft', he assured himself, 'you're imagining it.'

Like most under-powered B&B kettles, his took ages to boil and when it finally clicked off, his plan to make tea was interrupted by his phone ringing. He thought it was the white one, and he was correct. The previous day he had spent a happy half hour attributing a different set of call, text and email alert sounds to each phone. He'd also created a new email address; james451896@hotmail.com. This tickled him; the Daily Mail was first published on the 4th of May, eighteen ninety-six.

"Hi David."

"Jonathon, where are you; what are you up to?"

"I'm in Bournemouth, catching up with an old flame," said Jonathon, plausibly. David knew he used to have a girlfriend from down that way. He remembered her name was Olivia and that she was beautiful, as mad as a box of frogs and that she could talk nineteen to the dozen. In fact he had taken a shine to her himself and still had her phone number.

"Are you behaving yourself?"

"No," said Jonathon, truthfully.

"Good for you."

Just then the black phone starting to ring. This would be tricky.

"David, look, I've got to go," and he abruptly hung up.

"But…," said David.

Jonathon answered the other phone.

"Hello," said Jonathon, in his Birmingham accent.

"Evening, this is Brian, is that James?"

"Speaking," said Jonathon.

"I hear you might want to have a little chat with someone like me," said Brian, "and I hear there might be some money in it."

"There might indeed," said Jonathon, "possibly a lot of money." Without giving too much away, he proceeded to describe the kind of team he needed to put together and the various skill sets they would need to have.

"But Eddie told me you were some kind of journalist."

"I lied."

"This all sounds like it might be something illegal," said Brian, "is it?"

"Very much so," said Jonathon, "have you eaten yet this evening?"

"Sorry James, but I'm not your man," said Brian.

"Twenty thousand pounds," said Jonathon.

"I'm your man," said Brian, "there's a decent Chinese on Grosvenor Road. I'll text you the address. Meet me there in half an hour."

"How will I recognize you?" asked Jonathon.

"I'll be the bloke who looks like he needs twenty grand."

Jonathon decided to lay down again and go over the precautions he was going to need to take. First, he decided that if Brian did turn out to be the kind of man he needed then he wouldn't have to see him ever again after this first meeting. All communication could be via phone, text message and email. Neither would he ever have to meet any of the men that Brian might recruit for the sharp end. So if Brian or any of his buddies got caught, all they would be able to give the police would be an untraceable mobile number and an untraceable email. And of course Brian could be immensely helpful in assisting a police artist put together a photo-fit of a man with long dark curly hair, a dark moustache and glasses. And he'd be able to swear blind that the man who paid him came from Birmingham and was called James. All payments would be made in cash either by mail, using recorded delivery, or by using the dead letter box system that had been used by spies all over the world. If by mail, he would simply get a train to random towns a long way from London, go to the nearest post office and get the next train back. And either way, he would either wear gloves when handling the bundles of cash, or simply hold them by their edges.

What could possibly go wrong?

Jonathon was still comforting himself that he would leave nothing to chance and that he would be diligent in covering his tracks when the black phone made a sound like a train, which signaled the arrival of a text message.

His clothes had barely had time to dry but he put them back on anyway, straightened his moustache, gave his wig a quick comb over and donned the spectacles which he didn't need to wear.

The Chinese wasn't far and thankfully it had stopped raining by the time he again hit the streets of Aldershot. He strode confidently and rehearsed his opening gambit to Brian. On entering the restaurant he saw there was only one table with a lone diner; a large man who had deliberately chosen a table well away from the others so that he might be spared the customers' chatter, and so that they wouldn't be able to hear any details of what promised to be an earnest conversation about something seriously dodgy. He was so busy studying the menu he didn't see Jonathon approach.

"Can I interest you in a quick twenty grand?" asked Jonathon.

Brian looked up from the menu. "James?"

"Yes," said Jonathon, sitting down and signaling for the waiter, "what would you like to drink?"

"I'll have a beer thanks."

The waiter soon arrived.

"Two Tsingtao please," said Jonathon.

"So what's all this about?" asked Brian.

"The media," said Jonathon, "and in particular, at least to begin with, the Daily Mail."

"Vile rag," observed Brian.

"I think we're going to get on rather well," said Jonathon, and he decided to trust this man from the outset. After all, there was no way he would be able to track him down after they had left the restaurant.

Brian, too, sported a moustache, albeit his was genuine and was pretty much the only hair on his head. He looked mean, calculating and vicious. He certainly wasn't the kind of individual anyone would relish being cornered by in a dark alley. It transpired that he had risen to the rank of Captain in the army, had spent a total of eighteen months in Afghanistan fighting the Taliban and had seen three of his mates get blown to smithereens by a roadside bomb not ten metres away from where he stood. Brian himself still had shrapnel buried deep in his left thigh and suffered painful twinges that could wake him from the deepest sleep. He also still suffered the anger and the indignity at being let go by the MOD exactly one month after returning to Britain, shell-shocked and shattered. And he was broke.

They ordered and Jonathon briefly described how he felt about the media; that much of it was worthless tripe and that he had decided to bring the guilty parties to their knees. Brian not only saw his point but had tremendous sympathy with it, and he liked the idea of having a different kind of enemy to fight. "But this won't be easy," he said, "and it'll take me time to assemble a willing team. Remember this is all highly illegal. If anyone gets caught it'll be prison for sure."

"Take as long as you need," said Jonathon, "how many men do you think it'll take to pull this off?"

"A minimum of two," said Brian, "including me."

"There's fifty grand in it for each of you."

"What? And how can I trust you?"

Jonathon reached into his inside jacket pocket, took out a wad of ten thousand pounds and placed it on the table at the precise moment that the waiter arrived with their starters.

"Won Ton soup?"

"Thank you," said Jonathon.

"And the hot and sour is for you sir?" said the waiter, eyeing the money on the table.

"Yes," said Brian coolly, picking up the cash and keeping his eyes on Jonathon, "the hot and sour is for me."

The waiter retreated, satisfied that these two customers were unlikely to do a runner.

"This feels like only ten grand James," said Brian, "you promised twenty."

"We haven't finished talking yet," said Jonathon.

As they ate, he described roughly what he had in mind and Brian listened intently, interjecting only when necessary and with salient points. Jonathon knew instinctively that he had made the right decision to choose men from the military to help him achieve his aims. Career criminals would probably lack the discipline he sought and would surely be less trustworthy.

"But there's one vitally important detail," said Jonathon.

"And what's that?"

"I do not want anyone to get hurt," he continued, "nobody at all; not a soul; not a hair on their heads."

"Fair enough," said Brian, "in fact I'm glad to hear you say that; it's not like the media have been going around killing people."

They finished eating and called for the bill. Jonathon took

out the other wad of ten thousand and lay it on the table. "Your fifty will be on top of this twenty; if you're going to put together a team and oversee the operation, and also be my only point of contact, then I think that's only fair."

Brian thought this was extremely fair; probably the fairest thing he'd ever heard in his life. "And where are you going to get hold of all this money?" he asked. "You're committing to coughing up another hundred grand."

"I've already got the money," said Jonathon. "I'll pay twenty-five upfront to each of you and the rest when the job's done, but only if nobody gets hurt. You can use some of this twenty as a sweetener if you need to."

"Can I trust you?" Brian asked.

"Absolutely; can I trust you?"

"Does the Pope shit in the woods?" said Brian. "Do bears wear funny little hats?"

5 | Team building

The following morning, as Jonathon drove back to London, Brian sat up in bed and drank the cup of tea his wife had brought him, like she did every morning. He hadn't yet told her about the money and wasn't convinced that he should, knowing how she had reacted the time he shoplifted a pair of trainers. Penny had had a very strict upbringing and the thought of being on the wrong side of the law was anathema to her. It had occurred to him that he could just keep the twenty grand and forget all about James and assembling a team of saboteurs, but the lure of an extra fifty thousand pounds had inevitably won the day. After all, he was unemployed and was likely to remain so, and seventy thousand represented a good deal more than he might earn in two whole years. Also James had said there might be even more if the first operation was successful. He wondered how much more, and for doing what.

His mind made up, he leapt out of bed, grabbed his dressing gown, peeled a thousand pounds off the wad of money in his jacket and wandered through to the kitchen, where Penny was preparing breakfast. He placed the cash on the counter next to her. "There you are love; go and buy yourself something nice."

"What's this?" she asked.

"It's a grand," replied Brian proudly, adding with all honesty "and before you ask, I haven't done anything illegal." 'Well, not yet,' he thought to himself.

Penny looked at him. "Really?"

50

"Really."

"You haven't been gambling again have you?"

Why hadn't he thought of that before? He had a history of betting and ever since the army had got rid of him he'd been giving into the temptation at least once a week. She wouldn't be happy about it, but at least it was an easy way out for now.

"You could say that, yes."

Penny pleaded with him. "For God's sake Brian, don't go back to your old ways; I couldn't bear it. Just because you got lucky for once means nothing; nothing at all."

"I promise," said Brian, "now why don't you go into town and treat yourself?"

They ate breakfast and Penny showered and dressed. The sooner she was out of the house the better, thought Brian, for he had some phone calls to make and some people to see.

As soon as she was gone he grabbed his mobile and dialed Terry, who was in a similar position to himself.

"Brian?"

"Yes, I need to talk to you about something and it can't be done over the phone."

"Can't you give me some idea?" asked Terry.

"How would you like to earn a quick fifty grand doing what you do best?"

Within half an hour they were sitting on a park bench, feeding the ducks on some chunks of bread that Brian had brought along.

"And what would I have to do?" asked Terry. "Fifty grand doesn't come easy."

"You would have to blow up a printing press," said Brian, "think you can handle that?"

Brian knew the question was unnecessary. Terry's specialism was anything that went 'bang' that hadn't first come out of the barrel of a weapon. He was an expert with dynamite, Semtex,

C4, TNT, gelignite, Tovex, the lot. As a boy, Terry's favourite time of year was always the fortnight or so that led up to November the 5th, during which he would do anything he could to lay his hands on as many fireworks as possible. But rather than use them as the manufacturers had intended, he habitually dismantled them and reassembled them in any way that took his fancy, using any number of types of containment vessel. It was for this reason that Terry was minus his left earlobe and still bore heavy scars all over the left side of his face and over the entire length of his left arm. He was fortunate not to have also lost a finger or two, or the army would never have accepted him.

"You're kidding me," said Terry, incredulous, "what kind of nutter would want to blow up a printing press?"

"The kind of nutter who'd be prepared to pay you fifty grand," said Brian, "twenty five upfront and twenty five once it's done, provided nobody gets hurt."

He described to Terry the meeting he'd had with a man called James; a man Terry would never have to meet and who Brian might never meet again either. "So, are you up for it?"

"Whose printers is it?"

"The Daily Mail," said Brian.

Terry hooted with laughter. "It's starting to make sense," he said.

"The printing presses are the easy part," Brian continued, "this guy also wants to take down their computers and their internet servers, comprehensively and permanently. He doesn't want them to be able to access a single retrievable byte of data from the very first day they entered the digital age."

"I wouldn't know where to start," said Terry.

"Me neither," said Brian, "but he's happy to pay for it to be done; all we have to do is find someone who can do it. But you haven't answered my question."

"Which was?"

"Are you up for it?"

Terry slumped back on the bench, stretched out his legs, tossed some bread for the ducks and reflected on his life. He too was unemployed and likely to remain so, given his scars. It wasn't enough for potential employers that he was phenomenally bright, skilled and capable; the way he looked put everybody off, although of course they could never admit that it was his appearance that was the barrier to them hiring him. For the same reason, his relationships with women had been few and far between, with most of his experience limited to the kind of brief trysts for which he had to pay. He sighed to himself and concluded that he had nothing to lose and fifty grand to gain.

"Yes, I'll do it," he said at last.

"Good man," said Brian, giving him a thump on the back and a sealed envelope, "here's a grand to cover your expenses."

They agreed their next steps, shook hands and went their separate ways; Terry to research a printing facility and Brian to unearth a pliable computer geek.

Meanwhile Jonathon had driven home, remembering halfway to pull over to the hard shoulder, remove his wig and moustache and place the false plates under a blanket in the back. It wouldn't do for any of his neighbours to see a strange man getting out of his van, still less notice that the plates had changed. Once inside, the enormity of what he was planning made his head start to spin and he went for a lie down on the sofa. Closing his eyes, he calmed his breathing and went over the situation so far. He would give Brian twenty-four hours to get back to him with a progress report and if he failed to get in touch he would call him, or send a text. He remained sure that he could trust him, although he was slightly nervous about delegating so much to him. But then, what choice did he have?

It was imperative that he remain anonymous and well hidden in the background while using others to carry out the attacks. Besides, how could he coordinate this whole damn adventure *and* find and recruit the right people to carry it out? No, he had the money, so why not use it? Bugger; the money. He had been in such a hurry to get down to Aldershot and get the ball rolling that he never got round to hiding the bundles of fifty thousand, most of which were still in his flat. Yes, that's what he would do next. He would carry on hiding them, starting with using the left luggage facilities at Heathrow. He would also board a bus carrying a small lockable briefcase hidden inside a larger bag and upon disembarking he would hand the briefcase to the driver as lost property. Yes, he would do that twice, handing in two dissimilar cases that would be kept safe and sound at the lost property office. He would also visit the left luggage facilities twice, using two different disguises, and pre-pay a month's fee. That would take care of twelve bundles. He now felt a reassuring calm descend and he drifted off to sleep.

When he awoke he rustled up a quick bite to eat and having dulled his hunger he decided to first pay another visit to the theatrical costumier, where he would again tease Kenneth.

Upon arrival, he wandered up and down the racks of costumes, looking for another quick and simple disguise. Eventually, Jonathon having explained that he had just landed the title role in a touring production of Entertaining Mr. Sloane, an excited Kenneth provided him with a black leather waistcoat and a black biker's hat reminiscent of Brando in On the Waterfront.

"There you are sir," he purred, "wear these with your moustache and put on a simple white T-shirt and you'll look just the part!"

"I do believe you're right," said Jonathon, "but I suppose I'd better practice the right kind of walk. I've heard that clenching the buttocks on a coin usually does the trick."

"I'm sure you can mince with the best of them, sir," said Kenneth breathlessly, "I do believe you have the makings of a truly great actor."

"That's very kind. And do you have a reversible jacket of some kind?"

"Goodness me yes; oodles of them."

Jonathon chose one and assured Kenneth that he would very soon be requiring his assistance in helping him to learn his lines in any number of forthcoming productions, at which his devoted costumier let out a long sigh.

Back home, Jonathon tried out his new disguise and rehearsed switching quickly between d'Artagnan and Mr. Sloane, relieved that the former was only from the neck up and that he didn't have to wear a 17th century frockcoat. Dressed normally, he then left the flat, jumped into his van and visited several shops, where he bought a large hold-all and a selection of briefcases and small bags, all with combination locks.

He wasn't back home for five minutes before his white phone rang, slightly muffled. It was still in his overnight bag and he had to rummage for it before he could answer.

"Hi Jonathon."

"David!"

"Have a nice time with Olivia?"

"Yes," said Jonathon, "it was great to see her again."

"Lying hound."

"Excuse me?" said Jonathon, cursing himself inwardly.

"I tried calling you a few hours ago but couldn't get hold of you so I tried Olivia's number."

"And she told you I hadn't been with her?" asked Jonathon needlessly, remembering that he'd put both phones in his overnight bag and that it had been in the back of the van, the noise of which would have drowned out any incoming calls.

"She told me she hasn't seen you for over a year," said David. "Jonathon, what the hell are you up to?"

"I still can't tell you, I'm sorry," said Jonathon. "Listen, I'll call you in a couple of days but right now I really do have to go."

"I thought I heard another phone ringing yester…"

But Jonathon had hung up.

David was frustrated. He had wanted to tell Jonathon about his first helicopter lesson and that he had signed up for an intensive course and that if all went well he would be granted his licence within four months or so. What he didn't know was that, in the months ahead, his own helicopter was going to prove very handy in enabling Jonathon to flee from the police.

By the evening of the following day, the left luggage offices of all five terminals at Heathrow were each looking after two small locked bags, each containing fifty thousand pounds. Using his left hand to disguise his handwriting, Jonathon had taken care to jot down the sequences of their combination locks on the reverse of the ten receipts. He had then made his way to Richmond Library, where he hid them between the pages of ten books he considered safe from being borrowed anytime soon, including 'Brass Rubbings from Romanian Churches', 'Rare South American Frogs' and 'Interesting Tasmanian Geological Formations'. Meanwhile two briefcases were being safely cared for at the lost property office of London Transport. Preferring not to commit anything to a piece of paper, he had memorized the combinations and prayed to God he wouldn't forget them, for they would be the proof of ownership for whoever went to collect the money.

When he returned home, having switched between d'Artagnan and Mr. Sloane all day, Jonathon felt he deserved to open a bottle of La Lagune, and as he settled back with a large glass, the black phone rang.

"James?"

"Brian, how are you?" said Jonathon, nearly forgetting to adopt his Birmingham voice.

"Fifty-fifty," said Brian.

He went on to explain that while it had been a doddle to recruit an explosives expert, he'd drawn a complete blank finding a willing computer nerd. "Everyone I spoke to either didn't want to know or said it couldn't be done without someone on the inside."

"Shit," said Jonathon, and then "why?"

"Because even if someone managed to get inside the building and even if they managed to locate the server and even if they managed to damage it in some way there's no guarantee the hard drive would be affected. And even if it was affected, all these servers have at least one mirror site that is automatically synchronized with the main server and is always kept in a separate location, sometimes overseas."

"Shit," repeated Jonathon.

"But," Brian continued, "if I can get to someone senior in the IT department; someone with the access codes to the main server and the main host site, then maybe they can be gently persuaded to help."

"You mean with money?"

"Of course," said Brian, remembering that James had stipulated no violence against anyone.

"Well, you'd better start hanging out at The Greyhound; it's the nearest pub to their head office," said Jonathon.

"You'll cover my expenses, yes?" asked Brian, "I'll need to stay in a hotel somewhere."

"Consider it done," said Jonathon, "and what's the name of the explosives guy?"

"Terry."

"You'd better text me his and your addresses; I'll post each of you the first twenty-five tomorrow by recorded delivery. Or if you prefer you can collect it from left luggage at Heathrow."

"Eh?"

"I've got a lot of cash available and I didn't want to keep it all at my place, so I spread it around for safekeeping."

"The post will be fine," said Brian, buoyed by the promise of a nice fat envelope landing on his doormat.

As Jonathon sat back with his wine, a delightful thought occurred to him. If Brian could make contact with a bribable IT guy then maybe he could play some games with the content of the MailOnline before deleting everything. He could maybe execute a find/change command across the entire website. The possibilities were endless and Jonathon started to chuckle. And then he remembered about David. He had twice cut short his oldest friend on the phone and he owed him some kind of explanation. After all, if it wasn't for David's generosity none of his plans would be possible.

He picked up the black phone, put it back down, picked up the white one and dialed.

"Jonathon!"

"David, I think I should explain myself a little."

"You should explain yourself a lot," countered David, "what the hell has got into you?"

"Er, well, you know I've got a bit of a thing about some aspects of the media?"

David knew all too well. Time and again Jonathon had banged on at the Ferret's Knees about how the trashy media were affecting people, especially weak and impressionable people, leaving them with a skewed view of the world and a damaged value system. To Jonathon it was a very real problem and he claimed it had a negative effect on large swathes of society. And, to be fair to him, he had backed up his theories by naming several convincing studies carried out by people with doctorates and professorships at respected universities the world over.

"Yes Jonathon; I do have a vague idea."

"Well, thanks to you I can now do something about it!"

"Like what?" asked David.

"It's best if you don't know too much detail, in fact any detail; suffice to say I'm going to teach a few of them a lesson."

"Whatever it is you're up to, are you being careful?"

"Yes, very," Jonathon assured him, "nobody will find out that it's me behind it all."

"Eh? Behind what?"

"Never you mind," said Jonathon, "but I expect you'll hear all about it."

"Good grief; this sounds ominous."

"Enough about me," said Jonathon, "what's your news; how's dear Bertie?"

"Bertie is a sheer delight; tell you what, why don't you hop in and come with me to Redhill Aerodrome on Saturday?" said David. "Maybe they'll let you sit in the back of the chopper while I have my lesson."

Jonathon was excited by the idea. "I'd love to; and how's the hunt for Yogi; any progress?"

"Yogi has been found and is in Southampton, being fitted out to my specifications; she's an absolute beauty."

"I'm sure she is; and is she sail or a gin palace?"

"Sail of course," said David.

"I'm very relieved to hear it."

"Boo-Boo is the gin palace," David added. "I couldn't resist it; thought I'd keep Yogi down at Hamble and Boo-Boo somewhere nice in the Med."

Jonathon chuckled, "I assume you've resigned by now?"

"Oh yes," said David, who had been a junior partner in a law firm. "I've got far too much to do to without worrying about any pesky work nonsense; as soon as I've done the helicopter thing I'll be going on a sailing course, even though Yogi will have a full crew. And it wouldn't hurt to learn how to handle a ninety-foot powerboat, too."

"Only ninety?' Jonathon chuckled again. "Okay, see you Saturday."

He hung up and remembered about a piece of paper he had stuffed into his jacket pocket. Within a couple of hours he was having dinner with a very pretty young bank cashier, who was still feeling a little bit sore and who, every now and then, couldn't help giggling, wriggling in her seat as she pretended to be cross with him.

6 | The pieces take up their positions

The next morning, while Jonathon was busy returning his bedroom to some semblance of order, Terry was hiding in some undergrowth in Oxfordshire, studying through binoculars the comings and goings at a large printing works. Meanwhile Brian was checking into the Royal Garden Hotel in Kensington. He reasoned that since everything was on expenses he might as well make the most of it and once he settled in he had room service send him up a breakfast he could hardly step over.

Brian had decided to do two stints per day at The Greyhound, one from noon to three o'clock and one from 5.30 onwards. He was going to do this for as long as it took to get talking to the right person. His cover was to be that he was a budding journalist who had long admired the writing and the editorial stance of the Daily Mail and that he was hoping to find employment at the paper. If he could carry that off, he thought, he deserved a second career on the stage. He was just polishing off a very fine Cumberland sausage when Terry rang.

"Hi," said Brian.

"This place is fucking huge," said Terry, "I had no idea."

"Don't worry about it, we're not blowing up the whole building, just the printing presses."

"There are four of them; four printing presses!"

"Who cares, you can get hold of enough Semtex surely."

"Yeah, no problem," said Terry, "but when am I going to see some proper money?"

"James says he's posting off the first twenty-five today; I gave him your address."

"No, I'll text you the address of the place I'm staying at; I'll still be here tomorrow. I need to work out the levels of activity at different times of the day."

Human nature being what it is where the receipt of money is involved, it was only two minutes later that Jonathon received a text from Brian asking him to send Terry's cash to the Premier Inn in Didcot. Having reflected on it, Brian swiftly followed suit and asked him to send his money to him at the Royal Garden Hotel. That way he would avoid having to field any tricky questions from Penny.

Given that both men were clearly taking the job seriously, Jonathon was only too happy to comply and it amused him that their respective lodgings were at different ends of the spectrum. Donning gloves, he prepared two padded envelopes, printed out two address labels and wondered where he might like to go to in order to post them. It was a lovely day and since he lived near Clapham Junction he decided to treat himself to a Dover sole at English's in Brighton. He even bought a first-class ticket, despite the fact that the difference between first-class and second-class had become negligible, with only a sign saying 'First Class' providing any real clue. It was no wonder so many people found themselves sitting in First by mistake, having genuinely not realised their error nor indeed noticed any evidence of an increased level of comfort, for there was none. Jonathon very much wanted to meet the man who had designed these new carriages and to have a quiet word with him.

That lunchtime at The Greyhound, in the hope of being able to eavesdrop on a wider variety of conversations, Brian decided to stand at the bar rather than sit at a table. True to what happens in pubs and bars the world over, he was not disappointed by the number of snippets he heard of folk complaining about their bosses and indulging in brazen politicking. But he didn't pick up any clues that any of them might be working in an IT department. Hoping for better luck that evening, he wolfed down a pie and chips and returned to his hotel for a kip.

In Brighton, having first been to the post office, Jonathon dined on Iranian sevruga caviar with two shots of ice-cold vodka, followed by Dover sole meunière and a half bottle of Puligny Montrachet. He nearly didn't order a pudding but in the end the bitter chocolate marquise with macerated cherries won him over. But his mentality still reflected more of the jobbing gardener than the multi-millionaire and he felt a tinge of guilt when he ordered the '98 Yquem. But upon drinking it, he forgave himself.

Tipping the waiter more than necessary, Jonathon decided to pay many more visits to Brighton and he began to stroll slowly back to the station, stopping only to pity the handsome old Clock Tower, surrounded as it now was by mainly ugly, garish shops which were keeping the tide of consumerism ticking over. Shopping had become the new religion, with people so desperate for bargains they would queue for hours, often overnight, waiting patiently, pathetically, for the doors to open. Then they would surge like pack animals and grab whatever it was that marketing campaigns had told them they needed. Even worse was that Britain had imported the idea of Black Friday from America, a country where people claim to be God-fearing but where the main object of worship was really the dollar. On these days people would actually get hurt in the frantic, sometimes violent stampedes for the latest flat-screen TVs and games consoles. On several occasions the police had to be called. Department stores and giant shopping malls had become the new cathedrals, where people went to offer prayer, and to offer money with which they couldn't afford to part.

Jonathon strolled, Brian snored, and Terry got increasingly excited about the prospect of reducing some printing presses to tangled piles of useless steel.

And in London, Wendy was convinced she'd just seen David driving a Bentley down the Fulham Road. She ran after it and knocked on the passenger window, which David reluctantly lowered.

"David!" said Wendy.

"Wendy, what a lovely surprise," said David, disingenuously.

In truth, David had had little time for Wendy ever since she'd broken the heart of his best friend, reducing him to an emotional wreck and causing him to lose over two stone in weight, but nonetheless he found himself agreeing to go and sit with her in a nearby café. Given that Wendy had not only seen him in a Bentley but had now actually sat in it, and given that David was a lousy liar, it wasn't long before he admitted to her that he'd recently had a bit of luck.

"How much? she asked.

"Don't be vulgar," he told her.

He knew what she was thinking; that he was so close to Jonathon he would almost certainly have looked after him and that, in turn, Jonathon might be generous to her. He doubted that he would, because six months after Jonathon lost his job, she had confirmed the old adage that when poverty walks through the door, love flies out the window. If she had stayed with him, and had been supportive, he had no doubt that Jonathon would have picked himself up and made a success of something else, but she had lacked both patience and the belief that her husband could or would ever again achieve very much.

In Oxfordshire, Terry had finished his day's surveillance and had returned to his hotel to write up his findings, which were to be of far more use than he had hoped. Trying his luck, he had walked up to the building pretending to be looking for work and, instead of being turned away, a kindly soul had granted him some time and had even allowed him to look round for a few minutes. It was plenty long enough, as Terry just needed to have a mental image of where the presses were located in the general layout, so he could draw a diagram and share the knowledge with Brian. He could study the actual machines in pictures he could find on the internet. This would be essential in working out the most effective positions to place the explosives, once James had given the order to go ahead. Crucially he had also managed to place undetected a small, mostly transparent, radio-controlled device on the fire alarm nearest the main large loading doors. It was a risk but Terry had reasoned that people tend to look at fire alarm buttons only when there's a fire.

Meanwhile, having picked up a fillet steak and a few other essentials, Jonathon had arrived home and Brian was back on duty at The Greyhound, enjoying the first of several pints of Young's Ordinary, one of his favourite beers, in what was to prove a highly successful session.

Jonathon decided to have a quiet evening in and he wrestled with the nagging doubt that had been torturing him for days. Was it all worth it? There he was, with countless millions in the bank, millions that meant he never had to do another day's work in his life, yet he was fixated on carrying out an act of sabotage on a national newspaper, and maybe more. Why wasn't *he* treating himself to some big boys' toys and living it up? He consoled himself that he had in fact recently had a most delicious lunch and he sat down at his computer. What he found on MailOnline removed any lingering misgivings about his intended actions.

There was a piece about an actress who had once appeared in a popular soap opera. This poor woman had recently lost not only both her mother and father but also her own son and she had sought comfort in alcohol. Some repulsive photographer had taken pictures of her in the street drinking from a small bottle of white wine and the Mail had dutifully snapped them up and written pathetic, desperate captions calculated to add to them some drama. The piece had attracted well over a thousand comments, most of them furiously condemning the public humiliation of a woman who should be left alone to battle her demons. In a cowardly fashion, the writer had hidden behind the byline 'MailOnline Reporter'. The abhorrent piece about this woman was similar to how they regularly posted embarrassing photographs of a once fine footballer who had played brilliantly for England but who had since fallen victim to his own battle with the bottle. And of course hardly a day went by without them publishing pictures of a 'nip-slip', or 'an embarrassing wardrobe malfunction' or a 'sideboob'. Such was their obsession with their opinions about what people looked like, they also regularly appointed themselves judge and jury on what so-and-so was seen wearing at some premiere or other. And, perhaps worst of all, they would regularly state that a woman was unrecognizable, simply because she had been seen popping to the shops 'make-up free'. It was beyond pathetic.

'No,' thought Jonathon, 'you people deserve what's coming. And you're not the only ones.' He gave serious consideration to dealing with *all* the red tops, a classification which, to Jonathon, included the Mail and the Express, for he considered them to be just red tops whose mastheads didn't use red ink. Collectively, they were a largely homogenous bunch of papers and websites all fighting for attention by using the same kind of blatant shock-horror reporting, shameless soft porn and mindless, puerile twaddle about miniscule celebrities. Such was the dearth of original thinking and writing, there were often days when two or more of them would choose the exact same tired old pun to headline yet another piece about a banal, tired old subject. If someone was pictured wearing something made of leather it would be 'goes hell for leather!'. If someone was pictured lying on the sand, it would be 'life's a beach!' or 'alright for sun!'. And if a woman, any woman, wore anything with a low neckline, it would be 'takes the plunge!'.

Every now and then, one of these papers would be taken to court and challenged by their victims over a piece they had published without thoroughly checking their facts. Often, guilty as sin, the sloppy perpetrators would settle out of court for an undisclosed sum and be forced to publish an apology, which was always tiny and which was buried somewhere where few people would ever see it.

In the kitchen, while he par-boiled some Maris Pipers, Jonathon melted some butter in a small saucepan and in his pestle and mortar ground a handful of green peppercorns, which he then softened in the butter for five minutes before adding a small tub of single cream.

Sitting down to a dinner of fillet steak, crispy roast potatoes, broccoli and mange tout, he wondered how anyone in their right mind could face eating steak without a sauce au poivre vert.

He washed it down with La Lagune and it would have been a perfect evening had Wendy not called and started to ask him searching questions about his financial status.

"Hi, it's me," said Wendy.

"Hello you."

"Guess who I bumped into today?"

"Elvis?"

"Stop it," said Wendy, "your friend David."

Jonathon instantly had the sinking feeling one gets when one suspects someone has learned something one would rather they hadn't.

"He bought me a coffee at Café Nero," she added.

"How nice," said Jonathon, who reckoned David could probably have splashed out on the entire chain of cafés.

"Has he told you?"

"Told me what?" asked Jonathon, enjoying the tease.

"Stop playing games Jonathon; he was driving around in a bloody Bentley!"

"Oh, so you didn't see him in his helicopter, or on his yacht?"

"Jonathon!"

"You're not getting a penny Wendy, sorry."

"So he did give you some money?"

"Yes, and I'll happily increase the child allowance and pay for them to go to private schools if we jointly decide it would be best for them."

"But nothing for me?"

"No, just for Nicholas and Jackie."

To Jonathon's surprise, Wendy hung up. He had thought she would have displayed more tenacity in trying to prise some money out of him, but maybe her conscience had told her it wouldn't be worth the effort, considering what she had done to him a few years earlier.

He turned to reading the latest Private Eye, which was a publication that would always be safe from him. He admired the way it had stuck to its roots by refusing to become glossy; instead preferring to keep to its rather basic presentation on what was little better than thick loo paper. Then the black phone rang, but he didn't get a chance to say hello.

"Bingo James!" said Brian, "I hope you don't mind me calling this late."

"It's only 11," Jonathon reassured him in his Birmingham accent.

"Guess what, I think I've found our man," Brian continued, "he's deputy head of the IT department."

"Go on."

"He's frustrated as hell. Wants the top job but they won't give it to him. Hates his boss, too. Says he'll do it. But not for fifty thousand. He wants to talk to you about the money."

"What's his name?"

"Spencer."

"What's his number?"

"He wouldn't let me have it but I gave him yours and mine. Says he'll get another phone tomorrow and be in touch. Something about his usual mobile being work-connected."

Jonathon liked the sound of him already. "That's fair enough; I've heard there are certain people who use different numbers for different purposes."

"I'm going to get back to Aldershot tomorrow; I'll leave as soon as your parcel arrives."

"Cool."

"And there'll be an update from Terry, too, ok?"

"Cool, sleep well."

Jonathon didn't doubt that Brian would sleep well that night, for it was obvious he hadn't been drinking tonic water all evening.

Jonathon slept well too, after turning over in his mind the encouraging progress and comforting himself that there was no way anyone could ever discover his identity.

He was woken in the morning by David calling to warn him that Wendy might be in touch, asking questions about money and that he was sorry he couldn't keep his mouth shut. Jonathon laughed and told him it's hard to disguise that you're driving around in a Bentley unless it has tinted windows. After reconfirming Saturday's jaunt in a helicopter he went through to the kitchen, brewed coffee and wondered how long it would take for Spencer to get in touch. The thought had barely subsided when the black phone rang.

"Hello?"

"Is that James?"

"Speaking," said Jonathon in his Birmingham accent, "and I'm guessing you might be a man called Spencer."

"We should meet."

"Yes we should; today is good."

"How about noon on the steps of the Albert Memorial, facing the Hall?"

"Ok," said Jonathon.

"How will I recognize you?"

"Dark curly hair, moustache, glasses, and I'll be carrying a black briefcase."

"Jeans, Timberlands, leather flying jacket and I'll be wearing a backpack."

"Good, you'll need it."

"Eh?"

"Never mind, see you at noon."

Jonathon stored and named the number in the black phone and went about preparing some breakfast. He'd eaten so much the day before that cereal and a boiled egg would suffice.

Having showered and dressed he put on his gloves and placed one of the bundles of fifty thousand pounds in his briefcase. If Spencer was indeed his man there was no point in making him wait for some money and besides, he wanted to get things moving sooner rather than later. Also, Spencer was going to earn it. Jonathon had lots of mischievous ideas of how he was going to mess around with the MailOnline before he deleted everything. The very thought made him laugh out loud. He threw in his disguise, stepped outside and walked to the bus stop.

Jonathon considered bus travel to be the most civilized method of getting around London, especially when he had time on his side. While he was in no way claustrophobic, there was something about the underground that made him shudder, especially having nothing to look at but grim, expressionless faces and dozens of armpits, smelly or otherwise. But peering from the top deck of a bus he could watch the world slide slowly by, admire some of the architecture and, in the summer, he could study the breasts of the women on the pavement without them knowing.

He left the 170 at Victoria, ducked into the gents' lavatories to don his disguise and then jumped on the 52, which took him directly to the Albert Memorial.

Again it was a beautiful autumn day and as he sat on the steps opposite the Albert Hall he now and then peered towards the west, towards Kensington, where the Mail had their offices and from which direction he expected Spencer to appear. And then he spotted him. The closer he got, the younger he appeared to be and when he finally arrived by his side, Jonathon put his age at somewhere in the mid-twenties. It was true what they said about these computer folk and Jonathon reckoned Spencer was young enough to be his own son.

He sat down and held out his hand. "James?"

"Spencer," said Jonathon, "how long have you got?"

"An hour or so."

"Good, I've got a lot of things to talk over with you."

"I got a rough idea last night."

Spencer nodded along as Jonathon explained what he wanted to have happen, and the reason for doing it. It soon became clear that Spencer was indeed thoroughly disenchanted with his employers, and he relished the ideas that Jonathon was presenting to him.

"The question is," asked Jonathon, "can you remotely access the web servers?"

"Yes, I'm one of only a few people who know the access codes to the servers and the host site; the question is," continued Spencer, "what's it worth?"

"One hundred thousand; fifty upfront and another fifty when it's all over."

"Done. It'll need to be a Cron job. I'll need to clone the site, store it in the Cloud, make all the changes you want, switch the sites and later execute the delete. You'll need to provide me with a laptop."

Jonathon opened his briefcase and offered Spencer a fat envelope. "Here, you can choose your own laptop from the first fifty; why do you have to clone the site, and what's a 'Cron job'?"

Taking the money, Spencer explained that if he made changes to the real site in real-time, it would be spotted before he had finished, and a Cron job was where you give instructions to a computer system and dictate that they should be carried out at pre-determined times, as in 'chronology'.

"And will the changes be passed on to the mirror sites?"

"Yes, they'll sync with the main site automatically."

"And you can definitely do a find/change thing?"

"I can code anything in, yes," said Spencer, "but you'll need to be one hundred percent precise about exactly what you want to find and change; computers still only do exactly what they're told."

"So if I asked you to change, say, 'car' to 'vehicle' across the entire website, how long would that take?"

"Seconds," said Spencer, "but I hope it'll be more fun than that."

"Don't worry, it'll be a lot more fun than that; set up a dedicated email address and I'll send you the full list."

"When do you want to do all this?"

"Sometime soon," said Jonathon, "I'll let you know; I need to coordinate things with Brian."

"Who's Brian?"

Jonathon smiled inwardly. "He's the bloke you met at The Greyhound last night."

"He said his name was Kevin."

"Can you describe him?"

"He was a big bloke, brown hair…"

"Hair?" Jonathon laughed out loud. "And did he have a moustache?"

"No, but I remember thinking his upper lip seemed a little pale."

Jonathon was impressed that Brian was taking care to make sure there was no comeback, even though he wasn't being particularly thorough.

"There's just one thing," warned Spencer, "you need to think very carefully about how long you want the delay to be between playing around with the site and deleting it."

"Why?"

"Because even though I'll have changed the access codes I can't do anything about someone deactivating the server before it executes the delete command."

"Why?"

"James, these things aren't powered by a wood-burning stove," said Spencer, "they run on electricity; all someone would have to do is go and unplug the bloody thing."

"Hmm, good point."

Before they went their separate ways, Spencer promised that within the following 24 hours he would obtain a new laptop specifically for the purpose and that he would provide Jonathon with a dedicated email address to which he could send his list of find/change instructions. In turn, Jonathon undertook to email his list within a couple of days and also to confirm the day and the time he wanted Spencer to carry out the cyber crime.

"Oh, and Spencer," added Jonathon, "one more thing; I don't know how much you earn in a year but I'm guessing a hundred grand is going to make a considerable difference to you."

"Yes, it will."

"Then don't go flashing it around, even a little," Jonathon counseled, "people might start putting two and two together."

As Spencer wandered back to his office, Jonathon caught the 52 and the 170 back home, where he started to compile his list of find/change commands for Spencer to put into practice.

where 'cleavage' change to 'tits'

where 'ample cleavage' change to 'big tits'

where 'impressive cleavage' change to 'huge tits'

where 'plenty of cleavage' change to 'massive tits'

where 'curves' change to 'tits'

where 'assets' change to 'tits'

where 'goes topless' change to 'shows off her tits'

where 'derriere' change to 'arse'

where 'pert derriere' change to 'incredible arse'

where 'posterior' change to 'arse'

where 'pert posterior' change to 'incredible arse'

where 'toned pins' change to 'spreadable legs'

where 'the thigh's the limit' add '(yes, that one again!)'

where 'life's a beach' add '(you could be reading The Sun, couldn't you?)'

where 'sextape' add '(this is why we write about her)'

where 'TOWIE' add '(why the hell do you watch this confected crap?)'

where 'Made in Chelsea' add '(why the hell do you watch this confected crap?)'

where 'Apprentice' add '(why the hell do you watch this confected crap?)'

where 'Keeping up with the Kardashians' add '(if you watch this shite you should be taken out and maimed)'

He was just getting into the swing of it when he realised that the coming weekend was his turn with Nicholas and Jackie and he had promised David he would come along to Redhill Aerodrome. Picking up the white phone, he dialed him.

"David," he said, "I've just remembered; I've got the children this weekend."

"Then bring them along; they'll love it," said David, "I'll pick up the three of you at ten."

"You're sure you don't mind?"

"Of course not; I'm their Uncle David."

He was right of course; having never married, nor had any children of his own, David looked upon Nicholas and Jackie as his default family and had always been extremely kind and generous to them. In turn, the children had always loved his daftness and his love of tricks. The truth was, David was just a big kid and he found it easy to connect with youngsters, especially when they were a captive audience.

Jonathon considered calling a pretty young bank cashier to see if she was free that evening but decided against it, instead preferring to work on his list of find/change and to get in touch with Brian.

At that precise moment, Brian was back in Aldershot with Terry, each of them twenty five thousand pounds richer and having a quiet celebration at the Crimea Inn before going on to get something to eat.

"So what did you tell Penny?' asked Terry.

"I said I was sick of it and felt like a change," Brian replied, "and I told her it was starting to tickle too much."

"I thought you'd never, ever, shave it off."

"Neither did I," said Brian, "but this business is too tricky to take any risks; I wore a bloody wig too."

Terry went on to explain that he too had been as careful as he could, wearing a tracksuit top with a hood that he kept on all the time, the cord pulled tightly round his neck to keep it drawn over his face to hide his scars. He took from his pocket a rough sketch of the layout of the printing works and laid it on the table.

"Like I said, there are four printing presses," he said, pointing with his finger, "I'll take care of these two and you'll handle these two."

"How long will we have?"

"I drove from the nearest fire station and it took me eleven minutes without breaking the speed limit."

"So we'll have about nine?"

"No, less than that," said Terry, "don't forget we have to wait for the place to be completely evacuated after we set off the fire alarm; we'll have maybe four minutes tops."

"Are you happy with that?"

"Yeah I guess so," said Terry, "the bombs will already have their blasting caps inserted so all we have to do is place them and get the hell out."

"And how will we detonate them?"

"By remote control," said Terry, "we can wait until the very last second, even until the fire brigade arrives; and then 'boom', it's bye-bye to millions of pounds worth of state-of-the-art printing presses."

"You're enjoying this aren't you?"

"I sure am," said Terry, "I haven't had this much fun since Helmand."

He took out a photograph that he'd printed off the internet and laid it on the table. "This is one of the actual presses," he said, again pointing with his finger, "we need to place the charges right here, where they'll cause the most damage."

"Understood. When are you picking up the Semtex?"

"Tomorrow."

"Am I allowed to know where from?"

"It's best you don't."

Heading to the best restaurant in Aldershot, they argued the toss over who would pay for dinner. Previously they had always split their meal bills, but now they were each insisting that they should pay for everything.

Later, walking home, Brian called James.

"Hello?" said Jonathon, only just remembering to switch accents, "I was about to call you."

"James, we're all set; all you have to do is name the day and the time."

"You got your money then?"

"Sure did," said Brian, "did you meet up with Spencer?"

"Yes. Bit of a smart arse, isn't he, Kevin?"

Brian laughed. "I just wanted to be careful."

"Very wise," said Jonathon, "I'm sure a disguise was a good idea."

"So when do you want us to go ahead?"

"I'll need to make sure Spencer is all set up and ready to go, but I was thinking very early next Tuesday morning; nothing ever happens on a Tuesday."

7 | Redhill Aerodrome

"Wow!" said Nicholas, "Dad, you're kidding me!"

Jonathon was impressed. His son was not yet fifteen and like many of his peers he had become proficient at using grunts as his preferred method of communication. This was one of his rare excursions to the land of proper sentence construction, and Jonathon hoped he had finally turned a corner.

"No, we really are going up in a helicopter; a proper chopper."

"Have you told Jackie?"

"No I called you first; you tell her."

"Oh wow; a bloody helicopter."

"Language," said Jonathon. "I'll pick you up at six as usual. Have a think about where you'd like to go for dinner tonight. Anywhere; anywhere at all."

"Okay."

Jonathon knew full well what they'd choose. It would be dim-sum. He booked a restaurant in Chinatown and a cab to pick them up at seven from his flat. He usually either drove everywhere with them or took the bus, but there was no point in hiding the fact that he finally had a bit of money to spend. Besides, no doubt their mother had already mentioned it. He then called David.

"My dear old thing," he said, "Nick and Jack and I are going out for dinner this evening; want to join us?"

"I'd love to Jonno but I really shouldn't," said David, "it would be too tempting to have too much of a good time and I absolutely must have a clear head tomorrow or I'll get all the controls muddled up."

"Don't call me Jonno."

"I'll pick you up at ten."

In the years since the split, and later the divorce, it had become difficult keeping the children entertained. Poorer parents faced a constant battle to manage the expectations of their offspring, who were under relentless pressure from the media to either do this or do that; or own this or own that. He was going to have to be careful if they weren't now going to turn into a pair of spoiled brats. He would have to ration the treats and the good times, but not this weekend.

Arriving at Wendy's in his beaten-up old van, he honked the horn and waited.

Nicholas and Jackie came bounding out with more enthusiasm than usual, swinging their weekend bags and racing to get to the van first. Jackie got in, followed by her brother and they all waved goodbye to Wendy, who had appeared at the door.

"Dad?" said Jackie. "Are we really going up in a helicopter?"

"Well," said Jonathon, "it wouldn't be much fun just sitting in one on the tarmac."

Nicholas grunted his approval. He was by no means a one-grunt teenager and had developed a variety of grunts from which he could select the most appropriate for the situation, imbuing them with a range of tonalities with which to convey his emotional attitude to the subject.

"I've booked us a table at a dim-sum place in Chinatown."

At this, Nicholas's grunt was considerably more positive than the first, and he even managed to follow it up with some speech.

"Yay!" he said.

"Dad," said Jackie, "mum said something about you having some money at last; is that true?"

"I've had a bit of luck darling, yes."

"So does that mean we can go in a helicopter every time we see you?"

Bless her heart, thought Jonathon. His daughter was just 10 years old and she still had the delightful ability of children of that age to assume that exciting experiences could and should be repeated as often as possible, to the exclusion of any other activities.

"Well, perhaps not *every* time," said Jonathon, reflecting that in fact he could go out and buy them each a helicopter without batting an eyelid.

"So, what else will we be able to do?" asked Nicholas, putting together yet another complete sentence.

"Wait and see."

Arriving at Jonathon's flat, the children dumped their bags in the spare bedroom and raided the fridge, where they found some chocolate éclairs and a good supply of orange juice. Meanwhile their father poured himself a glass of La Lagune and sighed with pleasure.

The taxi soon arrived and forty minutes later they were dropped at the end of Gerrard Street, from where they walked to the Golden Dragon. It wasn't the finest dim-sum place in Chinatown but the food was nevertheless excellent. It was also huge and mostly full of chattering Chinese folk enjoying a Friday night out. This, accompanied by the endearing, incessant rudeness of the waiters and waitresses, gave it an impressive air of far-Eastern authenticity. It wasn't the first time the three of them had dined there but it had been two years' prior and the children had harped on about it ever since. Jonathon had found himself on the receiving end of a small error committed by Her Majesty's Revenue and Customs and had decided to broaden

Nicholas' and Jackie's appreciation of different cuisines.

The children pointed gleefully at the various dim-sum that were wheeled around on trolleys and ate heartily, occasionally having to strike bargains with each other when there was an odd number of something. Jonathon also chose a few treats from the trolleys but not before ordering some pak choi and some Cantonese roast duck. Mischievously, he requested that the skin was to be really really crispy and he took great delight in asking the waitress to repeat what he had said.

This went over Jackie's head but Nicholas cottoned on.

"Da-ad," he said, "that is just SO bad!"

Even though he wasn't going to be at the controls of a helicopter, Jonathon decided that a joy-ride should be exactly that; joyful, and not marred by the kind of panic attack that can be brought on by even the mildest of hangovers, as had once happened to him at a depth of sixty feet on one of his scuba dives many years before. He therefore stuck to drinking Chinese green tea, reasoning that the wine list wasn't really up to much anyway.

God was still being kind with the weather so rather than go straight home, Jonathon suggested they went for a ride on the London Eye. It was far more enjoyable than the last time they had done so, when it had been a dull, grey afternoon with hugely disappointing visibility. Now, it was perfectly clear in all directions and the huge expanse of London by night looked genuinely beautiful, studded as it was by lights of all colours and sizes; some inert, some gliding gracefully along as they traced the paths of the roads. Jonathon felt good as Jackie gave him a big hug.

Nicholas then excelled himself. "Tell you what Dad; this is the best time we've had with you for ages and ages and ages and ages."

"Really?"

He then reverted to normal and gave a warm, positive grunt. "Just you wait until tomorrow."

Back at the flat, they played a few hands of rummy before calling it a day.

Before sleeping, Jonathon first checked his black phone and was relieved to see no texts and no missed calls. Good, he thought, all that can wait until Sunday evening, when he would finish his list of find/change and email it off to Spencer, with instructions on when to go ahead.

In the morning, David's Bentley rolled up majestically just before ten and Jonathon noticed a few curtain-twitchers getting busy on the other side of the road. To be fair to them, it wasn't often they saw a car worth six figures in the neighbourhood, let alone in their own street, and he took pleasure in ostentatiously waving to them as he climbed into the passenger seat. The children sat in the back and gazed with awe at the car's interior.

"Uncle David?" said Jackie. "Is this really your car?"

"Yes Jackie, it is."

Nicholas let forth a special grunt that he reserved only for those things which truly impressed him. "Cool," he added.

As they rolled away, Jonathon couldn't help teasing the curtain-twitchers with the kind of royal wave that involved resting the elbow on the window ledge and slowly rotating the vertical forearm while keeping the fingers loose and slightly splayed.

"Idiot," said David.

Despite the opulence of their transport, this was nonetheless just another car journey and it wasn't long before Jackie asked if they were nearly there yet. Jonathon and David kept the children entertained with a succession of daft jokes and they were particularly impressed by the 'what do you call a man…?' series.

"What do you call a man with a rabbit on his head?" asked David.

"Don't know."

"Warren," cackled David. "What do you call a man with a spade on his head?"

"Don't know."

"Doug," he hooted. "And what do you call a man *without* a spade on his head?"

"Douglas!" said Nicholas, feeling rather proud of himself.

Such was the effectiveness of the Bentley's sound insulation, Jonathon felt the outside world had assumed a kind of surreal mime quality, with all the other vehicles being eerily quiet. Then, when the A3 finally began it's long sweep round to the left and David stood on the accelerator, he and the children caught their breath, pressed back into their seats as the needle rapidly shot up to 120mph. It could have gone on to over 200mph but David was going to wait until a trip to Germany before treating himself on the autobahns to that kind of thrill. As it was, he brought the speed back down to 80 or so and decided to treat his passengers to the amazing sound system. Rated at 1100 watts, which was way more than most people have in their living rooms, and driving no fewer than 15 separate speakers, it was as if they were right next to the stage at Wembley, and despite some mild protests from Jackie, they feasted their ears on Led Zeppelin IV all the way to Redhill Aerodrome.

David had done his homework and had discovered that, no, he couldn't invite a passenger along for the ride on his lesson, still less three of them, and had suggested to Jonathon that they come along anyway and go on a separate pleasure flight, which he had taken the trouble to book. While David wandered off to the training school, Jonathon and two excited children were ushered onto the tarmac where a 4-seater Robinson R44 sat waiting for them as it underwent its final pre-flight checks.

"I want to sit in the front," said Jackie.

"No, I want to sit in the front," demanded Nicholas.

Reaching into his pocket, Jonathon took out a coin and said "this is the only way."

"Heads," said Nicholas, as the coin spun in the air.

"Heads it is," said Jonathon.

"Yay!" exclaimed Nicholas, and then he saw his sister's bottom lip begin to tremble. "Oh, alright then, you can sit in the front."

As Jackie gave her brother a hug, Jonathon felt a surge of pride at his son's unexpected and admirable gallantry. They piled in and the pilot showed Jackie how to do up her seatbelt, which was of a typical aviation design, anchored at four points with two over-the-shoulder straps that met two waist straps at a round buckle that was positioned over the stomach.

"My name's Mike," said the pilot as he handed his passengers a headset each, "put these on or you won't be able to hear each other speak."

"Will it be safe?" asked Jackie.

"It had better be," said Mike, "my wife's expecting me home for tea and crumpets at four o'clock."

He started up the engine and as the rotors began to turn lazily round, Jackie gripped her seat tightly with both hands and Nicholas and Jonathon both stared out of the window with huge grins on their faces. The rotors gathered speed and soon the aircraft was at the point where the skids left the ground, allowing Mike to turn it into the wind to complete the take off.

Having first exchanged messages with air traffic control, Mike announced that they would be flying due south, then turning west to fly along the south coast and then all the way around the Isle of Wight before turning back.

"How long have you been flying helicopters?" asked Jackie.

"This is my first time young lady," said Mike with a wink, "but it doesn't seem too difficult so far."

Mike gave his passengers a flight to remember, cruising not too low to cause concern, yet not too high to make them feel out of touch with the terrain. Along the way, he had to field a lot of questions, mostly from Jackie.

"How does it stay up in the air?" she asked at one point.

Mike explained that the beveled shape of the upper sides of the leading edges of the rotor blades caused the air passing above them to move faster than the air passing beneath them, which meant that the air beneath the rotors had a greater density than the air above them and therefore the air pressure beneath them was greater than the air pressure above them, which caused the helicopter to lift, just in the same way as the shape of the wings on a fixed-wing aircraft work. Jackie sat there open mouthed and she clearly wasn't going to have any of this nonsense. "Yes, but how does it stay up in the air?"

"Beats me," said Mike, who knew when to give up. "I think it must be some kind of magic."

Jackie folded her arms and gave him one of the looks she reserved for people who had displeased her.

At the Isle of Wight, they circled The Needles twice and, between them, Jonathon and Mike explained the principles of erosion.

"So you mean, like," began Nicholas, "some rocks are softer than others so the water washes them away more quickly?"

"Yes," said Jonathon.

"Yay!" said Nicholas.

On the way back, Mike gave his passengers a quick look at Devil's Dyke near the Sussex coast, where there were often dozens of hang-gliders out in force when the wind was favourable. Taking care not to be directly above them, he circled a couple of times to give everyone a good view of what seemed like multi-coloured butterflies with wings that did not fold or beat, slowly turning and gliding; turning and gliding, until they ran out of updraft and had to land in the valley below, where their trackers were waiting with the cars.

Later, nearly back at Redhill, Mike asked if anyone was interested in experiencing a quick demonstration of stunt-flying. All three of his passengers agreed and Mike gave them his impersonation of an eagle diving to catch a lamb, descending frighteningly fast and pulling up at the very last moment at what seemed like only twenty feet above the ground, but which in fact was more like fifty feet. Jonathon tensed, Jackie screamed, and Nicholas said "fucking hell!"

Touching down gently on the tarmac, Mike switched off the engine and the rotors gradually slowed to a stop.

"Thank you for flying Mike airways," said Mike, "I hope you'll join me again one day."

"Enjoy your crumpets," Jonathon winked at him.

Their return was nicely timed and they were greeted at the main building by David, who had recently finished his lesson.

"So how was it guys?"

"It was amazing," said Jackie, "I need the loo."

They grabbed a snack at the Aerodrome's café and on the way back to London, both children fell deeply asleep while David and Jonathon indulged in some quiet conversation.

"Jonathon," said David, "what are you up to?"

"I can't tell you."

"Why?"

"Because if I told you, you might try to stop me."

"Is it illegal?"

"Yes," said Jonathon, "but in a fun way."

As Jonathon yawned and drifted off to sleep himself, David wrestled with the concept of breaking the law 'in a fun way'.

Bertie the Bentley purred his way back to Clapham, where Jonathon invited David in for a drink.

"No I'd better not," said David, "I've got a date tonight."

"Fair enough," said Jonathon, who wondered when he might next see a certain pretty young bank cashier.

Later, Jonathon, Nicholas and Jackie wandered round the corner for a pizza, where they talked excitedly about flying in helicopters and other adventures. Jonathon suggested they went go-karting the next day, which was an idea that went down very well.

Before going to bed, he checked his black phone and found a text message from Spencer, giving him the email address to which he should send his list of find/change instructions. He texted back: 'will send tomorrow late PM. Be prepared to execute late Monday night; will advise time to do so.'

The imminence of the execution of his plans made it hard for him to get to sleep and he crept to the living room for a nightcap. Sipping a Glenlivet, he wondered what the jail term might be for someone who was behind the act of blowing up a few printing presses and deleting the entire contents of a national newspaper's computer systems. He also imagined the glee with which several hundred thousand people, perhaps millions, would receive the news that an habitual purveyor of piffle had been wiped out.

On the Sunday, Jonathon and the children took breakfast at a cafe in Chelsea before going go-karting, after which they went to the movies before returning to Wendy.

"Thanks Dad," said Nicholas, "that was the best."

"Yes thank you Daddy," agreed Jackie, "I love you so, SO much."

"And me you," said Jonathon, "don't forget to concentrate on your mathematics."

Nicholas gave a mocking grunt.

"As for you," added Jonathon, "I want to see a marked improvement in your French."

Nicholas grunted again, but with less enthusiasm. "Oui Papa," he offered.

Back home, Jonathon sat at his computer and refined his list of find/change instructions for Spencer, giggling to himself as he did so, before hitting 'send' and retiring to bed.

8 | Semtex in the works

Waking at six in a cold sweat, Jonathon wandered through to the kitchen and made himself a cup of tea. His sleep had been fitful, and he was scared. He was scared of himself; scared of what he was about to do. Scared of being found out.

Sitting at his computer, he clicked on 'MailOnline'.

Even though he had visited the site a million times, it still struck him as incredible the way they relentlessly served up the same kind of mindless, vacuous, puerile content, constantly using exclamation marks where none was either necessary or deserved. A reality show 'actress' wore a lacy dress: 'lovely in lace!'; a couple went shopping for saucy lingerie: 'frill seekers!'; a footballer's wife wore an orange bikini: 'tangerine dream!'

Jonathon's resolve was again redoubled and, picking up the black phone, he issued instructions to Brian and Spencer by text message and asked them to acknowledge and confirm.

He was half-way through a bowl of cereal when his white phone rang.

"Is that Mr. Taylor; Mr. Jonathon Taylor, the gardener?"

Jonathon agreed that it was indeed him speaking. "Yes," he said, "what can I do for you?"

The caller was a Mr. Matthews, a kindly old soul who lived not half a mile away and who wanted someone to clear out his greenhouse, prepare it for over-wintering and to plant some hardy salad crops indoors ready for planting-out come the spring.

"Yes I can do that for you," said Jonathon, "would you like me to come round today?"

"Yes please," said Mr. Matthews, and he gave Jonathon his address.

This job was just what he needed, for two reasons. He had reached the point in his plans where he couldn't do anything further, for everything was now in the hands of Brian, Terry and Spencer. It would be good to busy himself and take his mind off what was about to happen and also it might be useful to be seen that he had been continuing his life as normal.

As it turned out, Mr. Matthews found all manner of other things with which to keep Jonathon busy and he returned home exhausted and eighty pounds better off. Too tired to cook, he fetched some fish and chips and slumped down in front of the TV.

Glancing at his watch once he'd eaten, he saw that it was T minus 5 hours before the attacks and, picking up the black phone he called Brian, taking care to slip into his Birmingham accent.

"Hello, Brian?"

"James," said Brian, "what can I do for you?"

"Just wanted to make sure everything was in place, that's all," said Jonathon.

"Yes it is," said Brian, "at 1 am tomorrow we're going to make history."

"And you're sure nobody will get hurt?"

"Don't worry James," said Brian, "remember, Terry and I have got another twenty-five grand depending on it."

"True," said Jonathon, and then he called Spencer.

"James?"

"Everything ok for tomorrow?"

"Yes, I've been laughing myself silly at your list," said Spencer, "I don't know how I'm going to keep a straight face at the office."

"Well, you'd better," said Jonathon, "for God's sake don't let anybody suspect you."

"I'll try my best."

"Do the find/change at midnight and then delete the whole site at 1 am, ok?"

"Don't you think an hour is a bit risky?"

"Maybe," said Jonathon, "but it'll give the rest of the world plenty of time to have a laugh. And I'm hoping a few thousand people will save a few of the pages on their computers."

Jonathon listened to the radio and had another few glasses of wine before going to bed, where he lay with his eyes wide open and again had second thoughts. Unable to sleep, he wondered if maybe he should contact Brian and Terry and call the whole thing off.

But eventually he did get to sleep, so he couldn't call it off.

At 12.30 am, Brian turned off the lights and the engine of the car and he and Terry rolled quietly to a stop in a muddy lay-by opposite the Daily Mail's printing works. Each carrying a holdall, they crept over the road, bent at the waist, and ghosted into the grounds, where they lay low and watched the activity.

At 12.50 am Terry took a small transmitter from his pocket, switched it on, extended its aerial and pressed a small red button.

Inside the building, the glass covering a fire-alarm shattered and the sirens went off, piercing the calm of the night with their relentless, urgent intensity. Terry started the timer on his watch and signaled to Brian to be ready to get moving in 5 minutes.

They watched as scores of workers, some running, some just walking quickly, left the building and assembled outside. In the confusion, nobody noticed two figures, each carrying a holdall, slip inside through the main doors to the warehouse area. A few minutes later, nobody noticed them come out again, minus their holdalls, and slip out of the main gates. Back in the car, satisfied that there was nobody left in the building, Terry removed another device from his pocket, extended the aerial and pressed a button just as the first fire engine arrived and started to disgorge several firemen in bright yellow jackets.

The four bombs exploded simultaneously with massive force, rocking the building and sending the firemen and the assembled workers scattering. In the still of the night the noise was immense, easily camouflaging the sound of Brian starting up the engine of his car and engaging first gear.

"Let's stay and watch for a bit," said Terry.

"Get real," said Brian, and he slowly drove away, safe in the knowledge that everyone would be facing the building and not the road.

Meanwhile, Spencer had cloned the website, carried out Jonathon's list of find/change instructions and uploaded everything to the host. He entered one last command, then closed the laptop and went to bed, completely unfazed by what he had just done. The only thing that kept him awake for a while was the thought of how he was going to spend a hundred thousand pounds.

9 | One down, four to go

Jonathon was woken by the black phone and received confirmation of his newly acquired status as a major criminal.

"James?" said Brian. "Seen the news?"

"No, I'm still in bed," said Jonathon, "how did it go?"

"It went bang; and it's the lead story everywhere, and I mean *every*where!"

"Nobody hurt?"

"Nobody at all; we evacuated the building before setting off the bombs."

"Good."

"When can we get the second twenty-five?"

Jonathon explained that he would need to go to Richmond Library, where he would find a left-luggage receipt from Heathrow hidden between the pages of a book, the title of which he would send to him by text message.

"The bag is locked and the combination number is written on the back of the receipt. There's fifty grand in it. You can split it with Terry."

"You don't take any chances do you?"

"No, I don't; I'll be in touch. This isn't necessarily the end of it."

Hanging up, Jonathon couldn't wait to turn on the news and get on the internet and he didn't even bother to make coffee before sitting at his computer, where first he clicked on

MailOnline only to find a holding page which read: 'Sorry but your daily dose of nip-slips, toned pins, wardrobe malfunctions, incredible post-baby bodies and Z-listers' pouting selfies is currently unavailable. How hilarious is that? The value of your house will not be affected. Nemesis.'

'Well done Spencer,' thought Jonathon, and he began to trawl through some other websites.

'Who's got it in for the Daily Mail?'

'Daily Mail ceases to exist.'

'Printing presses bombed; website hacked.'

Exploring further, he was delighted to find a few examples of what he had hoped would happen. News outlets constantly monitor each other and several of them had captured and uploaded to their own sites a few examples of Spencer's find/ change activities before the delete command had kicked in.

'So-and-so displays her tits at film premiere.'

'So-and-so flashes her impressive tits at star-studded event.'

'So-and-so displays her spreadable legs on Dubai beach break.'

He decided to call Spencer, who picked up, but only briefly.

"James I can't talk now; I'll call you later."

At that precise moment, Spencer and his boss were on their way to be quizzed in the boardroom of a major national newspaper; a major national newspaper which had just been the target of some unprecedented and embarrassing attacks.

"How the fuck could this happen?" demanded the MD. "We're a bloody laughing stock!"

'So what's new?' thought Spencer, who had never really cared much for his employer's product.

"I er,..." began Jason, who was Spencer's boss.

"Shut up."

"If you remember sir," began Spencer, "I recommended six months ago that we introduce a rolling rota of regular changes to the access codes. Without doing that, it would only be a matter of time before a determined hacker could eventually stumble across the codes using automated search algorithms."

"And why didn't you?"

Spencer looked at Jason, who shifted his weight uneasily from one leg to the other.

"Jason?"

"Sir?"

"You're fired."

In his kitchen, Jonathon switched on the radio and made coffee, chuckling as he did so. The media couldn't help having a go at each other at every opportunity and this latest turn of events had unleashed a torrent of theories, most of them rather unkind and the vast majority rather amusing. Nobody seemed to be too upset about it all and Twitter was at boiling point with sarcastic comments.

"But who would want to do such a thing?" asked the host of a live phone-in show.

"Good question," said Gareth, from Islington, "I can't imagine it would be more than just a couple of hundred thousand people."

"Good riddance," said Julie, from Liverpool.

Jonathon was tempted to call in himself but decided it probably wouldn't be very wise.

Taking the black phone, he texted to Brian 'Richmond Library: The Magic of Old Tractors'.

He reflected that it was only twelve days prior that he had met David at the Ferret's Knees. There's no substitute for money, he thought, and he turned his attention to preparing some breakfast. He noticed he was feeling perfectly calm, which he partly put down to the fact that, according to all the reports, nobody had been injured in the bomb attacks; not a scratch. News outlets were always quick to report people's deaths or injuries so he was confident Brian and Terry had done their job as he had demanded. But what was he going to do about the other four red-tops, including the other one that didn't use red ink? Would they step-up their security? Maybe yes, maybe no. But one thing was certain; if he hit just one more, then the other three would definitely fear there was a concerted attack on the low-end tabloids and would introduce the kinds of security that might be impossible to overcome. No, if he was going to get the other four, it would have to be carried out simultaneously. He wondered if Brian would be able to put together the necessary people. But there was no hurry; indeed, given enough time, the more at ease the other papers might feel and the more convinced they might be that the only target was the Mail.

Not surprisingly, it didn't take Spencer long to call back.

"Happy? he asked.

"Very," said Jonathon.

"James, when can I get hold of the second fifty?"

Jonathon told him he could get it that day if he wanted and described to him the same procedure he'd outlined to Brian.

"You're kidding me?"

"No, I'll text you the title; all you have to do is go to the library, get the receipt, then go to Heathrow."

"Ok."

"And Spencer?" added Jonathon. "I might have another job for you."

"Excellent!"

Jonathon hung up and texted him 'Richmond Library: The Anger of Aubergines.'

Meanwhile, Scotland Yard had sent detectives and bomb experts to the Mail's printing house and had also begun investigations into the cyber attack, in which their computer crime division would be helped enormously by a very accommodating young man called Spencer, the recently appointed Head of Information Technology. Outside both the printing facility and head office, TV crews were still hanging around, desperate for information about the blasts, but there was none forthcoming. In the manner of TV crews and reporters the world over, they did what they always do; resort to endless repetition and wild speculation, including filling in time with completely irrelevant information and re-running the same old archived film clips, many of them many years old and only tangentially related.

After a light breakfast, Jonathon returned to his computer and started to read, in-depth, the reactions from the other papers. There was a lot of speculation across the board, including that maybe a wronged Mail celebrity victim was behind it, or that it had been the work of an affronted organization of some kind. Nobody speculated that it had been orchestrated by just an ordinary member of the public who had been driven to distraction by the paper's output. But they had all reached the same incorrect conclusion; that the website had been taken down deliberately, voluntarily, in reaction to someone hacking in and sprinkling 'tits' and 'arse' all over the place. At least two of the quality papers observed that this had not increased in any way the frequency with which the MailOnline reported on cleavages and derrieres; it had simply amplified the effect. Interestingly, none of the tabloids echoed this observation, for they were all just as bad as each other and they would simply be pointing the finger at themselves and their own predilection for attention-craving reality-show celebs, soft-porn, nip-slips, wardrobe malfunctions, tits, and arses, pert or otherwise.

Detective Inspector Foot kicked over some of the wreckage of an unsalvageable printing press. "Whoever did this meant business," he said sagely, trying to sound in control, "the only thing this is good for is the scrap yard."

It was true that Terry had perhaps been a bit over-enthusiastic with the amount of Semtex he'd decided would be right for the job, but he was being paid a lot of money and he wanted to be thorough. The other reason he wanted to be thorough was that Brian had told him their paymaster might have more work for them if the first operation went well. Terry had never met this James character but he didn't care; he already had half his money and he had no reason to believe he wouldn't get the rest.

"Look," said a member of the bomb squad, holding up a fragment of the device Terry had planted the previous week, "this must be how they set off the fire alarm; it's clever stuff."

"At least we're not dealing with murderers," said Foot, "whoever did this had a conscience."

"Do you read the Mail, sir?"

"No but my wife does; well, she did."

Detective Inspector Foot told his team there was no point in looking for prints but he insisted that there be carried out a full study of the CCTV recordings from the past couple of weeks, from the cameras both inside and outside the building.

In London, David had risen later than usual, having had a wild night out with a couple of friends at a gentlemen's club. He put his feet up and switched on the television, where news of the bombing and the hacking had been the lead story for many hours. Fragments of conversations floated lazily through his mind and it took a few minutes for the thought to form in his hazy head, but then it crystalised and he was sure.

Jonathon picked up the white phone and answered the call.

"It was you wasn't it?" demanded David.

"What was me?"

"You know damn well," said David, "have you had breakfast?"

"Only a little."

"Meet me at the cafe in thirty minutes, ok?"

Jonathon knew there was no point denying his involvement

and was grateful to him for being wise enough not to go into any detail on the phone, although in fact it had been just luck that David hadn't mentioned what he was on about. "Okay, I'll see you there."

They ordered bacon sandwiches and mugs of tea and sat down at a corner table, far away from the workmen in paint-spattered overalls and the dusty road crew who had been busy digging a hole in the pavement outside. Jonathon noticed that most of them were reading either The Star, The Sun or The Mirror.

"So what makes you think I had anything to do with it?" asked Jonathon.

"You told me yourself," said David, "twelve days ago at the Ferret."

Jonathon racked his brain.

"You said; and I quote, 'I'm going to get the Daily Mail'."

"Really?"

"And later, when I asked you what you were up to you, you told me I'd be able to read about it, but not everywhere."

Jonathon nodded. "Yes I can see why you'd jump to conclusions."

"Dammit Jonathon," demanded David, "I haven't jumped to any bloody conclusions; I know it was you, or at least that you were behind it."

Jonathon realised there was no point in hiding the truth; David knew him too well and, after all, he was sure he wouldn't turn him in. There was a long pause, during which David's eyes never left his friend's face.

"I paid some people to do it," said Jonathon at last.

"And that's why you needed all that cash?"

"Well no, not all of it," said Jonathon with a wink, "it turned out that the going rate for this kind of thing is far less than a million."

David couldn't help but smile. But then he got serious again. "Do you know why I'm not going to turn you in?"

Jonathon knew David as well as David knew Jonathon. "Because nobody got hurt."

"Yes," said David, "but what about all those poor people who *like* the bloody Daily Mail?"

"Fuck 'em", offered Jonathon with conviction, "they'll get over it."

"You do know you're trying to play God, don't you?"

The thought had occurred to Jonathon before. "No, I'm not; I'm playing Parent."

David listened as Jonathon extrapolated the role of a responsible and caring parent to that of a responsible and caring media or, at least, what he believed *should* be a responsible and caring media but large swathes of which were just a bunch of amoral bastards.

"The fact is David, these people don't give a flying fuck about what they put in front of people; about the shit they force them to consume. All they care about is readership and ratings and pulling in the advertising pound. And if that means constantly appealing to people's baser desires and feeding them dross then that's what they're going to continue to do."

"And you think sabotaging the Daily Mail is going to stop the rot?"

Jonathon ignored the question. "How many people do you think it would take to reverse the decline; the ever-increasing rate of dumbing down; the worry that if they don't cater for the lowest common denominator they'll lose the interest of the masses?"

"I've never thought about it."

"Then think about it now," said Jonathon, "I have, and I reckon it's probably just a couple of hundred people."

"And they are…?"

"Newspaper editors, magazine editors, TV program

commissioners, creative directors in advertising agencies; anyone who has the power to govern and select what is put in front of the public."

"You're forgetting the power of the advertising pound."

"True, I know it's just a dream; it's big corporations that are behind it all."

"Meanwhile, you think that what you did last night is going to make any difference?"

"I haven't finished yet."

"Ye Gods."

"David, let's change the subject."

It was uneasy, but the next half hour was spent discussing David's life, which for the time being revolved around his Bentley, learning to fly a helicopter and the progress being made on Yogi down in Southampton.

"I'm flying down to the Cote d'Azur on Friday to check out some berths for Boo-Boo at Antibes; want to come along?"

"I'd love to but maybe another time; with any luck I'll be taking a certain young lady to Italy this weekend."

"Surely criminals like you would feel more at home on the Costa del Sol?"

"Very funny; thanks for the bacon sandwich."

Back home, Jonathon called Bianca, a pretty young bank cashier, and asked her if she could take Friday and Monday off from work.

"I could take Tuesday off too if you like," she said, "and maybe Wednesday."

"Even better; I just need your surname and your passport number."

"Sounds exciting!" she said. "But I must go; I'll message you."

That afternoon his white phone beeped with a text that confirmed she could indeed take the four days as holiday and it was signed off with her surname and passport number.

Keen to get out of the country for a few days, Jonathon booked BA flights to Venice from Gatwick and managed to secure for himself and Miss Bianca Bennett a room at the Danieli. To hell with the money, he thought, again forgetting that it didn't matter; if ever there was a girl in the world worth spending thousands on it was the delightful Bianca Bennett, a pretty young bank cashier who had a most appealing peccadillo.

Jonathon spent the rest of the day and the Wednesday studying the news about the events for which he was ultimately responsible. While on one level there was widespread condemnation for the atrocities, there was also a good deal of tittering going on, mostly from the chattering classes who, like himself, considered the gutter press to be guilty of far worse crimes. To his relief, police were reporting that they did not, as yet, have anything to go on but were awaiting the results of an examination of CCTV footage. He suddenly remembered that the following day he was again due at Mrs. Wilson's at number 37. He had a nightcap of a small glass of port, with which he washed down three water-biscuits topped with Stilton and walnut halves, then went to bed and plotted how he could make further use of Brian, Terry, Spencer and anyone else they might be able to tempt into their fold of saboteurs.

"Jonathon," said Mrs. Wilson the following morning, "before you start work on the garden, would you mind going to the newsagent for me?"

"Not at all, why?"

"I've been without a newspaper for three days and I can't bear it any longer."

"Oh dear, so you take the Daily Mail?"

"Yes."

"I'm sorry to hear that," said Jonathon, genuinely, "it's a terrible thing, isn't it Mrs. Wilson?"

10 | Venice

On his way home from Mrs Wilson, Jonathon bought £200 worth of top-up vouchers for the black phone and coded them in. He had remembered that mobile phone companies were required by law to assist the police in tracing people, so to help eliminate the possibility of anyone discovering his identity, he had taken care not to link a credit or debit card to the black phone's number. It didn't matter that only Frank, Eddie, Brian and Spencer knew the number; he didn't want to take any chances.

Gardening is physically demanding and Jonathon rested for a while on his sofa, happy in the knowledge that he had now successfully buried two waterproof packages, each containing fifty thousand pounds, in Mrs. Wilson's back garden. He had been tempted to write a list of the whereabouts of all the bundles of cash he had squirreled away but decided that would be foolhardy and instead committed everything to memory, including the list of book titles he had chosen at Richmond Library.

The white phone rang and it was a bubbly Bianca.

"I need to know where we're going," she said, "I don't know what to pack!"

"We're going to Venice," said Jonathon, I think you'll…"

He had to hold the phone away to protect his eardrum from her shrieks of excitement. Once she'd calmed down a bit, he risked bringing it back a little closer.

"So, you're pleased then?"

"Oh my God, oh my God, oh my GOD," she exclaimed, "I am so, SO excited!"

"Look, I'd suggest we have dinner tonight but I've got to put a few things in motion before I go away; you don't mind?"

"No not at all," said Bianca, who was still a bit breathless, "it'll take me all evening to go through my wardrobe and choose stuff."

"We're staying somewhere a bit posh," offered Jonathon.

"Mum and dad want to know exactly where I'll be."

Jonathon had forgotten that she lived at home with her parents. "Tell them it's the hotel Danieli; you'll be perfectly safe there."

"Ok."

"Except from me," he added. "The flight is at 12.30 from Gatwick and I'll pick you up in a cab at around 10, so be ready, ok?"

"Ok," said Bianca, who was already imagining herself in various lovely outfits, hopping in and out of beautifully garlanded gondolas, "I promise I'll be ready."

Jonathon turned on the news to find that the attacks on the Mail were still the lead item and that, so far, the police were none the wiser. They did however have two potential leads; both of which came from the examination of the CCTV footage taken at the scene.

Jonathon held his breath as he watched a grainy and stuttering image, time and date-stamped, of a hooded character surreptitiously placing something on what was said to be a fire alarm on a wall inside the building. 'Oh Christ,' he thought, 'that must be Terry.'

The news footage then cut to another grainy image, this time an exterior night shot of a car parked opposite the printing works; a car which, without turning on its lights, moved off shortly after the explosions. It was difficult to make out the make and model or the number plate but the reporter stated that the police were busy working on enhancing the image.

'Oh Christ,' thought Jonathon again, and he picked up the black phone.

"Brian?" he said in his Birmingham accent. "Are you watching this?"

"Hello James," said Brian, "yes I am but there's no need to worry."

"No need to bloody worry?!" Jonathon shouted. "They've got you on camera; of course there's a need to bloody worry."

"James, calm down, it's not my car."

Brian explained that he and Terry had driven half-way to the printing works in his own car, parked and then hot-wired another. After doing the job, they had simply returned the stolen car and driven his own back to Aldershot. It was then about two in the morning and he had taken great care to replace all the wiring back in the steering column. If anyone was going to get a visit from the police it was whoever owned the other car; someone who probably didn't even know it had been stolen but who might have been a little surprised by the petrol gauge reading. He also emphasized that there was no way Terry could possibly be identified from the CCTV images.

"Did you wear gloves?"

"Does the Pope shit in the woods?"

Jonathon relaxed. "Look, I want to press on with the other four," he announced, "and they have to be done simultaneously."

"When?"

"About three or four weeks from now," Jonathon continued, "do you think you can find enough men?"

"If they have to be done simultaneously then I'll have to find them," said Brian, who smelled more money coming, "Terry and I can't be in four places at once."

"Of course, but it has to be this way," said Jonathon, "if we hit just one more paper by itself then the other three might start to get too well prepared and the element of surprise would be lost forever."

"Just remind me which four we're talking about."

"The Sun, the Star, the Mirror and the Express.

"My wife reads the Mirror."

"And is that going to stop you?"

Brian laughed, "I suppose not."

"There's another two hundred thousand in it."

"But we got a hundred grand for the first one," Brian protested, "now you're offering only twice that for four times the work."

"I'm not made of money," said Jonathon, "and you can be in charge of how it's split."

Brian rapidly did some sums. Was it really necessary to have two men for each hit? Maybe not. And anyway, he and Terry deserved larger slices of the total; himself for orchestrating things and doing the recruiting, and Terry for being in charge of the bombs. He was sure he could come out with another thirty or forty thousand at least. It was still pretty lucrative for what was really only a few hours' work.

"Ok," he said at last, "leave it with me."

"Good man," said Jonathon, "I'm now going away for a few days but I'll be contactable if you have any news or any questions."

"I've got one now James," said Brian, "do you also want me to find the IT guys again?"

"No," said Jonathon, "leave that to me; I'll text you the names of another couple of books at Richmond Library so you can go and pick up half the money tomorrow."

He hung up and dialed Spencer.

"James; what can I do for you?"

"You can persuade a few of your peers to do the same as you did."

Jonathon told him that he wanted to hit the other four tabloids and that it had to be done simultaneously, albeit there would be no need to carry out more find/change games first.

"I understand," said Spencer, "and when do you want this to happen?"

"I'm thinking three or four weeks from now."

"Same money as before?"

"I've earmarked another two hundred thousand to cover it and you can be in charge of how it's split and between whom. I'll text you another couple of book titles to get you started, ok?"

"Ok," said Spencer, "and is there anything else?"

"Actually yes," said Jonathon, "there's no hurry but you can start to have a quiet think about how to interfere with television broadcasts."

"Bloody hell," said Spencer, "I won't ask why."

"Good, because I haven't decided yet; I just want to find out if it's possible."

"Oh it's sure to be possible; it's just a matter of finding the right person."

"There'll be even more money for you if you do."

Jonathon decided to get his chores out of the way before relaxing for the evening. He first sent a text to Brian, 'Fancy Coffins to Make Yourself' and 'The Joy of Knitting'. Next, to Spencer, he sent 'The Book of Marmalade' and 'Rats for Those who Care'.

Having not had a simple pie and a pint for a while, he took himself off to the Ferret's Knees and was relieved that there was no sign of Bobble Hat and his gang on the streets. He settled at his favourite table near the fireplace and was delighted that the landlord had thought it wasn't yet cold enough to light the fire, but had nonetheless chosen to do so. Jonathon stared into the flames as he drank his pint. Gazing at a fire, like looking at waves or watching other people working, is immensely calming and therapeutic and Jonathon was in a semi-trance when his pie and chips arrived. It was beef and ale and he asked for some English mustard on the side.

Having eaten, he crossed to the table on which the pub kept a selection of the day's papers, picked up The Times and settled back in his chair, where he turned to the letters page.

'Sir,

While the attack on one of your competitors was of course a criminal offence, I find it difficult to see how anyone could do anything but applaud the perpetrators for ridding us, albeit probably only for a while, of one of this country's main providers of bile and balderdash. Please forgive me for referring to them as a competitor of yours.'

LtCdr (Rtd) Frederick Grimes, Suffolk

'Thank you kind sir,' thought Jonathon, who was pleased to see that, of the five letters printed on the subject, only one was in any way negative about the act. Still winding down, he fetched himself another pint of bitter and a large Laphroaig and scanned the letters pages of some of the other papers. Encouragingly, most of the contributors seemed to agree wholeheartedly with LtCdr (Rtd) Frederick Grimes.

Back home, he felt too exhausted to bother with packing and, given that it only ever took him a couple of minutes he decided to leave it until the morning. Instead, he had a small nightcap and collapsed straight into bed.

At 10.00 am, Jonathon's taxi rolled up outside Bianca's place and he and the driver waited patiently for her to appear. At 10.10, he suggested they honk the horn. Nothing. At 10.15, he got out, strode up to front door and rang the bell. Still nothing.

And then finally the door opened. "Oh I'm so sorry," said Bianca, "I'll only be another couple of minutes."

She pointed to a suitcase the size of a small car and said "here, can you take this for me?"

Muttering under his breath about how Miss Bennett might pay for this, Jonathon wheeled the case to the taxi and only just managed to heft it into the boot, whereupon he stood and drummed his fingers on the roof and looked repeatedly at his watch.

She appeared moments later and Jonathon now looked at her properly. She had clearly had her hair done specially for the trip and what he remembered to be long blonde straight hair was now gently curled and it fell beautifully over the shoulders of a short white leather jacket, with which she wore a pair of tight blue jeans and which afforded a tantalising glimpse of arguably her most alluring feature as she turned to shut the gate, bending over slightly to close the latch.

"Hi," she said breezily.

"Hurry up and get in."

"Am I in trouble?"

"Yes."

"Oh goodie."

The traffic was kind enough and they arrived at Gatwick's north terminal not much later than Jonathon had estimated. British Airways seldom quibbled about just an extra kilogram or two, but Bianca had managed to ensure that Jonathon found himself paying for excess baggage. After checking in, they still had half an hour or so before they needed to get to the gate.

"I need to quickly get a new pair of sunglasses," said Bianca, "mine are horrid."

"Trust me," said Jonathon, "wait until we get there and we'll get you a classic pair by Persol; you'll look fabulous."

"You mean I don't look fabulous now?"

Jonathon wasn't going to get caught that easily. He knew how men the world over managed to fall into this kind of trap. 'Which do you prefer?' a woman might ask, holding up a blue dress and a red dress. 'Er, the red one,' says the man, innocently. 'Oh,' demands the woman, 'so you don't *like* the blue one?!'

"Bianca," he said with a grin.

"Yes?"

"Watch it."

They killed some time in the bar before heading to the gate and it soon became clear that Bianca had been studying their destination, for in quick succession she rattled off a dozen things she wanted to do and places she wanted to see, starting with the Rialto bridge. She had even downloaded a travel guide app to her phone, which she proudly waved at Jonathon.

"See?" she said. "It's all on here – what to do in Venice!"

"And how's your Italian?"

"Oh, you'll have to do all the talking."

"This should be interesting," said Jonathon, "my Italian's pretty crap."

On their way to the gate, it was not purely out of chivalry that he let Bianca walk ahead of him. 'Sweet Jesus,' he thought, 'it's like two hard-boiled eggs in a condom,' and he remained mesmerized all the way to the holding area, as did a few of the other male passengers.

The flight was uneventful, save for a short spell of nasty turbulence during which Bianca held on tightly to Jonathon's arm and nuzzled her head into his neck. Reassuringly, he pressed his cheek onto the top of her head.

"I'm scared," she said, truthfully.

"It's ok," he said, "we're in safe hands."

He remembered his first experience of turbulence, which had been in his early twenties on a flight back to London from Frankfurt. The plane was being tossed around like a cork in the surf and he was genuinely in fear of it crashing. But when he looked around at the other passengers, most of whom were businessmen returning home, they appeared not to have a care in the world. Obviously frequent fliers, they had learned to pick up their drinks from their tables and allow their arms to move up and down, left and right, as if on gimbals, to soak up the buffeting. It seemed to Jonathon that their biggest concern was spilling their gins and tonic, not dying, and he himself had then relaxed.

They arrived at Marco Polo airport and after a brief struggle getting Bianca's case off the carousel they began the long walk to the various pontoons. Dutifully, Jonathon again allowed her to walk ahead of him until they reached the private water taxis, where he rejected the painted Rivas in favour of one with immaculately varnished yet otherwise bare mahogany. The driver winced as he lifted Bianca's case onto the vessel.

"Is yours Signorina, yes?"

"Si, Signor" said Bianca, who on the flight had been studying the phrase section of her travel guide.

"Mamma mia."

Jonathon shrugged, palms out, in a gesture of male camaraderie, at which the driver winked, started the engine and slowly reversed away from the pontoon. The sun had not yet begun to set and with its rays glinting off the water, Jonathon reflected that there was no finer way to approach Venice. He had been twice before, once on a school trip and once with Wendy and on neither occasion had he arrived in such style.

Once out of the speed restricted channel, the driver opened up the Riva and Bianca let out a whoop of delight at the sudden acceleration. As he turned into the wake of another vessel, she held on tightly and whooped some more.

Before long they were at the lagoon and slowly inching up the narrow canal which led to the side entrance of the Danieli, where the driver happily let a porter deal with Bianca's case.

Jonathon had spared no expense on their accommodation. Even a standard room at the hotel was swimming in luxury but he had opted for a room with a balcony, overlooking the lagoon.

Bianca gasped as she walked in. "Oh Jonathon, this is amazing."

"Yup," he said, "it's not too bad is it?"

The porter placed their luggage on the suitcase racks, handling one case with far more ease than the other, then paused so that Jonathon could tip him before he left. Bianca was already out on the balcony with her arms stretched out wide and turning in circles on the spot as she drank in the cool crisp air. Jonathon stopped her spinning by placing his hands on her waist.

"Happy?" he said.

"I'm in Heaven," she said, "absolute Heaven."

"How would you like to do me a favour?"

"Anything," she said, "anything at all."

"I hate unpacking. Would you mind doing it for me and putting my clothes away?"

She thought about it for a moment. "On one condition," she said.

"And that would be?"

"I do it naked on high heels."

"You little minx."

He lay on the bed and watched intently as Bianca went to her case and took out a pair of her stilettos. She then peeled off her jacket and T-shirt, slipped out of her jeans and panties and briefly sat on the edge of the bed, tantalising him as she leant forward to put on each shoe.

Now dressed appropriately, she began to unpack Jonathon's case, provocatively bending over as she removed each item, and it was a surprise to both of them that she managed to get as far as hanging up a third shirt before he pounced on her and gave her what she both deserved and desired before they frantically formed the beast with two backs.

Returning to her task, the glow slowly faded and Jonathon was already beginning to look forward to round two, whenever that might be.

Bianca finished unpacking his case and turned her attention to her own, whereupon he couldn't help but blink at what he saw.

"You're kidding me," he said as she calmly removed two pairs of dumb-bells from her case and placed them on the floor, "that explains a lot."

"They're for my morning exercises," she said, oblivious.

"How much do they weigh?"

"These two are 3 kilograms each and these two are 5 kilograms."

"You brought 16 kilograms of solid steel all the way to Venice?"

"Yes," she said innocently, and Jonathon burst out laughing.

"You didn't think that, maybe…oh, never mind."

"And look how clever I am," she said, waving at what was otherwise a half-empty case, "there's plenty of room to take back lots of lovely Italian clothes."

They felt they didn't have the energy left to roam the streets and explore, and instead decided to take dinner on the terrace, but not before strolling along to St Mark's Square for an aperitif. They chose Caffè Florian, not least because of the ambience created by the string quartet playing outside. Jonathon ordered a negroni and Bianca, a glass of prosecco. When the drinks arrived, Bianca asked for a taste of Jonathon's.

"Ugh!" she said. "It's so bitter; what's in it?"

"Gin, Campari and vermouth," he replied, "and it really does stimulate the appetite; these Italians know a thing or two."

By now the sun had set, the front of the Doge's Palace was bathed in moonlight and the arches all around the Piazza were illuminated. If anyone had the need to take yet more publicity shots of Venice, this was the time.

As they strolled back to the hotel they kept close to the water, where dozens of gondolas bobbed up and down, as if in competition with each other to look the most enticing.

"I know what you're thinking," said Jonathon.

"What?"

"You can't wait to go in one," he said, "tomorrow, I promise."

Dinner was as excellent as Jonathon had expected and as the coffee and liqueurs arrived, the black phone made a sound like a train. It was a text from Brian: 'Good news. Can you talk?' Jonathon replied 'No. Will call when I can.'

It wasn't long before he could, for Bianca decided to take a shower before sleeping. As soon as he heard the water running and the bathroom door close behind her, he called Brian.

"Brian; James," he said, wondering how he would explain his accent to Bianca should she ever overhear him.

"I've got one more," said Brian, "a bloke called Graham."

"Ah, the one from Exeter."

"How did you know that?"

"Frank and Eddie mentioned him in the same breath as you."

"Ok, well he never got in touch with you because he didn't want to talk to any journalists."

"Fair enough."

"Anyway, now he knows what it's really about and that there'll be tons of money in it for him, he wants to play along. He's driving up to meet me tomorrow."

"Excellent."

"Also Terry thinks he knows of someone but hasn't managed to track him down yet."

"Ok, listen, I'd better go," said Jonathon, "you can text me anytime."

"There's one more thing," said Brian, "one of those books wasn't at the library."

"Fuck," said Jonathon, "which one?"

"The Joy of Knitting."

"You're kidding me," said Jonathon, "who the hell would want to borrow that?"

"I should think quite a lot of people mate, but you'll text me another title, yes?"

"Yeah, sure, bye."

He hung up and immediately texted Brian 'How to Find Your Car Keys'. He was lying on the bed, still turning over in his mind how to retrieve the missing left-luggage receipt when Bianca appeared, toweling herself dry.

"Is something the matter?" she asked.

"I may have just lost fifty thousand pounds," said Jonathon, unable to disguise his irritation, for he knew it was his own fault. After all, plenty of people are keen on knitting.

"Oh dear," she said sweetly, "is there anything I can do to help?"

"Oh yes," he said, "but I'm too tired for that now; let's sleep."

Before he dozed off, he sent another text to Brian: 'Find out from register who borrowed knitting book.'

In the morning, while Jonathon and Bianca wandered through the narrow streets to the Rialto bridge, Brian went once more to Richmond Library and Terry continued to try and get in touch with Neville, who he felt sure would be delighted to become a member of their motley crew.

"Excuse me," said Brian to one of the librarians, "I wonder if you could tell me when 'The Joy of Knitting' is due back in."

The librarian, a stiff woman in her forties wearing a tweed

suit, a high-necked white blouse and a string of pearls, regarded him with incredulity over her spectacles. Before her stood a giant of a man in a black leather jacket, completely bald and with the ragged beginnings of a moustache. Few people could look less likely to be keen on knitting.

"I'll have a look for you sir," she said, and she thumbed through the register of books that were out. "Actually it's due back in today."

"May I reserve it?"

"Yes, of course. Name?"

Brian flustered; he hadn't thought to prepare a name. "Er, Jeremy," he said, "Jeremy Higginbotham."

"I'll make a note sir," she said, cocking her head to one side, "will there be anything else?"

"No, no, thank you," said Brian and, feeling slightly foolish, he went off in search of 'How To Find Your Car Keys'. He removed the receipt and took up a position at a table near the front desk, where he sat and waited for someone who looked like they might be keen on knitting. There was no point in going to Heathrow again twice.

Meanwhile Terry finally made contact.

"Neville!" he said. "At last! You're a hard man to track down."

"Terry!" said Neville. "My phone's been on the blink; it's been a long time old friend."

"Yes it has. Listen, can you meet up? I've got a proposition for you."

"Well, I've got nothing better to do; what is it?"

"I can't talk about it on the phone."

Having agreed with Neville that they meet at the Crimea Inn that evening, Terry turned his attention to how he might spend some of the money he was earning. He had fifty grand and there was another fifty on the way and he had already decided it was time he treated himself to a new car. He now also gave serious thought to going under the knife of a plastic surgeon. He didn't care too much about the scars on his arm, but he longed to be rid of the scarring on his face, as he knew that most women couldn't bear to look at him and what he wanted more than anything else in the world was a steady girlfriend.

In Venice, Jonathon and Bianca were being textbook tourists, slowly negotiating the Grand Canal on what, for millions, had become the mandatory gondola ride. Jonathon was grateful that their gondolier hadn't broken into 'O Sole Mio', for he was sure he would simply get a fit of the giggles. When they turned off onto a small side canal, Bianca asked if she could have a go and to Jonathon's surprise their gondolier agreed. He allowed her to stand next to him on the stern and wield the pole, which endearingly she did with a very serious look on her face, as if she was now personally responsible for the safety of the vessel's other two occupants. Jonathon thought the gondolier had been ill-advised and not a little foolhardy at putting himself at risk of being cast into the water, but he seemed to know what he was doing and in fact only twice did he have to use his foot to fend off the gondola from the old stone walls. It was a moment that deserved to be captured and Jonathon shot several stills and also some video on his white phone. Bianca asked him why he had two phones, for she had seen him using the black one the previous evening.

"Ah," he said, "one is for business and the other is for pleasure."

In Richmond, Brian was carefully studying everyone who came into the library, in particular anyone who looked like they might have an interest in knitting. It seemed like hours but in fact it had taken only forty-five minutes for a likely suspect to arrive, cross to the returns desk and reach into her bag. And there it was. Brian jumped up and spoke to the little old woman.

"Excuse me madam," he said, "I've been waiting for this," whereupon he grabbed one end of The Joy of Knitting. But the woman refused to let go of the other end.

"Take your hands off it!" she said, and she snatched it from Brian's grasp.

"No, it's mine!" protested Brian, and he snatched it back.

The librarian looked on in bewilderment over her spectacles. She had seen many things in her time working at the library, but had never encountered a little old lady and a very large, violent looking man engaged in a tussle over a book about knitting. Brian leafed through the book and sighed with relief. The left-luggage receipt was still there.

"I've changed my mind madam," he said, and he handed the book back to her, "there, you have it." Then, waving a small piece of paper at both her and the librarian, he said "See this? It's worth fifty thousand pounds; that'll buy me a lot of wool."

The two women stared open-mouthed as Jeremy Higginbotham half walked and half ran out of the library, the ceiling lights reflecting in his shiny bald head.

Brian went to Heathrow for the second time in two days, collected another two bags and drove back to Aldershot, where he dropped in on Terry, who informed him that he was meeting up with Neville that evening at the Crimea Inn. With Graham on his way up from Exeter at that very moment, they agreed it made sense for all four of them to get together and work out their best plan of attack. Before leaving, Brian handed Terry fifty thousand pounds to split between himself and Neville. Apart from being a trained killer and now indisputably a criminal, Brian was a fair man and had abandoned his previous thoughts of taking for himself a larger cut of the money. There were four targets and four of them to carry out the attacks and they would each be facing the same risks. And besides, James had let him have an extra twenty grand at the outset.

In Venice, while Jonathon waited patiently in the chair reserved for men who were enduring shopping expeditions, Bianca tried on no fewer than eleven pairs of Persol sunglasses.

"What do you think?" she said finally.

Jonathon had in fact preferred an earlier pair she had picked up but these were perfectly fine and besides, it was nearly that negroni time of day.

"They really suit you," he said, "you look stunning."

"Clever you," she said, flinging her arms around his neck, "I'd have settled for something from Gatwick but these are truly lovely."

Unfortunately, Jonathon had to wait another two hours for his aperitif, Bianca having dragged him into a succession of clothes shops on their way back to St Marks Square. But with feminine guile, having noticed he was tiring of her endlessly coming out of changing rooms and giving him a twirl, she had grabbed him by the arm and marched him into a lingerie shop, in which, following some semi-naked and jaw-dropping twirls, he had ended up spending more on lingerie than on all the dresses and all the other clothes put together.

Having dropped off the shopping bags at the hotel they headed out again in search of refreshment and fell into Harry's Bar, where Jonathon finally got his hands on a negroni and where Bianca chose a bellini, the bar's signature drink.

Meanwhile, in Aldershot, four men were discussing Jonathon's requirements over a few pints at the Crimea Inn.

"Seriously?" said Neville.

"Seriously," replied Terry, "but we don't get the second twenty-five if anyone gets hurt."

"So who's this guy James?" asked Graham.

"I've only met him once," said Brian, "all I know is that he has long dark curly hair, a moustache, wears glasses, comes from Birmingham and has a fuck of a lot of cash."

"And a grudge against the media," added Terry, "well, the gutter press, anyway."

"So," said Brian, to Neville and Graham, "are you two in?"

"For sure," said Neville, who badly needed the money.

"I guess so," said Graham, "I've got nothing better to do."

Brian nodded to Terry and they each withdrew a wad of twenty-five thousand pounds and handed them to their new recruits. Brian then reached into another pocket and tossed four small screwed-up balls of paper onto the table. "I think this is the fairest way," he said, "who's going to go first?"

"What are they?" asked Graham.

"The names of the targets," explained Terry.

"Ok," said Neville, "here goes." He picked up one of the balls of paper and unraveled it to reveal the word 'mirror' scrawled in thick, inelegant writing. In turn, Graham picked 'express', Terry picked 'star' and Brian was left with 'sun'.

"So now what?" asked Graham.

"We each need to go and do a recce of the buildings and get the answers to these questions," said Terry, handing them all a checklist of the facts they needed to find out, "let's meet back here in 72 hours."

"But first I reckon we deserve a curry," said Brian and, to Terry, "is it ok if Graham kips at yours until this thing is over? It'll save any more awkward questions from Penny; she's already wondering what I'm up to, disappearing off all the time."

"No worries," said Terry, who would be glad of the company, and they all walked over to the Taj Mahal.

Meanwhile, Jonathon and Bianca had left Harry's Bar and wandered over to the outside area of the ground floor restaurant of the Londra Palace, where he ordered a very fine Nero d'Avola and a plate of spaghetti vongole. Bianca had chosen the seafood risotto and as they waited for their food, the wine was slipping down rather too easily.

"Let's get another bottle," said Jonathon, "this stuff is delicious."

"Are you trying to get me drunk you naughty man?" said Bianca.

"I don't think I need to."

The fact was that, prior to coming to Venice, they had spent only one night together, albeit a most enjoyable one, and over the next few days they slowly got to know each other in greater and increasingly emotional depth. Bianca, who to Jonathon looked to be only in her early twenties, was in fact coming up to her 30th birthday and she was living back at home after a disastrous relationship with a man whom she only narrowly avoided marrying. Her job at the bank had only ever been intended to be a stop-gap, but she had fallen into a rut and didn't know how to climb out.

"What would you *like* to do," Jonathon asked her over lunch one day.

She thought about it for some time before replying, "I'd like to get back to my ambition to work as a vet. I've got all the A-levels I need."

"Then do it," said Jonathon.

"But it's a five year course and I don't have the money and neither do my parents."

"Leave it to me."

"But Jonathon, we hardly know each other."

"I know you well enough already to know that I'd like to help you."

"Oh Jonathon; aren't you wonderful!"

"I'm serious," he said, "you're a very lovely lady."

By the time it came to leave Venice, where he had enjoyed much fine wine and fine food and also plenty of chastisement and penetration of the delightful and coquettish Miss Bennett, Jonathon had already decided that he would set her up in a flat of her own, in addition to funding her veterinary studies.

On their last night they visited the casino, where he gave her five hundred euros to play with and where she decided to concentrate on roulette. When she was about three thousand euros up she said "let's go; I'd like to buy you a drink somewhere," and they went off to cash in her chips.

"Have you played roulette before?" Jonathon asked.

"No, that was my first time," she giggled, "didn't I do well?"

Jonathon agreed that indeed she had done well, especially considering he had just lost about five thousand.

As they hopped on a vaporetto back to St Marks Square for a last nightcap at Caffè Florian, four rogues were again at the Taj Mahal in Aldershot, sharing their observations from their various reconnoiters of the printing presses of four UK tabloid newspapers.

11 | Fun on the river

Back in England, having dropped off Bianca at her parents' house, Jonathon returned home and decided to finally treat himself to a new car. It was nearly three weeks since he had become rich and he figured it was about time he splashed out a bit. In Venice, he had been monitoring the news stories about the attacks on the Daily Mail and had been relieved that the police were no nearer to solving the crime. The one lead they did have had proved to be a dead end. After their technicians had enhanced the CCTV footage of the car opposite the printing works, they had managed to identify the number plate and had carried out a dawn raid on the house belonging to the owner, only to discover that he had been out of the country at the time and could provide several alibis. A close examination of the steering column revealed that it had been tampered with but sadly there were no fingerprints.

Well done Brian.

Jonathon now scoured the news again and, satisfied, he turned his attention to finding himself a new car on the internet. Determined not to be too obvious or flash, he settled on a 1970 Bristol 411, which he arranged to go and test drive the following morning. The day after that, it was again his turn to have Nicholas and Jackie and he looked forward to picking them up in something, anything, that was not his tired old van.

Having not heard from Brian for a few days, he texted him to see if he could talk.

Within a few seconds the black phone rang.

"James," said Brian, "I've got some good news and some bad news."

"What?" said Jonathon. "Have you discovered that the Pope doesn't shit in the woods?"

Brian chuckled and went on to describe how the team now comprised himself, Terry, Graham and Neville and that they had each studied one of the four targets. The trouble was, they had yet to work out how they could pull it off.

"Leave it with me," said Jonathon, "I'll have a think."

"And by the way," said Brian, "I managed to get the other receipt," and he explained how he had risked life and limb battling with a little old lady at Richmond Library.

Jonathon then called a very clever computer geek.

"James," said Spencer, "I was about to call you; I've got some good news…"

"…and some bad news?" said Jonathon.

"Well, yes," said Spencer, "I've managed to hack into two of the other papers myself and I've persuaded the head of IT at a third to play ball for just twenty five grand."

"And the fourth?"

"He wants seventy five."

"Well that still leaves you with a hundred," said Jonathon, "same as before."

"True," said Spencer.

"It's lucky I've still got some money left," said Jonathon, "I've got to pay whoever might be able to interfere with television broadcasts."

"That's the bad news. I haven't even started on that yet," said Spencer, "one thing at a time, eh?"

"Agreed," said Jonathon, "but keep it in the back of your mind."

Next he picked up the white phone and dialed Bianca.

"Hello naughty one!" they said simultaneously.

"Listen," continued Jonathon, "I've been thinking; how would you like to move into a flat of your own somewhere?"

"Are you serious?"

"Perfectly," he said, "but nothing too fancy; a maximum of a thousand a week and it must have a car space."

Not for the first time, Jonathon had to hold the phone away from his ear and wait for her screams of excitement to subside a little.

"Have you finished unpacking yet?"

"Not yet," she said, "and I'm sorry about us having to buy another suitcase but I had no idea you were going to be so generous with all those clothes."

"It's my pleasure," said Jonathon, "you look wonderful in all of them."

"Thank you," she said.

"In fact you look wonderful out of all of them, too."

"You are so naughty."

After a few minutes of erotic exchanges, Jonathon remembered that he had very little to eat in the flat and he took himself off to the supermarket, where he had yet another infuriating encounter with one of the automatic checkout machines and he determined to himself that one day he would do something about them, if it were possible.

Back home, inspired by Italy, he rustled up a delicious linguine dish and opened a bottle of La Lagune. Knowing he would soon run out of it, he made a mental note to track down the Nero d'Avola he had found in Venice and to order a case or two, just to be on the safe side.

After dinner, he lay on the sofa and turned over in his mind how Brian, Terry, Graham and Neville might deliver a nasty surprise to four other tabloid newspapers. As had happened several times before, he eventually dozed off on the sofa only to awake in the early hours, shivering, whereupon he took himself off to bed. But this time, he missed the warmth of a certain Miss Bianca Bennett, whose delicious body he had discovered was a perfect fit in the spoons position.

The next morning he had a Full English at Joe's café and hopped on a bus to a classic car dealership in Chelsea. He fell in love with the Bristol straightaway and after a short drive with the salesman he bought it on the spot, but rather than go straight home he went for a spin down the A3 as far as Cobham, where he exited and rejoined the road back to London, breaking the speed limit nearly all the way. Having parked, he retrieved a few essentials from his van and put them in the boot of the Bristol before returning to his flat.

After making some coffee, he sent a joint text to Nicholas and Jackie: 'what would you like to do this weekend?'

Jackie replied immediately: 'can we go up in a helicopter again?'

An hour later, Nicholas texted: 'something silly'.

Jonathon thought about it for a while, did some research on the internet and decided on something in-between their two suggestions, whereupon he sent them another text: 'pack swimwear and towels and warm hats and gloves. I'll pick you up at six and it's going to be a four-hour drive.'

Jackie replied: 'can't we get there in a helicopter?'

Jonathon again turned his thoughts as to how his team of saboteurs could simultaneously wipe out the printing presses of four more desperate tabloids but he drew a blank and, seeking solace, he messaged Bianca to see if she would like to go somewhere for dinner that evening. She replied that she'd love to and he suggested that she first come to his place for a little hanky-spanky before they went out to eat.

Over dinner, Bianca updated Jonathon on her progress in both finding herself a flat and enrolling on a veterinary course and it was clear that she had wasted no time on either. It was also clear that, after spending five nights together in Venice, neither of them had much enjoyed sleeping alone the night before, which was a measure of how close they were becoming.

In the morning, Jonathon ordered a cab to take her to her bank and after she left he started to prepare for the weekend ahead. He still had his wetsuit from his old scuba-diving days and he bundled it into his bag, along with swimming shorts and towels, a bottle of La Lagune and a hip-flask full of Laphroaig.

At six o'clock, he rolled up in his new car and waited for Nicholas and Jackie to appear. He kept waiting until his patience ran out and he walked up to the front door and rang the bell, whereupon Nicholas appeared, looking surprised.

"Dad!"

"Correct," said Jonathon, "well done."

"We were looking out for your van."

"Ah," said Jonathon, "well come along, chop-chop and don't forget Jackie."

Returning to the car, he was soon followed by the children, both of whom demanded to sit in the front. As usual, Jonathon tossed a coin.

"Heads," said Jackie.

"Heads it is."

She poked out her tongue at her brother and climbed in.

"Cool car dad," said Nicholas, "what is it?"

"It's a Bristol."

"I thought they came in pairs, hahahaha," chortled Nicholas, who was still young enough to be amused by tits and bums humour.

It went over Jackie's head but Jonathon couldn't help breaking into a broad grin. "Very droll, Nicholas; very droll."

Nicholas grunted, not wanting to let on he didn't understand.

"Where are we going?" asked Jackie.

"North Wales," said Jonathon, steering them towards the M40.

"Why?"

"Because it'll be fun."

"What kind of fun?"

"Wet fun."

Jackie crossed her arms and gave him one of her looks. Jonathon had decided to keep secret from them that he had booked a white-water rafting trip, preferring them to find out only at the last minute when they rolled up to the base by the river. That would not be until around eleven the next morning and meanwhile there was a long drive to the B&B, where he had reserved three rooms for a couple of nights. They probably wouldn't get there until about ten that evening and sadly they would probably have to eat something revolting at a motorway service station. But it didn't matter. The Bristol had a six-litre engine and Jonathon was excited about making the most of it on a long journey.

"Dad," said Jackie, "you know uncle David?"

"Yes darling, I *do* know uncle David."

"Well, you know how he calls his new car Bertie; what are you going to call this?"

Jonathon was pleased to have a new game to play. "What do you think it should be called?"

"How about Flossie?"

"Don't be an idiot," piped up Nicholas from the back, "it has to begin with a 'B'."

"Why?"

"Because it's a Bristol!"

Jackie accepted this and gave the matter some serious thought. She was determined to come up with the name that her father would settle on.

At length, she offered "ok, how about Bernadette?"

"No sweetie," said Jonathon, "it has to be shorter than that and I think it should be a boy's name, too."

"Why?"

Jonathon had to tread carefully. He didn't want his daughter to think he had some kind of sexist approach to naming cars.

"Well, it's a big old brute of a car with a massive engine," said Jonathon, "it's not like mum's little Fiat."

"Brian!" said Nicholas. "Brian the Bristol."

"Not bad," said Jonathon, who had private reasons for not wanting the association. "Not bad at all, but I think there's probably something better."

They carried on in silence for some time, with only two of them determined to come up with the answer, Jonathon preferring to leave it to one of his children to name his new car. Suddenly there was a flurry of suggestions; Bernie, Bobby, Barry, Billy, Basil, but none tickled Jonathon's fancy.

"Boris!" said Jackie.

"Hmm," said Jonathon, "Boris the Bristol; yes I like that one. It shouldn't really work but somehow it does."

Jackie swiveled in her seat and poked out her tongue at Nicholas for the second time that evening. "Nah, nah, nah, nah-nah."

Nicholas gave her one of his angriest and most disapproving grunts.

About half way to north Wales, hunger got the better of them and they turned into a motorway service station to keep body and soul together. They trooped into McDonalds and after the children each ordered, it was Jonathon's turn.

"I'll have a Big Mac and fries please," he said.

"Is that a Meal?" said the youth behind the counter.

"Well, yes," said Jonathon, "it's a meal."

"So what drink would you like?"

"Nothing thanks," said Jonathon, "just a Big Mac and fries."

"So it's not a Meal?"

"Of course it's a meal," said Jonathon, "well, of sorts."

Nicholas stepped in. "Dad, you're being embarrassing; if you have a burger and fries *and* a drink, they call it a Meal, with a capital 'M'."

"Good grief," said Jonathon, who wished he was back in Venice, "how sad is that?"

Their appetites sated, they climbed back into Boris the Bristol and continued on their journey, playing the number plate game until Nicholas and Jackie fell asleep.

Arriving at the B&B, Nicholas was left in charge of all the bags while Jonathon carried a fast asleep Jackie up to her room. Tucking her in, he gave her a kiss on the forehead before sorting out his son and retiring to his own room, where he retrieved his multi-tool from his pocket and opened the bottle of La Lagune, from which he poured as much as he could fit into the glass meant for toothbrushes. Before going to sleep, he texted 'night night; missing you already' to the most appealing and lovely woman he had met in a long time.

In the morning, Mrs. Llewellyn gave them all a sumptuous breakfast, which was billed as the 'Full Welsh'. She was a stereotypical B&B landlady; hale and hearty with vast, liquid breasts that sloshed around beneath a simple flowery dress. She also had a mischievous streak, which she signaled by slapping her own thigh when she thought she had said something amusing.

"So with a bit of luck we might see you again later Sir," she said, "and your little ones, too; let's hope that that there wicked river is kind to you all." Slap.

"Dad," said Jackie, "what are we *doing* here?"

"Wait and see," said Jonathon, "you two go and get your stuff from your rooms; I'll be waiting in the car."

It was only a twenty minute drive to the rafting centre, during which time Jonathon noted that the Bristol was built more for straight-line speed than agility through tight bends on a winding country road.

Upon arrival, Nicholas and Jackie were issued with 5mm wetsuits and the three of them were instructed by Gareth, their guide, to listen very attentively to the standard safety measures and paddling instructions, as were another group of four who were to join them in the thick rubber dinghy. He told them that the river was usually a grade three, but recent heavy rainfall had pushed it up to a four, which meant their trip was going to be even more exciting, and even more dangerous.

"Are we going to get wet?" asked Jackie.

"Only from the tips of your toes to the top of your head," said Gareth, "the rest of you will be fine." She folded her arms and gave him a look.

The water was easy for the first few hundred metres and the eight of them paddled along steadily but, up ahead, they could make out the first signs of some white, bubbling water and they could see a giant granite block, the size of a double-decker bus, looming up in the distance.

As they entered these first rapids, Gareth told everyone to keep paddling. Then, when they were about ten metres from the granite block, he shouted "left back, right forward!"

Jonathon was impressed, and as they glided safely past the first major obstacle of their journey, he wondered how many times their guide had negotiated this particular stretch of the Tryweryn river.

The rest of their trip downstream varied between absolute calm, boiling rapids and unexpected, heart-stopping drops, at which Nicholas swore like a sailor and Jackie screamed like someone was coming at her with an axe, even though she was loving every second.

Gareth steered them to the exit point and after his happy crew had hauled the dinghy ashore, Jonathon noticed that, despite her assuring him that she was fine, Jackie's lips had actually turned blue. He gathered her up in his arms and went off in search of a towel, all their own being back in the car at the entry point to the river. One of the waiting team lent him a big fluffy robe and he wrapped her up and settled her into the large people-carrier that was waiting to return them to the base, before he, Gareth, Nicholas, and the man from the other group heaved the dinghy onto the roof and strapped it down, inelegantly but securely.

Back at the B&B, he asked the children if they'd like to do it again the next day.

"Yo!" said Nicholas.

Jackie said "well, yes, but it's *so* cold."

"Don't worry," said Jonathon, "we'll put you in a thicker wetsuit."

The next day's rafting proved to be even more exciting than the first, for the event that everyone was afraid of, yet secretly and perversely wanted to actually happen, happened.

Gareth was an excellent river guide and an accomplished rafter, but the increased height and speed of the water due to the recent rains caused him to slightly misjudge one of the faster and steeper drops; one which also required a sharp turn to the left to avoid colliding with a sizeable boulder. The raft didn't capsize completely, but it spent long enough at about 90 degrees vertical to turf Jonathon, Nicholas, Jackie, and two of the other party of four into the river.

"FEET FIRST!" shouted Gareth.

He had drummed in this essential safety advice at the initial briefing, but it didn't hurt to ram it home, now that five of his charges were being carried rapidly downstream. Although all rafters were required to wear helmets, it was far better to hit a partially submerged rock with your feet instead of your head. The only thing they could do was ride it out until the rapids gave way to slower, calmer water, and as Jonathon craned his neck to see if the children were ok, his worries were answered by their screams of joy and as they bobbled at speed down the river.

Reaching the next quiet patch, the five souls overboard ended up either clinging to low overhanging branches or scrabbling onto flat, moss covered rocks and Gareth and the remaining two rafters paddled to them in turn and hauled them back on board.

"Oh wow," said Nicholas, "let's do that again."

"Yes Gareth," echoed Jackie, her teeth chattering, "can we; *can* we?"

Gareth was simply relieved that everyone was safe, for a death on one of his trips would certainly be frowned upon by the rafting company, who took that sort of thing very seriously. "Well," he said, "perhaps not today, ok?"

Jonathon was determined not to subject himself to another visit to a fast food outlet and he was relieved to find a local Chinese restaurant, where they ate before beginning the long drive back to London.

Arriving at Wendy's house, both the children were fast asleep and he had to gently coax them back to consciousness before getting them out of the car. Wendy arrived at the front door and looked askance at the state of them; tired, happy, dirty, disheveled, and looking like the sort of things one would remove with a pair of tongs.

Jonathon saw her frowning and pre-emptied her. "But they had a seriously great time," he said.

Back home, he poured himself a large Laphroaig, checked the news, where he found nothing to concern him and went to bed, where he gave further thought as to how he could help Brian and his team carry out their assignments.

As he drifted off to sleep, an idea began to formulate in his mind and after fleshing out a few details, his confidence in it grew to the point where he didn't want to risk forgetting about it in the morning. Turning on the light and grabbing the black phone, he created a new note and typed a reminder to himself; 'warehouse, vans, suits, voice generator'.

12 | Appearances can be deceptive

When he opened his eyes in the morning he found there had been no need to write himself a reminder. The idea was still crystal clear in his head and, the more he thought about it, the more he got excited.

After breakfast he called Brian and ran it past him.

"That's very good James," he said, "what a conniving mind you have."

"Thank you," said Jonathon, "so you think it'll work?"

"I don't see why not; I'll organize a meeting with the other three and get back to you later."

"I want to do it two weeks from today," added Jonathon, "Monday night at 11pm sharp; do you think you can get everything ready by then?"

"I guess so; it's just the suits that might be a problem."

"You'll have to steal them," said Jonathon, "it's not like you'll be able to hire them from Moss Bros."

Brian chuckled.

"And one more thing," said Jonathon, "all four of you will need a smartphone that's capable of storing and playing a sound file."

"It all costs money James," said Brian.

"Add it to your expenses claim," said Jonathon, "you and Terry still haven't been reimbursed for your hotel bills, although I guess his will be just a fraction of yours."

Brian was glad that James was a man of his word, and Jonathon was glad that Brian liked the idea.

That evening at the Crimea Inn, Brian, Terry, Graham and Neville agreed that James' plan was good enough to go with and besides, they hadn't had any ideas of their own that didn't carry with them a severe risk of one or all of them being caught and sent to prison.

"Ok," said Brian, "I'll look after getting us a lock-up or some kind of warehouse; Graham, you can recce the suits manufacturer and buy four toolboxes and Neville, here's two grand; you get the overalls and sort out four smartphones and four pay-as-you-go sim cards."

Neville pocketed the money. "I'll get them from four different mobile shops; there's no point in risking anyone making a connection."

"What about me?" asked Terry.

"You just get the Semtex and then relax and look pretty for a couple of days."

"Fuck off," said Terry, although he had become used to the occasional references to his appearance and had learnt to take them in good humour.

The following morning Brian again shaved off his moustache and put into his knapsack the wig that he had worn when he met Spencer at The Greyhound. Penny assumed he was going through some kind of midlife crisis; first he'd shaved off the moustache he'd had for fifteen years, then he grew it back, now he'd shaved it off again.

Later that day in East London, Brian always made sure to park his car around the corner from the various lock-up garages and warehouses that he visited. The first two were too small, the third wasn't tucked far enough away from prying eyes and the fourth was way bigger than they needed. On an industrial estate, he eventually found a warehouse that was about the right size and was situated at the far side from the main entrance to the complex. Nobody would have any reason to go there unless they were delivering something and the four of them would have no need to have anything delivered.

Wearing his wig, he negotiated the rate with the landlord and gave him two weeks' rent in advance, in cash.

"So what are you going to do with it?" asked the landlord.

"Me and my mates are setting up a vehicle re-spraying outfit," said Brian, "we managed to get some funding so now all we have to do is make it work."

"Well, good luck with it mate," said the landlord and, trousering his cash, he climbed into his old Jaguar and drove off.

Graham was at that moment near Banbury, where he discovered that the suit manufacturer was open six days a week and closed on Sundays. It made sense to break in late at night on the Sunday immediately prior to the attacks and steal what they needed. There was no point in the company sounding the alarm and giving the police any extra time to try and track down the thieves. Using a 300mm lens, he took several pictures from different vantage points with which to brief the others. On his way back to Aldershot, he visited four hardware stores in two different towns and picked up four steel toolboxes.

Neville, having bought four smartphones and sim cards, made rough guesstimates of the sizes of Brian, Graham and Terry and, at a painters and decorators' merchant, bought four sets of overalls; two blue, one orange and one white.

They had all agreed it was probably unwise to keep meeting at the Crimea Inn and instead they hooked up with each other at the Red Lion, where they drew up a list of everything else they were going to need: twenty litres of white paint, two litres of both dark blue paint and yellow paint, a litre of red paint, spray guns, masking tape, a few square metres of cardboard, a cutting board and some sharp knives.

Of the four of them, Brian was the only one who needed to

give some kind of excuse as to why he was going to be away for so long and, to create his alibi, the others agreed that they would all pretend they were going on a long fishing trip, which would at least provide cover for why Brian was taking a sleeping bag with him. All he had to remember was to take his fishing and camping gear, too.

They divided up the list of the other items they needed and agreed to pick them up before meeting at the warehouse the following afternoon, after which they would get food and drink supplies and make themselves at home before spreading out across London in the early hours of the morning to do some stealing.

Brian had noted that the warehouse had a small kitchen area equipped with a kettle and a stove, and the next morning he loaded up his car with all manner of camping pots, pans, mugs, plates, and cutlery, in addition to his necessary sleeping bag and unnecessary fishing rods.

"Good luck angel," said Penny, waving him off, "I hope you land a big one."

They arrived at the warehouse and parked their cars inside, lined up side by side against a wall, away from the main vehicle entrance.

Neville was the last to get there. "Bloody hell," he said, "it's bloody freezing in here."

They looked around at the huge space that was to be their home for the next several days. It was ugly, it was soulless and it was empty, apart from their four cars and the various detritus that had been left lying around by the many failed business ventures that had used the warehouse in the past; businesses that had started in hope and ended in misery, bankruptcy and bullying bailiffs.

Graham kicked over a pile of wood off-cuts and sat on his haunches. "Let's get the kettle on," he said, "cheer up; we won't be here for ever."

While Neville prepared the tea, Brian located the boiler and lit the pilot-light. So far so good, and he prayed to God it would spring into life as he turned up the dial.

"I tell you what," he said, "let's have a cuppa and then bugger off and find a curry house somewhere before we go and pick up the vans."

Just then there was a 'whummph' from the boiler, much to Brian's relief, as Terry reappeared from the toilet and announced that they'd better pick up some loo paper while they were gone.

Leaving on foot, they soon found themselves on a high street where there were umpteen Indian restaurants to choose from. They ate, programmed into their smartphones the postcode of the warehouse and, using night buses, they each went to a different part of London to steal a van and drive it back.

By two in the morning they had all returned and it was agreed that Neville deserved the star prize, for the van he had stolen belonged to a bedding company and was full of mattresses. The warehouse could still not be described as warm, but the bone-numbing chill had disappeared and had been replaced by a temperature that was still very comfortable compared with the conditions they had all sometimes had to endure in their days in the army.

They lugged out four mattresses, grabbed their sleeping bags and had another brew before turning in for the night, or what was left of it.

In the morning, Terry said "I don't suppose anyone picked up any bog paper did they?"

It was agreed that none of them had, and it was also agreed that Terry should hop in his car and go and get some. It was then agreed that he shouldn't, for he was the most recognizable of the four of them, so Neville was despatched instead.

While he was gone, Brian and Graham cooked up a breakfast of eggs, bacon, sausages and baked beans and, given that there was no toaster, fried bread, which everyone preferred anyway.

They ate, washed it down with mugs of tea and then went about fulfilling their various responsibilities, dealing with the vans in a kind of production line and taking care to make sure they looked as convincing as possible. Graham seemed best qualified to cut out the stencils for the lettering and while he busied himself in one corner of the warehouse, the others wielded the spray guns and waited for the first coat of white paint to dry before applying two strips of masking tape down both sides of each van, ready for the yellow paint to fill the gaps.

The whole process took several days to complete and was not without its frustrations, but spurred on by the thought of getting fifty grand each, they weren't complaining.

Finally, they stood back and admired their handiwork, the vans lined up next to each other with military precision. There were now just two days to go before they had to break into the suit factory and three days before they were due to carry out the attacks.

"Well, they look pretty damn convincing to me," said Neville, and they all agreed they deserved another curry, but before they trooped off, Brian remembered one last detail and he went to each van in turn and tampered with the wiring to the indicator lights.

Jonathon and Spencer had also been busy.

Spencer had decided it would be better if he carried out all four cyber attacks by himself and had parted with sixty-five thousand pounds to obtain the two passcodes that he hadn't managed to find out by hacking in from his own laptop; fifteen to the IT guy who wanted twenty five, and fifty to the one who wanted seventy five. He promised them they would each receive the balance on the day after the job was done. He had also bought three further laptops and now had all four lined up next to each other, ready for 11pm on Monday night.

Earlier in the week, while his team had been busy preparing the vans, Jonathon took Bianca to a smart block of apartments not far from the Royal Veterinary College at the University of London, where she had been accepted onto a five-year course. Bianca had fallen in love with the flat the day before and Jonathon agreed to pick her up from the bank after she finished work. The apartment was tastefully furnished, there was a 24-hour concierge and it had its own dedicated car space in the underground car park. On the kitchen table, the managing agent drew up the paperwork in the name of Miss Bianca Bennett and Jonathon parted with a year's rent in advance, which he put on a card.

Bianca flung her arms around him. "When shall we christen it?"

It was Jonathon's view that there was no time like the present and, with the sap rising, he ushered the agent out of the flat as quickly as possible without appearing rude.

The following morning he drove her to the bank for what was to be her last day of work. "Are they having a leaving-do for you?"

"A few of us are going down to the local pub, that's all; it's not exactly going to be a wild night out."

"I'd join you but I've got a few work things to attend to."

"That's ok; I understand," she said, "when will I see you again?"

"I'm going to be busy for the rest of this week and I've got the children this weekend, so how about Monday evening?" said Jonathon. "Anyway, that'll give you the chance to put your stamp on the place; it's not really *you* yet."

"Ok, my parents have promised to help me move all my stuff in."

'Poor them,' thought Jonathon, and he wondered how many dumb-bells they'd have to lug over.

"Am I ever going to meet them?" she asked.

"Nicholas and Jackie?"

"Yes."

"Yes, yes I think you will, one day," said Jonathon.

Back home, he downloaded from the internet a text-to-speech application and typed out a short message which he then converted to speech, saved as a sound file and transferred to his black phone. He had experimented with a few choices and settled on a slightly sinister sounding, metallic American voice which, thanks to the limitations of the software, delivered the words in a slightly staccato and threatening manner. Pleased with the effect, he texted Brian and asked to be sent the numbers of the four smartphones he and the others were going to be using on the night. Upon receiving them, he sent over the sound file to each phone and turned his attention to what he was going to do with Nicholas and Jackie that weekend; something which he would prefer to involve an enjoyable journey in the Bristol.

Eventually he decided on a trip to Calais, where he booked three rooms in a small hotel in the nicest part of the town. He also booked tickets on the Eurostar and texted the children to tell them to bring their passports.

'Where are we going?' Jackie texted back.

'France,' texted Jonathon.

'Ooh-la-la,' she texted back, pleased with herself.

He picked them up at six as usual and they all had an early night at his flat, ready for an early start to drive down to Folkestone on the Saturday morning, where they put themselves and Boris the Bristol on the train.

Jonathon insisted that while they were in Calais the children should speak French as often as possible, to help them with their studies at school.

"Oh merde," said Nicholas, who didn't have a gift for languages.

"Quelle bonne idée papa," said Jackie, who did.

At lunch, studying the menus in a decent restaurant Jonathon was keen to try, Nicholas announced that he couldn't find anything he liked the look of.

"Quel dommage," said Jonathon.

"Eh?" said Nicholas.

"Don't you know what that means?"

"Er, is it something to do with cheese?"

"Imbécile," said Jackie.

Language problems aside, the three of them thoroughly enjoyed Calais, where they visited the second world war museum and the fine arts museum and ate in good restaurants. At Sunday lunch, Jonathon treated himself to a flash-seared slab of foie gras which was served with warm slices of apple and pear and with which he drank a good sauterne. He despised the way that most geese were force fed to increase production of this delicacy, but the menu had assured him that theirs was responsibly sourced and he couldn't resist it.

It was late on Sunday night by the time Jonathon returned the children to Wendy and as he drove back to his flat, Brian, Terry, Graham and Neville were breaking into the suit manufacturer's factory. There were no guards on the premises so all they needed to do was disable the alarm and force entry. Not wanting to waste any time trying them on, they each chose a suit they thought would be a good fit and made off back to the warehouse, where they shared a bottle of whisky before turning in for what was to be their last night in their temporary home.

In the morning, Jonathon texted Brian, 'all set?'

Brian rang back.

"James, we're nearly done here. We just need to place our cars and then wait for tonight."

"Feeling confident?"

"Yes, but bloody nervous," said Brian, truthfully.

"You'll be fine," said Jonathon, "just be brazen; I'll text you the fourth book title tomorrow morning."

The four men ate a large breakfast and then packed away their belongings into their cars, taking care not to leave behind anything incriminating. They also wiped down everything they could remember touching. The only things they left in the warehouse were a multi-coloured floor and a good supply of toilet paper for whoever next rented the place.

They each drove their cars to within a half-mile or so from the print-works they had picked at random from the four screwed-up balls of paper that Brian had produced in the Crimea Inn. They made sure they parked legally and then made their way by public transport back to the warehouse, where they waited until nightfall.

Spencer, who had taken the day off from work, opened up his four laptop computers and double-checked the validity of the four passcodes in his possession, two of which he had found out by himself and two of which he had paid for. Satisfied, he deleted the evidence of his visits from the sites' activity logs and prepared the text for the four holding-pages that he was going to upload before changing the passcodes to ones of his own choosing.

At eight in the evening, Jonathon drove over to Bianca's apartment block, stopping on the way to buy her a large bunch of flowers. He parked the Bristol in the bay belonging to flat 27 and summoned the lift. He didn't have to stop off at the ground floor, but he chose to. Exiting the lift, he walked the short distance to the concierge's desk. On the way, he had to walk up three small steps and he deliberately tripped over the top one and ended up sprawled on the floor, letting go of the bunch of flowers, which landed inelegantly on the floor in front of him.

"Oh my goodness," said the concierge, who wore the

cream and brown uniform so typical of men who performed his function the world over, "are you alright sir?"

Jonathon picked up the flowers and got to his feet. "Yes, yes, I'm fine thanks," he said, "I just wanted to ask if there was an off-licence near here?"

"Yes sir; out the door, turn right, turn right again and it's about ten yards along."

"Excellent; thank you," said Jonathon.

"Visiting young Miss Bennett are we sir?" enquired the concierge off-hand, having remembered Jonathon from the previous week.

"Yes I am," said Jonathon.

"Very nice girl, sir, lovely girl."

Jonathon left the flowers, made his way to the off-licence and couldn't help smiling at another universal truth about concierges and porters who looked after apartment blocks; that some of them took vicarious pleasure from imagining the naughty adventures of the people in their buildings.

He returned with two good bottles of red, picked up the flowers and gave the concierge a wink. "Not only is she very nice," he said, "she's very naughty, too."

"I'll have to take your word for that sir," said the concierge, who mentally filed away this interesting snippet of information, "have a pleasant evening sir."

"I'll try my best," said Jonathon.

He made his way up in the lift, confident that, if asked, there was no way the concierge would forget that Mr. Jonathon Taylor had arrived at about 8.30pm and hadn't departed until the following morning.

He had expected that they would order a takeaway, but Bianca had cooked a delicious casserole and a couple of hours later, as she lay naked over Jonathon's knee, Brian, Terry, Graham and Neville were each waiting in one of the four re-sprayed vans, which they had discreetly parked just a few hundred yards from their respective targets.

They had each programmed into their personal mobiles the phone number of their designated printing house and chosen 'withhold number' from the settings menu.

At precisely 10.45pm, all four of them dialed, waited for someone to pick up and then, holding their new smartphones close to their mobiles, they played the sound file provided by Jonathon; the file which played a slightly sinister, metallic American voice.

'This is a bomb warning. This is not a hoax. There is a bomb in the building which will explode at 11pm; fifteen minutes from now. You should evacuate immediately. This is not a hoax. Remember what happened to the Daily Mail.'

For good measure, they each played the message another two times and gave it ten minutes before they drove off.

At each of the printing houses, where the tannoy systems had soon sounded the alarm, scores of workers came running outside and didn't stop running until they felt they were at a safe distance from the building.

At each location, nobody thought it strange that a bomb-disposal vehicle arrived, its horn blaring and all four indicator lights flashing in unison. On the contrary; people were surprised and very impressed at the speed with which the emergency services had sprung into action.

Nobody thought it strange that there emerged from the vehicle a man dressed in a full head-and-body bomb disposal suit; a man who, carrying a toolbox, bravely entered the now empty building.

Nobody thought it strange that a few minutes later a man came running out of the building; a man wearing overalls the same colour as most of themselves and a man they assumed was just a foolish straggler, or who had been busy on the loo.

Nobody noticed the man put his hand in his pocket and place his finger on the button of a radio-controlled detonator, the aerial of which passed down through a hole in the pocket and rested again his leg.

But everybody noticed the massive explosion inside the building for, again, Terry hadn't stinted on the amount of Semtex he had used in each of the bombs, and everybody bowed their heads in respect at what had no doubt been the death of a courageous bomb-disposal expert.

Simultaneously, in their homes, thousands of people each noticed when the website they were browsing suddenly vanished and was replaced by a full-screen message apologizing for the disappearance of their daily diet of sensationalised news, exaggerated weather predictions, cancer scares, toned pins, incredible bikini-bodies, sideboobs, wardrobe malfunctions and vacuous, pouting 'selfies'. They were each signed 'Nemesis'.

Brian, Terry, Graham and Neville each slipped away from the mayhem they had caused and walked to where they had parked their cars earlier in the day, stopping on the way to remove their overalls and dump them. They then all headed back to Aldershot, where they had arranged to meet up at Terry's place for a whisky celebration.

Before driving off, Brian sent Jonathon a text: 'Job done!'

Meanwhile, one by one, police cars arrived at the four buildings and officers began poking around in the piles of metal debris. They were intrigued to find that, near each of the destroyed printing presses, there lay on the ground an empty and badly damaged bomb-disposal suit. Examining the four fake bomb-disposal vehicles, they found that one was full of bedding supplies, another contained metalworking paraphernalia, another was chock-full of old washing machines and the fourth housed a lawnmower and a multitude of gardening tools.

It also carried a set of false number plates.

13 | A nation doesn't mourn

Waking at dawn, Jonathon leant over and kissed a still sleeping Bianca on her forehead, before quietly slipping out of her flat. In the lift, he pressed the button for the ground floor and when the door opened, for the benefit of the concierge, he made an exaggerated show of how silly he was for not pressing the button for the car park.

When he arrived back at his flat he managed to park directly outside and he didn't notice four men sitting in a car parked on the other side of the road. They waited to see where he would go and only jumped out when they saw him approach his front door. They were on him in a flash.

"Excuse me sir," said one of them, "are you Mr. Taylor?"

"Who wants to know?" said Jonathon, flustered.

"Mr. Jonathon Taylor?"

"Who wants to know?" he repeated, inwardly panicking.

"Scotland Yard sir," said the man, holding out his ID card.

"And you are?"

"Detective Inspector Foot."

"So, Foot of the Yard, eh?" chuckled Jonathon, who couldn't help himself.

"Yes sir," said Detective Inspector Foot, who rolled his eyes because he had heard it more times than he cared to remember, "is this your car?"

"Yes."

"Very nice sir," said the inspector, "and can you tell me

where you were last night at about 11 o'clock?"

Jonathon's heart was thumping beneath his ribs as he frantically tried to work out how they had got onto him. "I was at my girlfriend's place."

"And can you prove that sir?"

"Yes, easily," said Jonathon, who was now glad that he had been through the rigmarole of making sure the concierge wouldn't forget him. He confidently gave the inspector the address.

"And do you own any other vehicles sir?"

"Yes I have a van too."

"And where is it sir?"

"It's parked around the corner," said Jonathon.

"Do you mind if we go and take a look?"

Jonathon said that he didn't mind at all and invited the inspector to follow him. As they walked to where he had last parked his van, which he hadn't used since getting the Bristol, the realisation dawned on him.

As they rounded the corner, his fears were confirmed. "Bloody hell," he said, "it's gone!"

"Where exactly was it sir?" asked the inspector.

"Right here," said Jonathon, pointing to a space that was now occupied by an old Land Rover.

"Have you seen the news this morning sir?"

"No, not yet," although that was what he was most looking forward to. At Bianca's flat he had deliberately avoided turning on the television for fear of seeming overly interested in the events of the night before.

"I'm afraid your van was involved in a bombing last night, sir."

"Nonsense," said Jonathon, "a bombing?!"

"Yes sir; one of four," continued the inspector, "it seems that the criminals stole four vans and yours was one of them."

Jonathon sensed that he was probably in the clear. It was obvious what had happened, even though the chances against it were astronomical. He could easily maintain that the bombings had nothing to do with him and that he was an innocent party.

He decided to play along. "So, has my van been blown up?" he asked as they walked back to his flat.

"No sir, it hasn't," said the inspector, "but on the outside it's still unrecognizable as your van."

Jonathon listened with interest as the inspector briefly ran through the events of the night before, and he thought he detected a hint of admiration in his voice as he described the subterfuge involved to gain access; the bombers using vans disguised as bomb-disposal vehicles.

"And from the contents of your van I assume you do gardening work, Mr. Taylor."

"Yes that's right."

The inspector waved his hand at the Bristol, "rather lucrative is it, sir?"

"Oh that," said Jonathon, "no that's a present from a friend of mine who had a bit of luck."

In the manner of cunning sleuths everywhere, Detective Inspector Foot had been saving the most difficult question until the end. "And can you tell me why there's a set of false number plates in the back of your van?"

Jonathon swallowed hard. He was sure he had always worn gloves when handling the plates but nonetheless he dreaded being asked for his fingerprints. But then, surely there was nothing to worry about; here he was, an innocent gardener who had had his van stolen by a gang of criminals; obviously it was more believable that it was they who had been responsible for the plates.

"I have no idea inspector," he said, "maybe when you catch these men they can tell you."

The inspector looked at him, studying his face intently. "Ok sir, when we've finished with your van at the pound, we'll arrange to have it returned to you."

"I think I'll ask you to deliver it straight to a spray shop," said Jonathon, who had now relaxed a little bit, "a lot of my customers are quite elderly and seeing a bomb disposal unit arrive might give them a funny turn."

The inspector laughed. "Right you are sir," he said, "I'll let you get on with your day."

Earlier that morning, three other police units had established that the other three vans had each been stolen from an innocent owner and Detective Inspector Foot had no reason to suspect that Jonathon wasn't simply the fourth victim of the gang. Nonetheless, there was something about Mr. Jonathon Taylor's demeanour that sat uncomfortably with the inspector and he got on the police radio to order a background check before driving to Bianca's to verify his alibi.

Jonathon watched as the unmarked police car drove off, then turned and went inside his flat where, despite it being only ten in the morning, the first thing he did was pour himself two fingers of Laphroaig. He threw back his head and gulped it down.

His pulse had still not returned to normal when he sat at his computer and scoured the websites of the newspapers that still had one.

'Four more papers attacked.'

'Who's got it in for the tabloids?'

'Maybe we'll be next.'

It was then that Jonathon remembered he should write an anonymous letter to the rest of the newspapers, but before he could start typing, the black phone rang.

"Hello James," said Spencer.

"I expect you're looking forward to a couple more book titles."

"Yes, that would be nice."

"Ok," said Jonathon, "I'll text them to you."

"Cool."

"Any luck with the television thing?"

"No, not yet, I haven't had the chance; I'll get onto it soon."

"Ok, I'll be waiting."

Jonathon texted to him: 'Taller Pygmies than Usual' and 'Great Italian Wartime Heroes', which he remembered was a rather slim volume. To avoid being interrupted further, he then called Brian.

"James!" said Brian. "Are you happy with the results?"

"I'm delighted," said Jonathon, "and I'm even more delighted that there have been no reported casualties."

"Funny how folk are so keen to scarper when they think a bomb's about to go off."

"I'll send you another book title," said Jonathon.

"Thanks," said Brian, "any more jobs in the offing?"

"Not that I can think of, but you'll be the first to know."

"It's been a pleasure doing business with you."

"You too."

He hung up and texted Brian: 'Things to do on the Falkland Islands', which was the last of the books in which he'd hidden the left-luggage receipts, before returning to his computer and writing a letter to the editors of some newspapers that still existed.

'Sir,

You may have been wondering why anybody would want to blow up the printing presses of five national newspapers and also to sabotage their websites. Well, the person behind it simply became sick and tired of their hypocrisy and the collective effect of them all, spewing out as they did a mindless stream of sensationalism, overt vulgarity and over-reliance on what various wannabes and D-list celebrities were wearing on their nights out and publishing endless photographs of them 'looking worse for wear' as they tumbled out of various venues. These 'newspapers' also had a nasty tendency to publically humiliate vulnerable people who are best left alone to deal with their problems, be they alcoholism, mental health issues or bereavement.

Perhaps you might agree that editors of national newspapers have, to an extent, a responsibility to their readers. It is arguably an extrapolation of the parent-child relationship. What parent would fill their children's minds with the kind of endless tripe that has become so prevalent in this country's media? What parent would, on the one hand, encourage their children to work hard at school and on the other hand subject them to the kind of influences that lead them to believe that all they have to do is take off their clothes for the cameras or win a talent show to achieve lifetime health, wealth and happiness?

You decide.

And please refrain from dumbing-down your newspaper any further, or you might be next.

Kind regards,

Nemesis.'

Jonathon printed out four copies and prepared and printed out four envelopes. Then, with gloved hands, he folded the letters, sealed them in their self-adhesive envelopes, affixed stamps, and put them all in a small plastic bag. Satisfied that there would be no traces of his DNA, he then sat back to think of a faraway place where he would like to go to post them and also to have a celebratory lunch.

It was now around 11 o'clock, which gave him comfortably enough time to get across to Whitstable, post the letters, have a Dover sole and get back in time to watch the evening news, by which time the stories of his escapades should be nicely fleshed-out.

Just then his white phone received a text from David. 'Very clever, you rogue.'

Jonathon replied 'Thank you.'

'An evening at the Ferret?' added David.

'See you there at seven,' texted Jonathon, who didn't want to miss the 6 o'clock news on the television.

As he sat on the train to Whitstable, an extraordinary coincidence was taking place at Richmond Library, where Spencer and Brian had converged simultaneously to relieve from between the pages of some books a few small pieces of paper; two for Spencer and one for Brian. Brian recognized Spencer immediately and kept his head down. Spencer, who had only ever met Brian once, when he had no moustache and was wearing a wig, studied him hard. Also studying Brian was the prim librarian who, not so long ago, had witnessed him and a little old lady engaged in an unlikely and animated altercation over a book called 'The Joy of Knitting'. It seemed to her very odd that Brian visited the library so often yet never borrowed any books. And she remembered him brandishing a small piece of paper at her, claiming it was worth fifty thousand pounds. 'The poor man,' she thought, 'perhaps he isn't very well in the head.'

Later, at Heathrow Terminal 4, Spencer couldn't believe it when he saw Brian again, and at the left luggage office, too. It was too much of a coincidence. It *had* to be him. James would be using the same method for getting money to all his cohorts, and he decided to say hello.

"Kevin?" he said to Brian.

Brian didn't react, for he had only used the name 'Kevin' when they first met at the Greyhound pub.

"Brian?" Spencer tried.

"Spencer," he said at last, "fancy seeing you here."

"I guess we're here for the same reason."

"I guess so," said Brian, "not bad money is it?"

"It suits me," said Spencer, "got time for a drink?"

Brian agreed that he did have time and the two of them made their way to one of the terminal's bars and ordered a couple of beers.

"I saw what happened at the printing houses," said Spencer, "it was cunning stuff."

"Yes but it was still nerve-wracking."

"Do you think he's mad?"

"James?"

"Yes," said Spencer, "our weird paymaster."

Brian quaffed his beer and thought about it. "No, I don't think he's certifiably mad but I do think he's a bit crazy."

"So, a bit crazy but not mad?"

"Yes," said Brian, "the thing is, he has a point; the papers he attacked, or paid *us* to attack, are a pretty despicable bunch when you think about it."

"True," said Spencer, who was the recently appointed head of IT at one of them.

"And anyway," said Brian, "I'm a hundred grand better off, so I don't give a shit."

Spencer wasn't going to take the bait. He knew Brian was fishing. The fact was, he was *two* hundred grand better off and there was no point in him showing his hand. Besides, he thought, he was a scalpel of computer technology precision whereas Brian and his crew were just explosive-wielding thugs. They couldn't possibly do what he had done; they didn't have the knowledge.

"Yes," he agreed, "a hundred grand comes in pretty handy."

"I need to go," said Brian, holding up a bag, "a couple of my team are waiting for the rest of their money."

"Me too," said Spencer, holding up his bags, "I also have people to pay."

"I guess we'll never meet again," said Brian.

"I guess not," said Spencer, "but with someone like James, you never know."

"See you around," said Brian.

"There is one thing," said Spencer, "if you come across anyone who knows how to mess around with TV broadcasts, I'd be glad to be put in touch." He scribbled his number on a piece of paper and handed it over. "You can reach me here."

"Sure," said Brian, "I'll see what I can do."

As they went their separate ways, Jonathon was coming to the end of a most enjoyable lunch in Whitstable, where he had rather overdone it on the oysters and the Parma ham and melon and had had barely enough room for his Dover sole and dauphinoise potatoes.

On the train home, he stared out of the window at the countryside rushing by and wondered whether it had all been worth it. No doubt the Mail would soon be up and running again and no doubt it would continue to pour out the same kind of thing as before. And the other four would do likewise. What would he have achieved, apart from the satisfaction of pulling off, and getting away with, some extraordinary crimes against some unusual targets? He wondered how the other papers would react when they received his letter the next day, and whether one or more of them might actually publish it. He hoped that they would; at least it would make public the reasons behind what he had done. It might stimulate some debate, too; it might even prove to be the catalyst for one of the BBC's in-depth, searching documentaries. He hoped so, for they would no doubt unearth some of the official studies that had been carried out into the effect on society of trashy, superficial media and how it was warping peoples' minds and perverting their value systems.

He worked out that he had so far spent six hundred and twenty thousand pounds. There were still two locked bags waiting at the lost property office, David was looking after two bundles of cash and there were also the two packages he had buried in Mrs. Wilson's back garden. Surely he had enough left to persuade someone to somehow hack into the output of a few television channels?

He also had best part of ten million in the bank. Perhaps it was now time to say goodbye to his flat in Clapham and buy himself a couple of nice properties; a flat in central London and a house somewhere in the countryside; somewhere unprepossessing and not too far from a crystal clear chalk stream, teeming with unsuspecting wild brown trout.

Jonathon spent much of the rest of the journey happily picturing himself wearing chest waders in the mayfly season and returning home to fry his catch in butter and black pepper only thirty minutes after it had been flapping around on the river bank before being despatched.

He was jolted out of his fly fishing fantasies by a call from Bianca.

"Jonathon," she exclaimed, "I've had the police round! They came this morning after I'd gone out and they waited for me all day!"

"Oh bugger," he said, "I didn't warn you because I didn't think they'd bother."

"It was about what happened last night with the papers and everything."

"I know; can you believe it?" he said. "One of the vans they stole was *mine*!"

"So it's nothing to do with you?"

"Don't be silly, it's just a weird coincidence."

To Jonathon, Bianca seemed happy enough as they rang off, but she couldn't help wondering why he would call it a 'coincidence'.

Once home he poured himself a glass of La Lagune and settled down to watch the early evening news. The bombings were the lead item and speculation was rife. The police had nothing whatsoever to go on and had stated that four people had had their vans stolen a couple of weeks prior and that there had been a break-in at a factory which made bomb-disposal suits; a break-in which in fact had been reported the day before but which nobody had been able to make head nor tail of until now. Thankfully there had been no casualties, the police spokesman observed.

'Well done team,' thought Jonathon.

Meanwhile, after a celebratory lunch of their own, his team had gone their separate ways. Brian returned home to Penny to announce that they were going to buy themselves a new car and go on a fabulous holiday to a destination of her choice. When she demanded to know how they could afford it he told her he had won a hundred thousand pounds on a lottery scratchcard that he had bought on impulse from a newsagent. She was too excited to question why he would suddenly buy a scratchcard, having previously maintained they were a waste of time and money. It occurred to her that her husband might at last be on a winning streak, for it wasn't so long ago he had handed her a thousand pounds in cash that he'd won on the horses.

Terry, Graham and Neville had no need to make up such stories, for each of them lived alone and they didn't have to explain how they had suddenly come into so much cash. Predictably, they had all decided to splash out on a new car but Terry had also decided to splash out on a new face and he was looking forward to his appointment with the plastic surgeon. The plan was to take some skin from one of his buttocks and apply it to the left side of his face. He remembered that he was obliged to make monthly visits to an extremely irritating aunt and he looked forward with pleasure to the day when she would be kissing his arse.

As Graham drove back down to Exeter, he was completely unaware of how his quick visit to an old girlfriend had led to a nightmare for Jonathon. He didn't get up to London very often and had arranged to meet her late one night at her place in Clapham where, after a very enjoyable hour or so, he had returned to the dark streets and stolen the first van he saw that he thought was suitable; a van that happened to be full of gardening equipment.

That evening, Jonathon was the first to arrive at the Ferret's Knees and he lined up beers and whiskies for himself and David before settling at his favourite table near the fire. David strode in a few minutes later and slapped him on the back before sitting down.

"Well," he said, tucking into his pint, "you *have* been a busy boy."

"It's very important to keep yourself occupied," said Jonathon.

"Indeed; but most people seem to do so without destroying half of the nation's newspapers."

"It wasn't the newspapers I destroyed," protested Jonathon, "it was the comics."

"And is that the end of your crusade against the press?"

"Yes," said Jonathon honestly, "I will not be attacking any more papers." He saw no reason to tell David that he was also nurturing plans to sabotage rubbish television.

"I've been listening to the radio most of the day," said David, "it seems you have a fair amount of support out there."

"That's nice to know."

"But you do realize that if you get caught they'll put you away for a very long time."

"I suppose so," said Jonathon, "but you're the only person who knows that it's me who was behind it all; none of the men I paid to help me have the slightest idea who I am."

"How many were there?"

"Five."

"And did you meet any of them?"

Jonathon switched to his Birmingham accent. "Yeah I met two of them, but I wore a dark curly wig, a moustache and glasses. And I called myself James and I spoke like this all the time."

David chuckled, "you really are a cunning old sod."

Without boasting in any way, Jonathon explained how he had hidden ten bundles of cash in locked bags at Heathrow's left luggage offices and then hidden the receipts in ten books at Richmond Library; books that he was fairly sure wouldn't be borrowed. He also admitted that he had made a mistake with one of his choices.

"Idiot," said David, "knitting is very popular."

"So it seems," said Jonathon, "I was lucky not to lose fifty grand."

"And whose idea was the bomb-disposal lark?"

"I cannot tell a lie," said Jonathon, " 'twas mine; it came to me late one night as I was drifting off to sleep."

David had genuine admiration. "And you're sure you've covered your tracks?"

"Yes, but I had a nasty scare this morning," said Jonathon, and he described how a million-to-one chance had led to a visit from Scotland Yard.

"Bloody hell," said David, "your own bloody van!"

"It's ok," said Jonathon, "they've got nothing on me."

"So what next? Now you've got all these shenanigans out of your system why don't you treat yourself a bit?"

"I shall," said Jonathon, "I was thinking about it only today."

Their conversation turned to matters of the heart and for the first time Jonathon told David all about Bianca and how he had spent a wonderful time with her in Venice and had since set her up in a flat of her own and was going to put her through veterinary college.

"You sound smitten," said David.

"I do believe I am," said Jonathon, "she's beautiful, intelligent, sweet, funny, charming, and basically a very lovely person."

"Is that all?"

"And she has a great arse, too."

David chuckled, "I've been seeing someone as well."

Jonathon was pleased at this news for it had been a long time since David had had anyone significant in his life. He listened with interest as David described her; how she was a single mother of a little girl called Charlotte, how she was very attractive, very kind and also a great cook, which was something of a necessity where David was concerned.

"And does she have a name?" asked Jonathon.

"Amy," said David, who decided to leave out the bit about meeting her at his favourite lap-dancing club, where he had tucked several twenty-pound notes into her panties as she gyrated in front of him at the edge of the stage.

"Maybe the four of us should get together sometime."

"Good idea," said David, "maybe even this weekend."

"Ok, let's sort something out tomorrow."

After another couple of pints and whiskies they decided to keep things simple and eat at the pub. It wasn't exactly a gastro pub but the food was unpretentious and heart-warming, there were some good bottles of red to choose from and besides, neither of them could be bothered to trek off to a restaurant.

"Jonathon," said David, before they parted for the night, "do you promise you're not going to attack any more papers?"

"I promise," said Jonathon, "I'm done with the papers."

14 | A good naughty boy

The next day, in the kitchen of a small terraced house in Shepherd's Bush, Mrs. Lawson finished ironing the last of her son's shirts and folded it neatly before placing it on top of the pile and patting it down. She had two reasons for visiting his bedroom; one to take up his freshly laundered clothes and the other to retrieve all the glasses, mugs, cups and plates which he never seemed to get around to bringing back downstairs. But he was a good boy, she thought, and she was extremely proud of him. He often had to work late into the night in his room and he needed endless drinks and snacks to keep him going.

Mrs. Lawson considered all his late nights to have been well worth it, for only the other week he had been promoted at work and he had given her five thousand pounds as a direct result. And he had finally bought himself a car. He had also announced that he was soon going to be able to put down a deposit on a place of his own. She and her husband would miss him terribly, but her son was now twenty-five and she knew he couldn't live with them forever.

Pushing open the door to his bedroom, she noticed that he had taken their old trestle table down from the attic and on it had lined up his four new laptop computers. He must be terribly important now, she thought, to need all this extra equipment in his new position. She had carried up his clothes on a tray and after hanging up things in his wardrobe and tucking things away in his chest of drawers, she used the tray to pile up his dirty glasses and crockery and return them to the kitchen.

Later, as she carried on with her chores, it was with only scant attention that she listened to a man on the radio describe the way in which he thought someone had brought down the websites of four newspapers two nights previously. His theory was that, because they had all been attacked within seconds of each other at around 11 pm, the deed had been done either by four different people with four different computers, and that they had synchronized their actions, or possibly it could have been done by just one person with access to four computers simultaneously. This person could have coded in the commands to each computer and then hit 'enter' in rapid succession, deleting the contents of each site.

At home, Jonathon too was listening. "It was the latter," he announced to his radio, feeling rather pleased with himself.

In Shepherd's Bush, Mrs. Lawson stopped dusting the sideboard and froze at the words 'four computers'. At first, she didn't notice that she had stopped breathing and, when she did, she sat down on the sofa and tried to compose herself. No, she thought, surely it wasn't Spencer!

At that very moment, Spencer Lawson was on his way to meet a man who knew everything there was to know about the sharp end of TV broadcasting; not how programs were made, but how the signals found their way into peoples' homes, and how it might be possible to interfere with them.

In Clapham, Jonathon was busying himself on the internet, looking at properties in Hampshire, when he heard his own words being read out on the radio. One of the newspapers to which he had written had shared his letter with the BBC, who had now hastily convened a panel of noteworthy people and also a bimbo reality TV 'actress' to pass comment.

People who work in media circles were notorious for

being highly interested in other people who work in media circles. It was a bubble of self-absorption and there was no wonder it was often referred to as a circus. The bombings and the sabotage of the websites had provoked a frenzy of intrigue in what was left of the media, which in fact was most of it, and the Twittersphere had likewise gone ballistic, with people using their 140 characters mostly to mock the tabloids and their readerships. It all seemed jolly good fun to most people.

On the radio, the host turned to a professor of media studies at Warwick University and asked her whether the writer of the letter had a valid point.

"Yes, but he's only just scratched the surface," she said, "well, I assume it's a 'he'."

"Please explain."

"Which bit?"

"About only scratching the surface."

"In my job I have to examine the media from all points of view and I can tell you that the tabloid press is arguably harmful to society."

"But that's just your opinion, yes?" asked the host.

"No, there have been carried out several formal studies, not just in this country, that have found, how can I put it, that the red-tops feed people, well, they feed people the sort of crap that skews their view, in a negative way, about what's important in life."

"Go on."

"Take that ridiculous house thing; Celebrity Big Brother."

"It's very popular."

"Yes but why?" continued the professor, "have you ever watched it?"

"I must say I haven't."

"Well, if you had, you'd know that it's just a collection of sensationalized, mindless and shamelessly concocted scenes between people who barely deserve the label 'celebrity'. The producers and the directors are so desperate for ratings that they issue so-called 'warnings' against the participants yet they're secretly delighted at what they deem to be their 'bad behaviour', be it swearing or being sexually suggestive. It's pathetic. It's soul-destroying."

"But that's television."

"Yes, but the tabloids can't get enough of it; they constantly whip up a frenzy about who's slagging off who, who's got their kit off and who's, well, that's about it actually."

"I'd like to bring in someone who's had a ring-side view of it all, as it were," said the host.

"Sharon," he continued, "you were once on CBB once, were you not?"

"Yeah, I was."

"And what did you get out of it?"

There was a silence.

"What do you mean?" said Sharon.

"I mean how did you enjoy it? How do you think it furthered your career?"

"I got my picture in the papers a lot," offered Sharon, giggling.

"Is that all?"

"And I launched my own brand of perfume – Heaven Scent from Sharon!"

"And this scent; did you create it at home, in your kitchen or somewhere, from ingredients chosen by yourself?"

"Nah, I was just asked if I'd put my name to it, so I said yeah, natch, 'course."

"I see," said the host, "but didn't you feel at all demeaned by the dozens of pictures of you in the papers, especially the ones which, ahem, showed you perhaps revealing more than you might have wanted?"

"What do you mean, demeaned?"

"I mean humiliated; disgraced."

"Oh no," said Sharon, "it's just a laugh, innit?"

"So you don't mind being seen scantily dressed?"

Sharon hooted with laughter. "Of course not; I used to be a glamour model didn't I?"

"Well," said the host, "we have, waiting in the radio car, Doctor Sofia Johansson, who while at the University of Westminster carried out an important and acclaimed study of the world of the tabloid press; she's on the line now."

"Good morning, Sofia?"

"Good morning."

"What is your opinion of the recent attacks on the tabloid press?"

"It's obviously a very serious crime, but I can't help feeling some sympathy with whoever's behind it."

"Why so?"

"I know all about the tabloids and their readers; I wrote a PhD thesis about it in 2007."

"So you don't approve of them?"

"I neither approve nor disapprove," said Sofia, "but I was saddened at my findings."

"Go on."

"If I may, I'd like to quote from the writings of Professor Bob Franklin, from his 1997 book 'Newszak and News Media' – is that ok with you?"

"Please do."

"He wrote: 'Entertainment has superseded the provision of information; human interest has supplanted the public interest; measured judgement has succumbed to sensationalism; the trivial has triumphed over the weighty; the intimate relations of celebrities from soap operas, the world of sport or the royal family are judged more 'newsworthy' than the reporting of significant issues and events of international consequence.'" said Sophia, "I think that about sums it up."

"I'm not sure I understood a word of that," said Sharon.

"I rest my case," said Sophia.

"Listen clever clogs," said Sharon, raising her voice, "I'm not thick you know; I've got three 'O' levels!"

The host intervened before the two women could get involved in a lengthy on-air spat and endlessly talk over each other, an event which is never good radio because listeners can't make out what either party is saying.

"We've got some callers waiting on the line; let's see what they have to say," he said, "hello Rachel from Portsmouth…"

"Good morning," said Rachel, "I'd just like to say good riddance to the lot of them; they're nothing but a bunch of low-rent muckrakers who use the word 'flaunt' too much."

"How do you mean?" asked the host.

"So-and-so flaunts this; so-and-so flaunts that; so-and-so flaunts the other; it drives me up the wall; that and their obsession with 'incredible bikini bodies' all the time," said Rachel. "I work in the health sector and I can tell you that thousands of young girls become deeply unhappy with their bodies and often anorexic, mainly because the gutter-press media force images onto them of unattainable so-called 'perfection'."

'Very well put,' thought Jonathon, who was starting to feel thoroughly vindicated.

"But now we have a caller from York," said the host, "who I understand takes a rather different point of view; Victor?"

"Yeah, good morning," said Victor, "what a load of old poppycock I'm hearing; if people want to read the tabloids then that's their choice; nobody's forcing anyone to read them and besides, they're just harmless entertainment."

"They're not harmless," interrupted Rachel.

"Of course they are," argued Victor, "how can a bit of newsprint be harmful?"

"Well, we'll have to leave it there," said the host, "I'm afraid we've run out of time."

Jonathon thought Victor sounded like a complete prat, and he turned off his radio and returned to his search for a nice house somewhere near a trout stream. He bookmarked a few pages with the intention of calling the agents later and arranging to visit them over the next couple of days.

Taking the white phone, he texted 'how are you?' to Nicholas and Jackie.

As usual, Jackie responded first, 'je suis tres bon merci mon pére!'

Half an hour later, Nicholas texted 'good thanks'.

Because he saw his children only every other weekend, he felt it important to send them occasional messages. Even though they were only basic two-beat exchanges, it still showed them that they were in his thoughts.

It occurred to Jonathon that Nicholas' paper-round must have become a whole lot easier and he hoped the newsagent wouldn't dock his pay too much, given the lighter load that he now had to carry.

Next he called Bianca, who was curled up on her sofa with a veterinary textbook.

Before he could speak, she felled him with one of her out-of-the-blue questions. Usually these were non-sequiturs in mid-conversation, but this time it was the very first thing she said.

"Did you know?" she said, "in theory, a single lady rabbit, along with her baby girls, and their baby girls, and their baby girls, and their baby girls, etcetera, can create literally millions of little baby bunnies within five years?"

Jonathon confessed that he was unaware of the cumulative

potential of reproduction in the rabbit community.

"Just imagine," she continued mischievously, "all that bonking!"

Jonathon paused momentarily to picture fields of rabbits having a good time, but he found it hard to hold the image steady in his mind. "Yes, that's all very nice, but listen; we might get together with my old chum David and his new girlfriend this weekend; what do you think?"

"That sounds lovely," she said, "what will we do?"

"I thought we might nip over to Amsterdam."

Bianca had never been to Amsterdam before and Jonathon yet again had to hold the phone away from his ear as she expressed her delight at the idea.

"Ok, I'll speak to David about it."

"Tell him it's Amsterdam or I'm not coming," said Bianca.

"Watch it," said Jonathon, "or I might have to teach you a lesson in manners."

"I'm willing to learn," she said, "well, a bit."

"Of course, you know the trouble with rabbits?" he said.

"No, do tell."

"They're all fur coat and no knickers."

He hung up and called David. "We're going to Amsterdam for the weekend," he announced.

"Oh, are we indeed?"

"Yes, Bianca has decided; what's Amy's surname?"

"Actually I have no idea."

"Well find out and text me and I'll sort it all out, ok?"

Meanwhile, over drinks at the Dog and Duck in Soho, Spencer Lawson had just apportioned three hundred thousand pounds of Jonathon's money; a third for himself and two thirds for Cecil, who was a man who knew a thing or two about television broadcasts. When he got home to Shepherd's Bush, both his parents were waiting for him and they didn't seem very happy.

"Come in and sit down," said his father.

Spencer went through to the living room, where he found his mother in tears. His father followed him and stood at the window with his arms folded, gazing out. "Do you remember what your grandmother used to tell you, Spencer?"

"Er, 'you must eat'?" said Spencer.

"NO!" shouted his father, whirling round, "she said 'you always get found out'."

"What do you mean?"

His mother spoke through her tears, "why are there four new computers in your bedroom?"

Spencer thought quickly. "They're to do with my new job."

"And is your new job to bring about attacks on the websites of national newspapers?" demanded his father.

Spencer laughed nervously. "No, no, after what happened a few weeks ago I was asked to test the effectiveness of some new firewalls and they each needed a dedicated computer."

His father knew what a firewall was; his mother didn't.

"So you had nothing to do with what happened to those papers two nights ago?" he said.

"What's a firewall?" asked his mother.

Spencer explained the ins and outs of internet security in terms that could be vaguely understood by a layperson; even his mother.

"See?" his father said to her, "I told you he had nothing to do with it."

But his mother knew when Spencer was lying.

"Let's go up to your room," she said, "I want you to show me."

"Can you just give me five minutes?" said Spencer, who needed to delete the evidence.

"No," his mother insisted, knowing how devious he could be, "I want to go straight up there. Now."

"Please?"

"What's your problem son?" said his father. "Surely you've got nothing to hide?"

Led by Mrs. Lawson, the three of them walked up the single flight of stairs and turned left into Spencer's room, where she folded her arms and demanded that he open the lids of the four laptops.

Spencer realised there was no way out and he did what he was told, flipping up the tops of the computers to reveal that they each still displayed the message he had uploaded to the websites before changing all the passcodes.

His mother went weak at the knees and would have fallen had her husband not steadied her. "So I was right," she said, "it *was* you!"

Spencer remained silent. His grandmother had been proven right.

"What have you got to say for yourself?" asked his father.

"I er, well, I don't really know."

"And did you have anything to do with the bombings, too?"

"NO dad, honestly, that had nothing to do with me; I was right here in my room when that happened."

"Yes, he was," said his mother, who remembered that Spencer had come down for a packet of biscuits at about the time the bombs were reported to have gone off.

"Well at least that's something," said his father.

"Listen," said Spencer, "I know this looks bad but nobody's been hurt and I've been paid two hundred thousand pounds so far and I can make even more."

"Two hundred grand!" said his father, who was not unimpressed. "Who the hell paid you that kind of money?"

"A man called James," said Spencer and he described in detail how they had met at the Albert Memorial, what he had asked him to do, and the method he had used to pay him most of the money.

"What do you know about this 'James'?" asked his mother.

"Only that he has long dark curly hair, a moustache, he wears glasses and he comes from Birmingham."

"You wait here for five minutes then come down," said his father, "your mother and I need to talk about this in private."

Spencer did as he was told and stayed in his room, quietly fretting about what his parents might decide to do with him. Downstairs, Mr. and Mrs. Lawson were examining their consciences. Although horrified about what their son had done, they were thrilled to bits at all the money he had brought into the household and they were pleased at the prospect of him being paid even more. And after all, he hadn't actually harmed anyone, so maybe it was best if they just turned a blind eye.

After exactly five minutes, Spencer cautiously went downstairs and reentered the living room, his head bowed.

"How *could* you?" said his father. "You know your mother reads the Express website."

It was then that Spencer noticed the twinkle in his father's eye and the smile on his mother's face. "So am I forgiven?"

"What you did was scandalous, but two hundred thousand is a lot of money," said his father, "it's difficult to be too cross with you."

Spencer relaxed. "And there's probably more on the way."

"Are you sure nobody could find out it was you?"

"Not a chance," said Spencer, "I set up a series of proxy servers based in different countries; nobody can trace anything back to me."

"Clever boy," said his mother, "whatever all that means."

"Where's all the money?" asked his father.

"Most of it's hidden in my room."

"And this James," said his father, "what else does he want you to do?"

Spencer explained that James had simply asked him to find someone who could help him play around with television broadcasts and that he wasn't going to be actively doing anything else himself; at least he didn't think so.

"And what's it worth to him?"

"I think I can squeeze an extra hundred thousand out of it."

"So that's three hundred grand just for being a clever son of a bitch."

"Dad!"

"What?"

"Don't talk about mum like that," said Spencer.

15 | Amsterdam

Spencer wasn't all that surprised but was nonetheless very relieved that his parents weren't going to shop him to the police and he suggested that to celebrate his new source of income he should take them out for dinner to their favourite French restaurant; the one they went to on their anniversaries when they could afford it. It wasn't particularly expensive, but it served several rich dishes from the Lot valley of which his mother was very fond. They were joined by Spencer's elder sister, Amy, who was kept in the dark about the source of his extra funds, and who, over dinner, proudly announced that she was off to Amsterdam for the weekend with her new rich boyfriend.

"That's lovely darling," said her mother, "but who's going to look after Charlotte?"

"I was hoping you would, mum," said Amy.

"It'll be my pleasure; I love spending time with my favourite granddaughter."

"Mum?"

"What?"

"She's your only granddaughter."

"Well, you know what I mean."

Before going to sleep that night, Spencer texted James, 'good news, I think I've found someone who can help.'

At the time, Jonathon was still busy on the internet, choosing a hotel for the weekend, and he replied, 'great, I'll be in touch on Monday'.

Spencer was slightly irritated by this, for that was five days away and he was keen to get his hands on the extra money as soon as possible, but all he could do was reply, 'cool'.

Eventually, Jonathon decided on The American hotel. It wasn't the best but nevertheless it was very luxurious and it wasn't too far from the red light district, an area to which he was sure he and the other three would gravitate more than once. He secured two of its best rooms and also booked flights for Bianca, Amy, David and himself before retiring.

In the morning, he climbed into his car and made his way to Hampshire to take a look at the few houses he had shortlisted the previous day. They were all very much to his taste, but the one that really took his fancy was a 19th century riverside property which featured a huge inglenook fireplace with plenty of room either side for large piles of over-wintered logs. Set in about an acre of land it also had a pool and he was tempted to snap it up on the spot, but instead decided to first investigate the history of flooding in the area. The estate agent pointed out that the house had been built a good fifteen feet above river level but Jonathon knew that estate agents had a tendency to say anything to secure a sale. Eventually he agreed to secure the property with a returnable deposit and to finalise the purchase the following week after he had made enquiries at the local water authority.

On the way back home, he stopped at a newsagent and bought copies of all four of the newspapers to which he had written a couple of days before. He was delighted to find that not one of them had published his letter on the letters page; instead they had all reprinted it on the front page. He had always known that what he had done would become big news, but it had turned out to be even bigger news than he had expected, and it was getting bigger by the day, thanks to the narcissistic tendencies of the media. At a press conference, a police spokesman admitted they didn't have any leads but were hopeful of making a breakthrough very soon.

"Hah," said Jonathon out loud, "fat chance," and he dozed off on his sofa for a while before waking and sending Bianca a text, 'be ready by 11 in the morning and don't bring any bloody dumb-bells'.

She texted back 'not even a little one?'

He replied with six images of an open palm followed by two of a bright red apple, a sequence which had become a familiar code for what she should expect the next time they saw each other.

The following day, the two couples met at Gatwick at around noon and the necessary introductions were made. Both Jonathon and David had been slightly nervous about their girlfriends meeting each other only at the start of a weekend away, rather than over dinner sometime beforehand, but their worries soon evaporated. Bianca and Amy were like peas in a pod, both of them prone to fits of the giggles and both delighted to poke fun at their respective boyfriends, who would simply look at each other, happy but bemused, and each with mischievous thoughts about what they might get up to in the naughtier of Amsterdam's nightclubs.

Arriving at Schiphol airport, the four of them piled into a taxi and made their way to the American hotel, where they agreed to meet in the bar a couple of hours later, ready for a couple of drinks before they went for a night on the town.

"Happy?" asked Jonathon of Bianca, as they were getting dressed in their room.

"Very, very happy," she replied, stopping short of what she really wanted to say, which, even after just a few weeks, involved naming a date, choosing a dress and making wedding vows.

As if he were reading her thoughts, he approached her gently from behind and, without being in any way sexual or proprietorial, he simply said, "me too."

The men were the first to arrive in the bar, each having persuaded their girlfriends that it was best they left them alone to finish getting ready, so that they could apply their finishing touches without feeling rushed in any way. It was disingenuous but neither David nor Jonathon relished the thought of twiddling their thumbs for half an hour or more.

"Amy's very nice," said Jonathon, sculling his first schnapps of the evening.

"So is Bianca," said David, who had started with a beer.

"They seem to be getting on very well."

"I saw your letter," said David, "to the papers."

"Ah, yes, well I thought I should offer some kind of explanation."

"It seems a lot of people understand why you did it."

"Thanks."

Before they could discuss it any further, Amy arrived, looking fabulous in a simple white dress slit to the thigh. The Daily Mail would have written that she had 'sizzled', 'dazzled', 'wowed', 'stunned' or 'smouldered'.

"What can I get you?" asked Jonathon.

"I'd like a Sidecar," said Amy.

Jonathon was instantly impressed and summoned a waiter.

"This is a really nice hotel," said Amy, "thank you so much."

Before Jonathon could reply, Bianca entered the bar, turning heads in her tight white jeans as she crossed the floor to join the other three.

"Hello you lot," she announced.

"What would you like to drink?" asked Jonathon.

"I'd like one of those cocktails with lots of fruit juices and different rums and things."

The waiter arrived and Jonathon asked him for a Sidecar and a Hurricane before turning to David and the girls. "So, anyone hungry?"

"Let's go straight to a club," said David, who was more interested in sampling Amsterdam's naughty underbelly than in eating, "the best ones serve some food anyway."

Bianca and Amy looked at each other, neither of them wanting to admit they were thinking along exactly the same lines.

"It's too early for a club," said Jonathon, "besides, I've already booked a restaurant."

"What sort of food is it?" Bianca asked.

"I have no idea," said Jonathon, "but whatever it is, it'll be excellent." He had stumbled across The Supper Club on the internet. It was seriously cool, he thought, and the girls would love it.

"What do you mean you have no idea?" asked David, who tended to prefer to have some idea of what he was going to be eating.

"They just bring you food," said Jonathon, "whatever the chef has decided to prepare that day."

"I like the sound of it," said Amy.

"And you're going to love the décor, too."

"Why?" said Bianca.

"Because there isn't any," said Jonathon.

Bianca punched him playfully on the arm. "Don't be ridiculous," she told him.

"Wait and see."

For the next hour or so, the conversation flowed easily between them, with Amy proving to be an impressive raconteur. She had no qualms about revealing how she earned most of her living, about which she had many amusing stories to share, and eventually it came out that she and David had met where she sometimes worked; at a lap-dancing club in the west end of London. Without mentioning Jonathon's involvement, Bianca revealed that she was soon to start a lengthy course in veterinary studies at University College London.

"I'm so envious," said Amy, "I absolutely love animals, especially really cute fluffy ones like David."

The small talk continued and inevitably got around to their respective families, with each of them offering a brief summary. When it was Amy's turn, she told them that she lived alone in a small flat where she and her little girl Charlotte had remained after the father had upped and left a year ago.

"And do you have any brothers or sisters?" asked Bianca.

"I have a brother who still lives at home but he seems to be doing incredibly well at the moment and he'll probably be getting a place of his own soon."

"What does he do?" asked Jonathon.

"He works in IT," said Amy, "it's all a bit dull if you ask me."

After another round of drinks they made their way by foot to The Supper Club, where Jonathon's earlier remark about its décor finally made sense.

"Wow!" said Bianca, "this is amazing."

The Supper Club was completely white; the floors, the walls, the tables and the two rows of raised soft seating that ran the entire length of the restaurant on both sides of the main floor.

"You blend in very well sweetie," said David, nodding at Amy's white dress, "don't go too far or we'll never find you."

They kicked off their shoes and made themselves comfortable around one of the low white tables on an upholstered white dais, adopting positions usually reserved for a sofa rather than a restaurant.

"You can go a la carte if you want," said Jonathon, "but it'll be more interesting if we keep with the spirit of the place and just let them do what they do."

Everyone agreed and Jonathon informed the waitress of their decision.

The food and the wine turned out to be as astounding as

Jonathon had hoped, with an elaborate array of exquisite courses ranging from fish to pasta to meat to vegetarian and finishing with a pudding that was worryingly but aptly called 'Death by Chocolate'. The wines, too, were impressive, and after a couple of hours the four of them were by no means sober.

"To a club," said David, "a naughty one!"

Jonathon settled the bill and the four of them made their way outside to find that, while they had been eating, some rain showers had left the streets glistening beautifully under the street lamps. But the wet cobbles were also hazardous, especially for people wearing high heels, and Bianca and Amy clung to the elbows of the men as they slowly walked to the red light district.

The closer they got, the more of Amsterdam's famous coffee shops they came across; the kind of coffee shops where different types of marijuana command their own separate menus, chalked up daily on blackboards and varying according to what the dealers had been able to supply.

"Let's have a quick spliff," said Amy, and the others agreed.

Twenty minutes later, with the four of them feeling like they were balanced on the ceiling, they tumbled back out onto the shiny cobbles, giggling like schoolchildren, hopelessly confused and each hoping someone else knew which way to go. The least silly of them turned out to be David, who used the map app on his phone to work out where they were and which direction to take.

"This way," he said, and the others tagged along like sheep, their minds fuzzy from the powerful Thai grass they had smoked, "at least, I think it's this way."

As they weaved their way along, the frequency with which they passed some of the city's window hookers palpably increased, until practically every other shop front was lit by a red light, creating seductive glows behind the scantily clad women who slowly writhed around, beckoning punters in with their forefingers.

"I'm just popping in here for a few minutes," said David, which was a mistake, because Amy didn't realise he was joking.

"Oh no you're bloody well not," she said firmly, and she yanked him away by the elbow, "how bloody dare you!"

David tittered and continued leading everyone to the Casa Rosso, a live sex club which, unbeknownst to the others, he had memorized and marked on the map in his phone. It was a good deal less seedy than some of the other clubs and David had thought it the perfect choice considering he and Jonathon had Bianca and Amy in tow.

They managed to get a table not too far from the stage and ordered some drinks before settling back and watching the various acts that had made the place famous. For the most part, the performers gave genuinely erotic performances, with only one couple appearing bored and listless as they laboured through their routine in a forced, mechanical manner, giving each of the positions they adopted what seemed to be a fixed period of time, before suddenly stopping and moving onto the next with a desultory air.

One of the acts which intrigued Amy and Bianca more than it did David and Jonathon featured a lithe young Hungarian woman, a few ping-pong balls and distances of several meters.

'*I* could do that,' thought Bianca.

'*I've* done that,' thought Amy, smiling to herself.

The last act of the night involved a beautiful redheaded woman and a muscular African American man who the compere introduced as 'Tripod', and with good reason.

After an energetic twenty minutes, exhausted and glistening, the performers eventually left the stage to enthusiastic applause, whereupon the house lights came up rather abruptly, leaving the customers in no doubt that it was time for them to leave.

"So that's how it's done," said David, winking at Jonathon.

"Oh, didn't you know?" said Jonathon.

Inspired by the show, the two couples walked measurably more quickly back to their hotel, keen to get up to their rooms and put into practice some of what they had just seen. In the foyer, Jonathon stopped at the front desk and had a quick word with the receptionist, gesturing to the other three with his hand. The receptionist studied them all briefly and jotted down estimates of their heights, mentally deducting a few inches to make allowance for the girls' high heels.

Jonathon took Bianca's hand and bade goodnight to the other two.

"Let's meet down here at around noon," he suggested, "I've arranged a surprise for you all."

In the morning, Jonathon was the first to awake and he found himself fantasising about how Spencer's new contact might be able to tamper with a few TV programs. It was difficult for him to do anything other than make contingency plans, for he still had no idea about what might be possible, but he imagined being able to superimpose titles on programs as they were being broadcast; 'Why are you watching this crap? It'll rot your mind.'

Jonathon disliked taking breakfast in hotel rooms and after showering he made his way down to the restaurant where he found David, who was similarly inclined.

"What a night," said David, who had gone on to attack his minibar with enthusiasm after making it back to his room, "I'm not at my best."

"Me neither," said Jonathon, "but it was worth it."

"How's Bianca?"

"I've no idea; she's still sleeping."

"So is Amy."

Preceded by two large glasses of freshly squeezed orange

juice, Jonathon ordered eggs Florentine and David opted for a grilled kipper and some brown bread and butter, which they followed up with strong cappuccinos.

"What's this surprise you mentioned?" said David.

"Wait and see," said Jonathon, "let's go and help the girls sort themselves out and meet up at reception."

"Better make it 12.30," said David, "give them a bit more sleep."

Jonathon went back up to his room and, without disturbing Bianca, he turned on the television, which the previous occupants had left tuned to CNN. The main news item was about the recent attacks on the National Enquirer and US Weekly, which were deemed to be copycat crimes of the sort that had recently been committed in the UK, except that the perpetrators had already been caught and were being held in police cells for questioning.

'Silly sods', thought Jonathon, 'can't you people blow up a couple of printing presses without being caught?'

Bianca groaned as she came to, reaching out for him with a limp arm. "Please, turn it down a bit," she whispered.

Jonathon complied and then began to slowly rub her lower back in an effort to reacquaint her with the land of the living. "Time to wake up," he said, "big day ahead."

"I don't want a big day," came her response, "I'd like a little day, or at the most, a medium-sized sort of day."

Jonathon smiled, called room service and ordered some coffee to revive her, then continued massaging, gradually increasing the pressure he applied as his hands moved slowly up her back towards her shoulder blades. The fact was that, despite their best intentions, they had both passed out the night before and had never got round to enjoying each other physically.

They were in the middle of rectifying this oversight when there came a knock on the door. Jonathon jumped up, wrapped a towel around his waist and suggested with some urgency to the waiter that he quickly leave the tray on the nearest available surface; whereupon he signed, ushered him back out of the door and jumped back into bed.

By the time they had finished, the coffee was still hot enough and Bianca sat up in bed and purred as she drank, nibbling tentatively on the fine array of Dutch biscuits that had accompanied the flask.

"I don't want to hurry you sweetie," said Jonathon.

"But you're hurrying me?"

"Yes, it's a lovely day and it would be a shame to waste it."

"Then please go downstairs', she said, "I don't want you hovering around up here, making me feel guilty."

"Wear your trainers and something casual," said Jonathon, before closing the door behind him and going off in search of David and Amy, who were waiting patiently in reception.

Jonathon took one look at Amy and suggested that she nip back up to her room and change out of her mini-skirt and into a pair of jeans. He then went to reception, signed some paperwork, and went outside to find the four bicycles that were awaiting their riders.

"Nice idea," said David, "I just hope none of us falls off."

"Don't worry," said Jonathon, "it's like riding a bike."

When the girls arrived, they were at first apprehensive but soon got into the spirit of things as they went for a short ride down the road and back. It was then agreed that, since none of them had been to Amsterdam before, they should just carry on and see where they ended up, with each of them taking it in turns to lead the pack.

As the four of them set off along the cobbled street, the redolence of a popular children's author was not lost on David and Jonathon.

"I say," said David, as they all cycled away, "did you bring the sandwiches?"

"Oh gosh yes," said Jonathon, "and *lashings* of ginger beer!"

Of all the world's cities, Amsterdam was the first to turn its streets into a haven for cyclists and, provided one was careful not to get the tyres wedged in the tram tracks, it was not only a delight, but reassuringly safe. The innocence of their afternoon's exploration was in stark contrast to the mischief of the previous night and they all felt a sense of calm and freedom as they slowly roamed the quiet little streets.

Quite by chance, they happened upon the Ann Frank museum, where they spent an educational hour or so before returning to the hotel and resting up for a while, in readiness for another wild night out.

While Bianca slept, Jonathon took the black phone and texted Spencer 'looking forward to speaking on Monday and making plans'.

Their second night, while not being a carbon copy of the first, nonetheless went along similar lines and they stumbled back to the hotel at around four in the morning, with Bianca still giggling about being over Jonathon's knee in front of a cheering crowd at the Moulin Rouge, a club which encouraged audience participation. If the quality of a night out could be measured by the number of things one wouldn't tell the grandchildren, then it had been truly excellent.

As they slipped into bed, too tired for any further games, Bianca snuggled up to Jonathon and stroked his chest with her fingertips.

"Jonathon," she said, "I need to tell you something."

"I know what it is," he whispered, "and I love you, too."

16 | Cecil

Having been out so late, they didn't have time to do much the next day before having to get to the airport, but they did manage to spend a while wandering around the Modern Art gallery, which they chose over the Hermitage Museum, having had their fill of history at Ann Frank's house the day before.

Jonathon was so taken by the work of Miles Aldridge that he bought three large prints, with the intention of giving one to Bianca to hang at her new flat. This was a cleverly colourised image of a woman lying face down on a carpet, her head resting on a pillow and fittingly, thought Jonathon, completely nude except for her panties, which were slightly pulled down.

He arranged for them all to be shipped to his flat rather than struggle with them on the journey home and, with an eye on the time, they returned to the hotel, gathered up their luggage and headed for the airport.

Back at Gatwick, it transpired that while Jonathon had driven there, David and Amy had taken a cab, so he offered them a lift back to London.

"Very nice," said David, who hadn't seen the Bristol before.

"Thanks," said Jonathon, "I thought it had a certain quiet charm; where to first?"

"Just my place," said David, "Amy's going to come in for a bit."

'I'll bet she is,' thought Jonathon.

He dropped them off and then drove over to Bianca's

apartment block, where he also went in for a bit, but not before nipping round to the off-licence to pick up a bottle of wine. When he returned, the concierge was keen to speak to him.

"The police came to see me last Tuesday sir," he said, "about you."

"Yes I expect they did," said Jonathon, "they wanted to make sure I had nothing to do with those bombings at the papers."

"Yes sir, I know; and did you?"

Jonathon laughed. "No, of course not, it's just that one of the vans they stole was mine! I mean, can you *believe* it?"

"Of all the luck, sir," said the concierge, who had privately wondered whether Jonathon had deliberately made sure he would remember him, "have a good evening, sir."

In apartment 27, Bianca was busy enjoying some slices of ham and some duty-free Gouda when Jonathon walked in. "Would you like some?" she said.

"Not of that, no," said Jonathon, "but of you, yes."

All that day they had both been conscious of how they had revealed their deeper feelings to each other the night before, but neither had wanted to refer to it and, after they had finished with each other physically, Bianca started to get emotional.

"Did you really mean what you said last night?" she said softly.

For a while, Jonathon lay there, still panting, and didn't say anything as he examined his feelings.

"Yes," he said eventually, "I do believe I did."

"Oh Jonathon!" she said, and she flung her arms around him.

"But I don't want to rush into anything," he added, "after all, we've only known each other for a short while."

"I understand," she said.

"I've got the children next weekend; I've no idea where we're going to go or what we're going to do, but how would you like to join us?"

"I'd like that more than anything," said Bianca, "will I see you before then?"

"I doubt it; I've got a lot on this week, but you never know."

"You're not working are you?"

"It's not exactly work, no, but it's a very important project."

Jonathon was torn. Half of him wanted to tell her what he had been up to; that it was him who had been responsible for all the recent attacks on the tabloids. Perhaps she would respect and admire him for what he had done. Perhaps she felt the same about all the crap that they pumped out. But no, to tell her, at least to tell her now, would be too risky, despite her obvious feelings for him.

"I wish I knew what you were doing," she said, "it's not as though you need the money."

"It's to do with media studies," he told her, and he left it at that.

He wanted to go home, to ready himself for what was going to be a day of preparation for the next phase of his crusade, but she was so lovely, so desirous of him, and he of her, that he decided to stay the night. Nevertheless, he sent another text to Spencer before he went to sleep, 'will text in the morning to see if you can talk.'

'I think you're going to be very pleased,' Spencer texted back.

Meanwhile, Detective Inspector Foot was at home with his feet up, watching one of his favourite reality TV shows. He pondered all the evidence he had, such as it was, and put together a couple of possible scenarios, but he had no faith in either. This case was important to him; if he solved it, he had been left in no doubt that a promotion would be pretty much guaranteed, and he desperately wanted to be a Chief Inspector and perhaps to buy a small caravan to take down to the west country.

In the morning, as Bianca slept, Jonathon quietly slipped out of her apartment and made his way home, stopping on the way to buy a few newspapers. What he saw in the newsagents didn't panic him, but he was nevertheless discomfited by it. The Daily Mail was once more in production and its huge front page headline read 'If the police don't get you, WE will.'

Nothing but desperate bravado, thought Jonathon, but he bought a copy anyway to see what they had to say for themselves.

At home, having also stopped off at the supermarket for a few basic provisions, and having had yet another fiasco with an automatic check-out machine, he made a pot of coffee, spread out the papers on the table and started with the Mail.

Predictably, it was full of indignant bluster about what they were going to do to find and prosecute whoever had humiliated them, reducing their printing presses to tons of useless metal wreckage and obliterating all the data on their website; data they had spent several years building up. Jonathon wasn't surprised that they had decided to mention the cash value of their printing presses, for they usually deemed it important to report what things were worth, like the value of the house in which someone had been murdered, or in which a baby had tragically succumbed to a cot death.

In the other papers, there continued to be several letters to the editors about the motives of the person called 'Nemesis', who had claimed to be the agent of the tabloids' woes. As before, most of them were in favour of his or her actions, but there were a few which condemned what was, essentially, an attack on free speech and the freedom of the press.

'Indeed', thought Jonathon; 'the freedom to inculcate their readers with a never-ending stream of sensationalist, mind-numbing crap, studded with the trivia of what D-list celebrities had been wearing the night before, as if it were somehow important or edifying.'

He cooked himself breakfast and then texted Spencer, 'are you free to talk?'

'Not yet,' he replied, 'give me twenty minutes.'

He used the time to get in touch with the Hampshire Water Authority, who were kind enough to immediately email him the flood records of the vicinity in which he was considering buying a house. The reports allayed his fears and he rang the estate agent to confirm he was ready to go ahead, pending a proper survey. Again he found himself imagining wearing his chest-waders, standing in the river and casting a fly directly in front of the nose of a wild brown trout, beguiling it with its realism.

The black phone rang.

"James," said Spencer.

"So, what can you tell me?" said Jonathon, in his Birmingham accent.

"I hope you're sitting down," said Spencer, "it's good, but it's complicated."

Spencer proceeded to recount his meeting with Cecil, who worked at London's largest TV distribution facility; a facility dedicated to providing TV stations with all their broadcasting needs. They handled the output of any channel in which Jonathon would likely be interested and Cecil could mess with any of their programs, if the price was right.

"How much does he want?"

"Two hundred grand."

"That I can do, provided you don't want more than fifty," said Jonathon, who wanted to keep some cash available for another plan he had up his sleeve.

There was a silence. Spencer had counted on there being another hundred thousand for himself.

Jonathon knew when he was being played. "What will be your involvement?"

"Nothing," admitted Spencer, "the technology of all this is way over my head; only Cecil can make it happen."

"Are you aware of what a headhunter makes these days?"

"Maybe fifteen; twenty percent," said Spencer.

"Right. And I'm offering you twenty five per cent," said Jonathon, "take it or leave it."

Spencer slumped back in his new Porsche and considered his options. He had already made two hundred thousand and there was now a choice between earning another fifty, or nothing at all.

"Ok," he said, albeit reluctantly, "I'll take it."

"All I want you to do is facilitate communication between Cecil and me and you'll get your money."

"He doesn't want to meet you."

"I don't want to meet him either; just give him my phone number and my email address and once he gets in touch I'll tell you how you can get your next fifty grand."

"Richmond Library, right?"

"No. It's buried in the back garden of a house in Battersea; I'll give you the address and the precise location of the package. All you'll need to do is wait until it's dark and then go and dig it up."

"Bloody hell James," said Spencer, "do I need to take my own spade?"

"No, there's one in the shed, but make sure you put it back."

"Ok."

"And Spencer, I'm planning on doing something else, for which I'll also need your help, so there'll be more money for you in the future; maybe another hundred."

"Cool."

Jonathon decided there was no point in sitting around just waiting for Cecil to get in touch and instead he sat at his computer and began to type out notes of the sorts of things he would ask him to do, assuming they were possible. First, he drew up a list of some TV programs he wanted to have fun with and wrote down a few ideas, smiling with pleasure as he imagined the reactions of millions of people, sitting on their sofas in their homes.

Next he found a conveyancing solicitor, gave the details of the estate agent and instructed them to proceed with the house purchase as rapidly as possible. Being a cash buyer was going to speed up the whole process considerably but nevertheless it would still be several weeks before he would get his hands on the keys to the property. In the meantime, he would have to shop for more furniture, as the contents of his two-bedroom flat would be nowhere near enough to fill a five-bedroom house. He closed his eyes and imagined Miss Bianca Bennett tottering around the pool the following summer, naked on high heels. He also pictured Nicholas and Jackie dive-bombing each other and splashing around in the water. They were going to love the new house, not least because they would each finally have their own room at their father's place.

The black phone startled him.

"Hello," said a voice, "is that James?"

Jonathon adopted his accent, "speaking; might this be Cecil?"

"Yes, I hear you want to get up to some more mischief."

"More?"

"It was you who did the papers wasn't it?" said Cecil.

Jonathon agreed that it was he who had been responsible and instead of being angry with Spencer for disclosing the fact, he assumed that he had also assured Cecil that the money side of things was very real and that James could be trusted to pay promptly.

Cecil went on to describe the complicated process by which TV signals end up in peoples' homes. All the producers of programs, of which there were dozens, supplied the footage to Quasar, the company for which Cecil worked, whereupon each was given a unique code and loaded onto central servers. Meanwhile the various TV channels prepared minute-by-minute schedules, including commercial breaks where necessary, to which Quasar would adhere. Using the appropriate codes, the programs were then extracted from the servers and packaged up in the correct order, with commercials inserted according to the TV channels' instructions.

"Now here is where it starts to get clever," said Cecil.

Jonathon had thought it sounded pretty clever already.

Cecil went on to explain that there were basically three ways in which television signals reach peoples' homes and that there were three separate feeds to accommodate them all; one to the cable network, one to a country-wide network of transmission masts and the third sent via uplinks to geo-stationary satellites, which in turn beam the signals down to the satellite dishes on the sides of peoples' homes.

"And at what point," Jonathon started, not sure how to phrase his question, "at what point can you interfere with the signals?"

"I can't interfere with the actual signals," replied Cecil, "but I can interfere with what's held on the servers and also the scheduling instructions."

"And would it be possible…"

Cecil cut across him. "What about some money, James?"

"I understand you want two hundred thousand pounds. You can pick up fifty thousand today if you like."

"Yes, I like."

"A few weeks ago I arranged for a couple of combination-lock briefcases to be held at the lost property office of London Transport. They each contain fifty thousand pounds."

"Sounds simple enough," said Cecil.

"Anything's simple compared to what you've just told me."

"And what about the rest of the money?"

"Don't worry, you'll get it," said Jonathon, "but you'll have to be happy with fifty for now until we've talked some more."

"Ok, so what kind of briefcase did I 'lose' and where and when did I 'lose' it?"

"It's a brand new, slim, burgundy leather case and you lost it on the 73 bus, probably somewhere along Oxford Street, about eight weeks ago."

"And how can I prove it's mine?"

"Who else would know the combination?" asked Jonathon. "I'll text it to you."

They agreed that Cecil would go and pick up his money and then call again later to discuss things further and to answer any questions.

Jonathon texted Cecil '759-363' and then proceeded to find some suitable furniture for his new house by the river in Hampshire. After the divorce, Wendy had made off with most of the nicer pieces they had collected and he was now determined to replace them. His taste ran to solidly built, darkish, hardwood furniture that he imagined would look good against the pale grey carpets he had already decided to have fitted before moving in. Given that he spent nearly a third of his life in bed, he began his internet search by looking for a king-size Lit Bateau and soon found a beautiful example in dark walnut, which he paid for and asked the vendor to hold for him until he could advise a delivery date.

Without having a fixed idea of what would go where in his new home, he carried on searching for good pieces of furniture in walnut, mahogany and teak and snapped up anything that pleased his eye. He was in the middle of paying for an eighteenth century chest of drawers when the black phone rang.

"Hi James," said Spencer.

"Yes, he did," said Jonathon.

"Eh?"

"Yes, Cecil did get in touch."

"Good, so I can go and dig up someone's garden?"

"Yes, I'll text you the address. Now listen carefully. Do it after 11 o'clock; the old woman who lives there is in bed by ten, so by eleven she'll be out like a light. To the left of the house is a gate which leads to a side passage to the back garden. By the fence you'll see a water-butt. Take exactly five paces from there and dig about eighteen inches away from the fence. And don't forget to put the spade back in the shed."

"Got it."

"And Spencer, thanks for all your good work."

"Thanks for all the money James."

Jonathon finished paying for the chest of drawers, texted Mrs. Wilson's address to Spencer and began hunting for some sturdy wooden sun-loungers to put by the pool. He had always admired the slatted kind used on the decks of luxury cruise liners and it took just seconds to find some, complete with integrated side-tables. He ordered six, together with some olive green cushions and also chose a large outdoor dining table with a huge sun umbrella. It would be months before any of it would be used, but Jonathon didn't care; he was on a roll.

He reflected on the difference between himself and David. While he was content with an unassuming car and a comfortable house in the country, David had dashed out and bought a Bentley, two incredibly expensive ocean-going vessels and, once he qualified for his pilot's licence, no doubt he would buy a helicopter, too. 'And why not? Bless his heart.' thought Jonathon. What he didn't know was that David would shortly be completing the purchase of both a mansion in Virginia Water and a large penthouse in Chelsea Harbour, conveniently situated opposite London's Heliport.

He also didn't know that it was from the Heliport that he would one day be having to make his escape and flee the country.

The black phone rang again, and this time it was Cecil.

"So James, where were we?"

Jonathon chuckled. "You got the briefcase then?"

"Yes; piece of cake."

"I think I was about to ask whether you could superimpose a title on an existing program."

"Not as a separate signal, no. First I'd have to duplicate the program on the server, put on the type, give it the same identifying code as the original and then switch the files."

"Sounds like a yes to me."

"But I would need to know exactly how long from the start of the program you'd like the title to appear and for how many seconds you want it to stay on."

"And would it be possible to do it to a live broadcast?"

"That would involve what we call a piggy-back; it's a bit more complicated but yes, it's possible."

"Excellent. And another thing; if I emailed you some original footage, could you use it to interrupt a program?"

"Yes, what kind of footage?"

"Footage of me, speaking directly to camera."

"Are you crazy?"

"Don't worry, nobody will know it's me."

"There's one thing you need to know," said Cecil, "everything you want to do will have to be done on the same night. Once Quasar realizes it's been compromised, they'll double-check everything that's held on the main servers."

"And you're sure you can do this without being caught?" asked Jonathon.

"Don't worry, I'll watch my back," said Cecil, "and besides, for two hundred grand I'm prepared to take the risk."

They talked some more and it was agreed that Jonathon would take his time to work out exactly what he wanted Cecil to do and then email the details the following week. Then, once Cecil had confirmed it could all be done, he would be told the location of another fifty thousand pounds, with the balance payable the day after the big night.

"You'll text me a dedicated email address, right?" said Jonathon.

"I'll set it up and send it over today."

Too excited by the prospect of playing havoc with some TV programs, Jonathon finished with his online shopping spree and studied the schedules for the next few weeks. He wanted to find an evening during which there would be several programs worthy of ridicule and he found one, a week on Saturday, which was just twelve days away.

Jonathon had a busy week, most of which was spent writing and honing the words that he would be instructing Cecil to have appear on the screen in certain programs. Using the built-in camera in his laptop, he also recorded himself delivering a short speech, for which he wore his long dark curly wig, moustache and glasses. Although he delivered it in his Birmingham accent, he nonetheless ran the soundtrack through some distortion software that he tracked down on the internet. He had also made sure to remove the pictures on the wall behind him, leaving it nondescript and untraceable.

Satisfied with his preparations, he turned his attention to what he, Bianca and the children might do at the weekend. He wanted the three of them to have a weekend to remember but, most of all, he wanted the children to like Bianca, and Bianca to like the children.

Eventually he decided on two separate adventures and advised them all to bring warm scruffy clothes and waterproof coats.

17 | Fishing and fighting

Jonathon usually picked up the children on the Friday evening, but he felt uncomfortable about them sleeping in the spare room, knowing that he and Bianca were in bed together on the other side of the wall. He thought it was too soon, so he arranged to collect them early on Saturday morning and spent the night at Bianca's flat.

"How scruffy?" she asked.

"Very scruffy," said Jonathon, "the oldest, scruffiest, shabbiest clothes you've got; and also you'll need shoes you don't care about."

"I wish you'd tell me what we're doing."

Jonathon dodged the subject. "Don't worry, you can wear something nice to meet Nicholas and Jackie and then get changed at the hotel."

"Where is it?"

"Deal, on the Kent coast."

They rolled up outside Wendy's house at eight in the morning and the children had obviously told their mother that their father was bringing his new girlfriend, for Wendy came to the door and strained to get a glimpse of Bianca in the passenger seat.

"Is she nice?" asked his ex-wife.

"No, she's pig-ugly with bad breath, a horrible personality and she *hates* children," said Jonathon.

"Idiot; well I hope you'll all have a lovely time together."

With Bianca in the front seat, there was no need to toss a coin to decide which of the children would sit there and they happily piled into the back while Jonathon fetched their bags and threw them into the boot.

Bianca turned round to greet them. "Hi, I'm Bianca."

"Hello, I'm Jackie."

"I've heard all about you," said Bianca, "you're very pretty."

Nicholas grunted a greeting. It was not a rude grunt, just non-committal.

"And you must be Nicholas."

"Yup, that's me."

"I've heard all about you, too," said Bianca, "you're very handsome."

Nicholas gave forth a special, appreciative grunt, and followed it up with a broad smile.

"In fact you're better looking than your father," added Bianca, "but whatever you do, don't tell him I said so."

With that one deft stroke; a simple, conspiratorial suggestion, Bianca had the children warm to her, with the three of them sharing a little secret that was hidden from the father.

The children stopped giggling as soon as Jonathon climbed in, and he immediately sensed something was afoot. "I hope you're not talking about me."

"Of course not dad," said Nicholas, "how's Boris behaving?"

"Who's Boris?" asked Bianca.

"Boris the Bristol!" said Jackie, proud to be in the know.

"What's 'the Bristol'?"

"It's the car you're sitting in, and not for the first time," said Jonathon, keen to cut short any further confusion, "it was made by a manufacturer based in Bristol."

Bianca laughed, "well thank God it wasn't made in Stoke-on-Trent, or Scunthorpe."

This began a game which lasted for several miles of their

journey out of London and onto the motorway through Kent, with each of them proffering ideas for unfortunately named, imaginary cars.

"And what do you drive?" asked Nicholas of himself. "Me?" he replied, "I drive a Huddersfield Hatchback."

"A Cardiff Car," offered Jackie, who hadn't quite got the hang of it.

Bending the rules, Jonathon amused himself by naming a few real-life vehicles which sounded as preposterous as any that the others were making up, and which Bianca and the children assumed he was inventing.

His favourite was the Mitsubishi 'Lettuce', a genuine vehicle whose name had presumably been chosen by a focus group; a focus group consisting mainly of salad enthusiasts whose opinions were blindly trusted by the manufacturer.

"And what do you drive?"

"I drive a Mitsubishi Lettuce."

"You get mayo with that?"

Predictably, by the time they were half-way to Deal, the children were asleep and Bianca was slowly nodding off, with none of them having any idea of what Jonathon had in store for the weekend. He had booked three rooms in a little hotel overlooking the sea and, after they had settled in, they gathered back at the car dressed in shabby clothes that didn't matter anymore.

"Excellent," said Jonathon, "you all look a right mess."

The road went inland from Deal, but as they neared Dover, with the sea now in view, Nicholas made an educated guess, preceded by one of his most positive and excited grunts. "Yay!" he said. "We're going to catch some fish!"

"We might do," said Jonathon, "we just might; we're certainly going fishing."

He turned into the marina car park and rolled the car

right up to the water's edge, whereupon they all leapt out and grabbed their wet-weather gear from the boot. Jonathon scanned the boats lined up next to the jetty and found the one he had booked. At eleven metres and with a broad beam, it was the largest and most comfortable recreational deep-sea fishing vessel he had been able to find and it was thoughtfully equipped with a few basic comforts. It also had immensely powerful twin inboard engines that reduced the amount of time it took to get to and from the best fishing grounds.

They strolled up and introduced themselves to a rotund, ruddy-faced man who wore oil-skins and who Jonathon assumed was the skipper.

"Hello there," he said, "we're the Taylor party."

"And I'm Alan," said the man, extending a meaty, weather-beaten hand, "climb aboard and I'll get the kettle on."

The two men warmly shook hands as Bianca and the children stepped onto the boat and started to acquaint themselves.

"Daddy", said Jackie, "will it be safe?"

"Oh, I dunno 'bout that young missy," said Alan, winking at Jonathon, "there be storms a rollin' in afore sundown."

Seeing the horrified look on Jackie's face, Alan dropped his pirate act and reassured her. "Only joking, little one. I've been taking folk fishing in these waters for nearly thirty years and I haven't lost anyone yet."

At this, Bianca smiled and Jackie folded her arms and gave Alan one of her most excoriating looks.

"The fact is," he went on, "if there were any storms on the way, we wouldn't even leave harbour; I don't take risks with peoples' lives, especially not my own."

While they waited for another party of people to arrive, Alan outlined the plan for the next few hours, which was basically a fifteen-minute trip to where he thought the fish would be, three hour's fishing and a fifteen-minute trip back.

"How do you know where the fish are?" asked Nicholas.

Alan tapped his bulbous nose with a pudgy finger. "Experience," he said, "and also I've got myself a little helper."

He guided Nicholas to the wheelhouse, showed him the sonar screen and explained how it worked. "It sends down signals which bounce off the sea-bed and come back, but if there are shoals of fish around, some of the signals bounce off the fish and take less time to get back to the boat."

"Cool," said Nicholas.

Alan made mugs of tea for Jonathon and Bianca and gave the children some orange juice before readying the boat for departure. He had an assistant, Lenny, a younger and similarly weather-beaten soul, who was there to help people get to know their rods and reels and also to bait-up the hooks for the squeamish, whom that day were to include Bianca and Jackie.

After a few minutes the other passengers arrived; a family of four with two young children and, after they were given some refreshments, Lenny cast off fore and aft and coiled the ropes neatly back on deck.

Protected by two massive, curved groynes, the water was perfectly calm as Alan reversed and then swung the boat round before putting both engines into forward gear and steering towards the mouth of the harbour, where the surface became gradually choppier as he opened up the throttle and headed out into open sea.

Making about 28 knots, which was well within the boat's capabilities, the eight passengers relaxed and enjoyed the fresh sea air and the occasional spray of water on their faces, while Alan kept his eye on the sonar until he felt it was worth cutting the engines and starting to fish.

Bianca and Jackie didn't much care for the sight and feel of lugworms and ragworms and cared even less for the thought of impaling them on sharp hooks and having their blood run out over their fingers, so Lenny did the honours, casted for them and passed them back their rods, which they handled with a mixture of hope and dread.

Jonathon and Nicholas had no such qualms about threading worms onto hooks and were soon fishing independently, gradually teasing their quarry some thirty feet below with a variety of short, sharp jerks, interspersed with longer, slower movements of the bait as they gradually reeled in.

For twenty minutes, there was nothing, then suddenly there came a squeal of joy from the six year-old boy in the other party.

"Fish on!" exclaimed Alan, and he went to see if he could be of any help, but the boy's father had already taken over and, after a short fight, he landed a nice sea bass of about 4lbs, which would make for a good supper for their whole family.

All was then quiet for a few minutes before Bianca felt a huge tug on her line, and Jonathon would have gone to her aid were it not for himself and Nicholas both hooking something simultaneously.

While Alan helped Bianca, Jonathon and Nicholas both reeled in a pair of equally handsome bass, from which they extracted the hooks and placed in the fish tub amidships.

To add to the drama, Jackie too then hooked something big and, startled, dropped her rod onto the deck, so while Alan helped Bianca, Jonathon helped Jackie, and he was taken aback by the force with which her catch was tugging on the line.

"I reckon that might be a conger," said Alan, seeing how Jonathon was struggling, "take it slowly and keep well clear of it after we get it on board."

Conger eels were renowned for not reacting kindly to being caught and were especially vicious once they had been gaffed and were thrashing around on deck. There were disturbing tales of how, their jaws snapping wildly, they had removed large chunks of flesh from people who had chosen to fish barefoot and in shorts.

While Alan eventually landed Bianca's 20lb cod, Jonathon was still struggling with Jackie's rod which, although short, thick and very stout, was nonetheless considerably bent over under the strain.

Alan was proved correct and after another five minutes of battling, he was able to gaff the conger as Jonathon drew it alongside the boat. Hauling it aboard, its jaws opening and closing convulsively, Alan wasted no time in delivering a massive blow to the top of its head and heaving it into the holding tub, where it took up a good deal of the space. Later, he measured it at 67lbs, which was only slightly less than Jackie.

"You must take it home to mummy," said Jonathon, with a mischievous glint in his eye, "she'll be *so* pleased."

Bianca thought this highly unlikely and she looked at Jonathon reproachfully.

"No, really," he said, "she *loves* conger eels."

"Yeah dad," said Nicholas, "sure she does."

For the next half hour, nobody landed another fish nor even reported a bite, so Alan ordered everyone to reel in, then started up the engines and went in search of pastures new. Five minutes later, with freshly baited hooks, everyone was fishing again and it soon became clear they had hit upon a shoal of sea bass, where they spent a satisfying hour before heading back to harbour.

The combined tally for the afternoon was eleven sea bass, three cod and one very large conger eel, which Jonathon hoped would fit inside the hotel's freezer. Alan and Lenny bagged up what their passengers wanted to take away with them and were happy to receive two cod and half a dozen sea bass as their tip for the afternoon.

Back at the hotel, over dinner, the talk was mostly of Jackie's conger eel and she felt very pleased with herself that she had hooked the biggest catch of the day.

"Sorry I was sick though, dad," she said.

"Never mind; at least you did it overboard," said Jonathon, "but let's not discuss it while we're eating, hmm?"

"What are we doing tomorrow?" asked Bianca.

"Yeah dad," said Nicholas, "you're not going to keep keeping it secret are you?"

"I'll give you a clue," said Jonathon, "it'll be very colourful."

After dinner, the four of them went to the hotel's small but comfortable living room and watched a bit of TV before getting an early night. Jonathon couldn't concentrate on the movie and instead found himself smiling at was going to happen exactly a week later, provided Cecil came good on all the promises he'd made about what he could do with TV programmes.

Jonathon packed the children off to their rooms and as he and Bianca lay in bed later, she snuggled up to him affectionately. "That was my first time."

"Really?"

"I mean deep sea fishing, you idiot," she said, "I really enjoyed it."

"Good, so did I."

"What are we doing tomorrow?" she tried once more.

"Wait and see."

Having breathed lungsful of ozone all afternoon, the four of them slept unusually deeply and awoke feeling thoroughly rested. They showered and gathered once more in the dining room, where they ate the giant breakfast which had been described on the hotel's website, and which had settled Jonathon's decision about where they should stay the night. Afterwards, he remembered to retrieve the bass and the conger eel that their hosts had kindly allowed them to store in their freezer.

Back on the road, there were several more demands to know what they were going to be doing that day, but Jonathon stood his ground and teased them with various suggestions.

ACCORDING TO THE DAILY MAIL

"We're going up in a space rocket."

"Wow, really?" said Jackie.

"No," said Jonathon, "unfortunately it was fully booked."

It was only when they passed a sign reading 'Paintballing 1 mile ahead' that the cat was finally out of the bag.

"Yay," said Nicholas, who had done it before at a friend's birthday treat.

"Oh dear," said Bianca, "I'm not sure I'm going to like this."

"Nonsense," said Jonathon, "it'll put some colour in your cheeks."

"That's what I'm afraid of."

"Will it be safe?" asked Jackie.

They parked up and Jonathon was surprised at the large number of people who had already arrived, forgetting how hugely popular the pastime had become, giving vent as it did to peoples' innermost desire to indulge in combat. After signing the various disclaimer forms, which basically absolved the organisers from any blame for any injuries that might occur to anyone, it was time for them to get kitted up in all the gear and to be introduced to their weapons, which looked like a cross between a machine gun and a sad attempt at an alien's death-ray from a 1950's sci-fi B-movie.

Bianca and Jackie were pleasantly surprised at the level of protection afforded by their head-to-toe combat suits, helmets and body armour and they started to feel nearly as gung-ho as the boys, whose predisposition to enjoying armed conflict came more naturally.

They were encouraged to try out their weapons in the practice area and, along with several other players, they all gleefully fired off dozens of balls of red, yellow, green, brown, orange and blue paint at classic military-style targets which depicted snarling, rifle-brandishing soldiers, positioned in the undergrowth some ten to twenty yards away.

There followed a mass briefing of all the participants, beginning with very strict safety instructions and going on to describe the various games on the agenda, with a break for lunch half-way through.

The surprise of the day was Jackie, who moved around the courses stealthily and mostly on her belly, using whatever cover she could take advantage of. She used her ammunition sparingly, sniper-like, and recorded the most 'kills' while being hit herself only twice.

By contrast, Nicholas might just as well have stood in the open, stock still, and invited everyone to throw tins of paint all over him, such was his habit of breaking cover with blind enthusiasm and forgetting that he too was a target. Unfortunately, there had opened up a gap between his helmet and the neck of his combat suit and the colourful contents of several paint balls had oozed out and dripped down inside.

"I'm very proud of you darling," Jonathon told Jackie as they all struggled out of their protective clothing, "I had no idea you would be so cunning."

"Someone told me they sting," she said, "the pellets; the paint ball thingies, so I didn't want to be hit."

"I wish I'd done the same as you," said Bianca, "I'm sure I must be covered in bruises."

"As for you," said Jonathon, turning to Nicholas, "you look like a Dulux colour chart; I want you to promise me something."

"What dad?"

"Never join the army."

As they drove back to London, it came as no surprise to Jonathon that Bianca and the children soon fell fast asleep and he felt a sense of deep contentment that they had all bonded so well. Bianca had taken care never to foist herself on Nicholas or Jackie and had instead mostly waited for them to initiate direct contact, to which she had responded in a friendly, affectionate manner, leaving them feeling increasingly comfortable about approaching her. He had been particularly touched at how, on the boat, Bianca had cuddled Jackie all the way back to the harbour, partly to warm her up and partly to comfort her after the ignominy of her throwing up over the side.

Arriving back at Wendy's, Jackie tapped Bianca on the shoulder, "when will we see you again?"

"I don't know darling; soon I hope."

"Me too," and she gave her a kiss on the cheek.

"Bye Bianca," said Nicholas, "you're pretty cool."

"You're not so bad yourself," she said, "but your father's right about you not joining the army."

Nicholas carried his and Jackie's bags to the door while Jonathon wrestled with a large black bin-liner containing a partially defrosted 67lb conger eel.

"Jackie's brought you a lovely present," he said to Wendy, handing it to her.

"What the hell is it?"

"It's a conger eel mummy," said Jackie, swelling with pride, "I caught it."

Why that's *lovely* darling," said Wendy, who with her free hand cradled her daughter's head close to her chest while shooting a withering glare at Jonathon.

"It'll make a delicious stew," said Jonathon playfully, "and it'll keep you going for weeks."

"Bye dad," said a technicolour Nicholas, "it was great."

As he settled back into the car, Bianca frowned at him. "I saw the look she gave you."

"I know, what fun. Let's get back to your place and bake one of those bass. I know a great recipe which involves completely encrusting them in salt."

"Will you stay the night?"

"I'd love to, but I'd better get home because first thing in the morning I've got to concentrate on that project I told you about."

But it was naive of him to think he would be able to tear himself away from her, for she was now under his skin, deep in the heart of him, and he in hers.

18 | Something odd on the television

When Jonathon awoke his thoughts immediately turned to contacting Cecil and briefing him on the following Saturday evening's mischief. He slid carefully out of bed but had no need to be quiet, for Bianca moaned softly and turned over.

"Good luck with your media studies," she yawned, "I'll be busy studying the physiology of guinea pigs."

And with that, she fell asleep again.

Back home, Jonathon revisited the preparations he had made the week before and tweaked a few words before emailing Cecil and attaching the video file of him speaking to camera. He followed it up with a text advising him to check his inbox.

Within five minutes, his black phone rang.

"James?"

"Cecil," said Jonathon, "what did you think?"

"It's very mischievous but it's all fairly straightforward; I'll make a start once I've got my second fifty thousand."

Jonathon told him the whereabouts of the other package he had buried in Mrs. Wilson's back garden.

"Got it," said Cecil, "after 11pm, eight paces from the water butt, eighteen inches from the fence, put the spade back in the shed."

"I'll text you the address," said Jonathon, "call me if you have any problems."

"With the money?"

"No, with fooling around with the TV schedules."

Jonathon sat back and wondered what he was going to do all week. He also wondered what he was going to do with the rest of his life, and with the eight million pounds he would still have left after the house purchase had gone through. And he wondered about Bianca; could she really be the next Mrs. Taylor? Did he want a child with her? He realised that the answer to both of those questions was 'yes'.

He decided to go on the internet and shop for a few more things for the house, but first he clicked on MailOnline to see what they were up to.

It was the same old thing, except they were no longer able to pad out non-stories about D-list celebs with irrelevant photographs taken by the paps years ago. Jonathon had put paid to that. But their preoccupation with the value of things was still plain to see, for he found an article about a very nasty car crash in which one of the vehicles was 'worth £250k' and that the accident had taken place 'in one of London's most expensive streets', as if that might have affected the severity of the injuries to the cars' occupants. In another piece, they had thought it important to mention that a mother who had killed three of her children had done so 'at her £1.2m family house'.

He was about to start looking for more furniture when it dawned on him that there would soon be just the other briefcase at the lost property office with which to pay Cecil the balance of his fee. He needed to free up another fifty thousand. He had it in his flat but thought it wiser to get back one of the bundles that David was holding for him.

"Hello, Jonathon!"

"David, I need to get hold of one of those packages."

"What packages?"

"Of fifty grand."

"Bloody hell, *now* what are you up to?"

"Nothing much, can I come over?"

"Have you had breakfast yet?"

"Actually no," said Jonathon, "and come to think of it, I'm starving."

"See you at the café in 15 minutes."

When they met, David handed over one of the same two plastic bags that Jonathon had prepared the day after their fight with Bobble Hat and his gang; the same day Bianca had slipped him her phone number.

"Is this the one from your place, or from Bertie's boot?"

"From my place; does it matter?"

"It might."

Over breakfast, they updated each other about what they'd been up to since getting back from Amsterdam, about Amy and Bianca, about David's mansion and penthouse and big boys' toys, and about Jonathon's new place in Hampshire.

"What do you need the fifty for?" asked David eventually.

"I have to pay someone."

"But I thought you'd finished tormenting the papers."

"I have finished tormenting the papers."

Back at his flat, Jonathon pondered the question of how he would get the fourth lot of fifty grand to Cecil. He could always hand in another bag as lost property, or use Heathrow's left luggage facilities again, but he wanted to find another method; he wanted to give himself a fresh challenge. But he had all week to think about it, so first he chased up the estate agent and the solicitor in the hope of speeding up the survey and the exchange of contracts, before going online and finding another chest of drawers. With Bianca in mind, he found and bought a very large one.

The following day, while he was still pondering where to leave another package for Cecil, his white phone rang.

"Jonathon?"

"Mrs. Wilson!" he said, "how lovely to hear from you."

"Jonathon, I hope you don't think I'm being silly, but do you think there might be any badgers here in Battersea?"

"I think it's highly unlikely," said Jonathon, "I'm sure they're much happier in rural areas."

"Well, the funny thing is, I'm having a little bit of lamb this evening."

"Er, yes," said Jonathon, who struggled to understand how a little bit of lamb might be in any way amusing, "that sounds nice."

"And I went into the garden to snip off a few sprigs of rosemary and I found two big holes in the flower bed."

"Good heavens," said Jonathon, "so you think there might be a badger about?"

"Well, I just wondered," said Mrs. Wilson, "anyway, we can talk about it on Thursday."

"Oh dear, I'm so sorry," said Jonathon, "I can't do gardening work anymore; I'm afraid I've been having trouble with my back. But don't worry, I'll find someone else who can help you."

"That would be very kind Jonathon; I wish you well."

He hung up and tittered to himself. At least Cecil had remembered to put the spade back in the shed, otherwise Mrs. Wilson would have been even more discombobulated.

Once again he started to think of an ingenious way in which he could safely convey the final fifty thousand to Cecil. He considered taping it behind the cistern of a lavatory somewhere, like in the way a revolver had been hidden for Michael in The Godfather, but he soon dismissed the idea on the grounds that it was not his. Leaving it in a rubbish bin would be too risky and besides, even though he had never met him, he didn't want to make Cecil go rummaging around among half-eaten hamburgers and goodness knows what else. And then it struck him. He would book a room in Cecil's name at the Dorchester hotel and leave a briefcase for him at reception. It was hardly brilliant, but in this way he could also treat himself to one of their excellent afternoon teas.

The following day he bought another briefcase, loaded it with the money, took the bus to Hyde Park Corner and walked up Park Lane to the hotel.

"And what's inside the case sir?" asked the receptionist.

Jonathon hadn't reckoned on being quizzed as to its contents, but he figured it didn't matter them knowing. After all, this was the Dorchester; women checked into this hotel wearing knickers worth more than fifty grand.

"It's fifty thousand pounds," said Jonathon, and he rotated the six-digit combination lock and opened the case to let the receptionist take a look.

"Very well," she said, without batting an eyelid, "obviously we have to be very careful about what we allow in our storeroom. And your friend will be here on Sunday, yes?"

"Or possibly Monday," said Jonathon, "I'm not sure of his schedule."

He wandered off and chose a table to the side of the Promenade; a position perfect for people-watching, and ordered the traditional afternoon tea. He had deliberately starved himself for the occasion and was soon gorging on an impressive selection of finger sandwiches, scones with strawberry jam and clotted cream and some delicious light pastries, all of which was accompanied by a pot of Orange Pekoe tea.

As he sat, he gazed around at the fabulously wealthy patrons, some of whom had never done a day's work in their lives. And then he remembered; he was fairly wealthy too, and he would never have to work again if he chose not to.

Feeling a bit bloated, the fairly wealthy Jonathon walked back to Hyde Park Corner and hopped on the bus home, where as soon as he walked through the door his white phone rang.

"Jonathon," said David, "I'm having a big night on Saturday; want to come along?"

"Er, well," Jonathon faltered, "I'm planning a quiet night in on Saturday."

"It's only Wednesday for Christ sake! How can you plan a quiet night in this far ahead?"

"There's something on the telly I don't want to miss."

"Oh I see; what is it?"

"Me."

After David had unsuccessfully tried to get his friend to explain himself, they hung up and Jonathon realised he was somehow going to have to manage Bianca's expectations. Their relationship was such that she now assumed he was hers at weekends. She was content that he might be too busy during the week, but Fridays, Saturdays and Sundays were different. They were her time. They were play time.

He called her and said that he could see her on Friday and Sunday but not on Saturday, because an old school friend had invited him to a Premiership late kick-off game in Manchester and he probably wouldn't get back to London until gone midnight.

"But you don't even like football."

"No, not much, but I like him and I haven't seen him in ages," said Jonathon, "and anyway a really good football match can be very enjoyable."

"When was the last time you saw one?"

"Fifteen years ago."

Bianca chuckled. "Well I'm glad you don't make a habit of it."

After they finished, Jonathon considered the implications of her statement. It was the statement of a woman who was thinking long-term; of a woman who could see herself spending the rest of her life with him, and he liked her train of thought.

With the exception of Friday night, which involved an evening at the theatre and a fabulous supper at J Sheekey, the next three days went slowly for him and he longed for it to be Saturday evening.

As the hour neared, he texted Cecil, 'all set?'

'All set.'

'I'll tell you how to get the rest of your money in the morning.'

Next he called the Star of India and ordered a lamb madras, some dahl, a brinjal bhajee and a few puppudoms. Then he opened a chilled bottle of Auslese.

He then turned on the television and watched the early evening news. With nothing fresh to report, the attacks on the tabloids had long since dropped off the news agenda and they wouldn't return until the police made some kind of breakthrough, a breakthrough which Jonathon was sure was never going to happen.

In Aldershot, Brian and Terry were having a couple of quiet pints at the Crimea Inn, where much of the talk was about Terry's new face.

"You look gorgeous," said Brian, "gissa kiss."

"Fuck off," said Terry, proffering his left cheek, "but you can kiss my arse," which was a phrase he had started to use a lot.

Meanwhile, while Brian was out, Penny was at home, hopping between the various desperate shopping channels, on which the presenters spoke ridiculously earnestly about the wonderfully fabulous and quite amazing and breathtakingly beautiful and fantastically elegant and simply divine examples of average goods that they were trying to pass off as bargains of the century. Many of them were made with inferior materials by empty-eyed young children who were paid a pittance somewhere in the third world. Despite this heinous profiteering, when there were no conventional comedy programs scheduled, the shopping channels guaranteed satisfaction.

'And remember this,' a presenter would exclaim, as if it were the most staggering fact in the world about an ordinary pair of emerald earrings, 'you can wear them with literally *any* colour!'

'Oh yes that is *so* true,' would add the co-presenter, 'and they're ideal for everything from an intimate dinner party to a trip to a school sports day or even just an afternoon's shopping!'

'Aren't they just *irresistible*? *And* you can buy them with just three easy payments of £29.99 – that's *under* £90!'

Penny was toying with the idea of buying a nine-carat gold necklace, which the presenters had breathlessly showered with glowing, insincere plaudits, when suddenly some words appeared on the screen of her television.

'You're not seriously thinking of buying this crap are you?'

They faded out and were replaced by:

'It really is a complete waste of money.'

Penny blinked, scarcely believing what she had just seen, but she nevertheless put away her credit card.

In Shepherd's Bush, Mr. and Mrs. Lawson had settled down to watch a talent show hosted by a pair of anodyne cheeky chappies who did little other than stand around making lame comments about the proceedings, each grinning at the other inanely as they waited patiently for their own turn to add nothing clever or entertaining.

Meanwhile the panel of judges, who sat imperiously between the audience and the stage, shared their bland pearls of wisdom concerning the merits of each act. Given the obscene size of the fees they were paid, these pearls were worth several thousand pounds each. Several thousand pounds for saying "Y'know what darlin'? I think you're going to go on to be a *massive* star; I really *really* do!"

Mr. and Mrs. Lawson, along with millions of others around the country, were taken aback when a message suddenly appeared on their television screens.

'Don't you wish you could just watch the acts?'

'You don't need these smug, overpaid judges to tell you how good the performances are.'

Jonathon chuckled to himself as he took another sip of his Auslese and followed it with a mouthful of lamb madras.

Later on there was an excruciating show which followed the self-obsessed goings-on in a Los Angeles-based family; a family with which the MailOnline had been besotted for many years and about whom they ran several dozen trivial pieces every week, each accompanied by plenty of photographs which, other than being taken from slightly different angles, were essentially the same. Helpfully, they added captions to the pictures describing in minute detail what the women were wearing, as if their readers couldn't see.

In the TV show, the conversations between the various family members was at best stultifying and it generally centred around the banal, mundane things they had been doing and what they all privately thought of each other:

"And then we went to the nail parlour and then we like, y'know, hung out at the mall."

"Don't get me wrong; maybe I wish she'd cut me some slack but I love my sister so *so* much, I *really* do."

"That bag is like, you know, just *awesome.*"

Jonathon didn't know that the bag was just awesome, and was surprised that anyone else might know that it was just awesome, because it was decidedly gaudy, but he didn't have to wait long before his messages appeared on the screen.

'Do you realise that watching this drivel will melt your brain?'

'Why do people worship these vacuous, talentless narcissists?'

But America did not hold a monopoly on reality TV shows that were largely made-up, scripted twaddle, and there was one such which took place in a UK county famed for the jokes about its female population, who were depicted as either slappers, or airheads, or both.

'What do Essex girls use for protection during sex?'

'A bus shelter.'

'How do you make an Essex girl laugh on a Saturday?'

'Tell her a joke on Wednesday.'

Unfortunately, the television show did little to prove that the dozens of Essex gags were an unfair representation of the residents of that county, featuring as it did a repetitious round of who's going out with whom, who's shagging whom, who's getting engaged to whom, who's breaking up from whom, who's going out to a party and who's wearing the most risqué outfits. It was superficial dross about one-dimensional people who could barely speak English properly, let alone attempt a sentence in which there were more than two clauses.

Nevertheless, it had plenty of fans who tuned in regularly, and who were surprised that evening to see a super fade up half way through.

'The only way is to turn it off.'

'Why? Because it's hollow, confected, scripted drivel.'

He flipped channels to where several alleged celebrities had agreed, for staggering sums of money, to share a house for a few weeks and to do little else but bicker among themselves and try to score points off each other. An annoying voiceover repeatedly told viewers what time it was that the following scene had been recorded, before cutting to footage of two people snarling and being horrible to each other. The producers of the show were always delighted when one of the inmates went too far, because they could then tell them off, in an attempt to sensationalise something, *anything*. One by one, the public voted the sad slebs off the show until only one remained, the one who was crowned the winner; although how they had succeeded in 'winning' was largely unclear.

'Why do you watch this trash?'

'There are much better programs on other channels.'

'Including the weather forecast.'

Jonathon was delighted with Cecil's work and he looked forward to the main event; a short film which he had timed to appear at 10pm across most of the major channels.

He finished off the rest of his curry, poured another glass of wine and sat back to ruminate on the evening's entertainment, happily picturing TV executives tearing their hair out in disbelief, determined that heads must roll. One person who would be safe from the inquests was Cecil, who had taken care to remove all traces of his digital footprint from the servers after he had made Jonathon's changes.

Big Ben dutifully struck ten o'clock and the image on the screens of millions of viewers cut to a man with long dark curly hair, a moustache, and glasses. Looking directly at the camera, he spoke in a Birmingham accent that had been slightly distorted electronically.

"Hello, some of you might have noticed some unusual things happening on the telly this evening. Well, that was just a bit of fun, but it was done to invite you to think. It was done to encourage you to think about what you watch, and the effect it might be having on you, on your values and on your view of the world. Let's face it, much of what's on television is worthless codswallop. What is the point of a quiz program in which many of the questions simply test a person's knowledge of who appeared in a reality TV show, or what happened in a soap opera? What kind of knowledge is that? Is it of any value? Is it of any importance? And what does it prove, other than demonstrating that one contestant watches more crappy telly than another?"

In Aldershot, Brian was raising his pint to his lips when he caught sight of the television above the bar in the Crimea Inn. "Bloody hell, it's James!"

"Eh?" said Terry.

"James, the bloke who paid us," said Brian, "looks like he found someone who can fool around with broadcasting."

"Reality TV might have some merit if it was exactly that – reality, using fly-on-the-wall cameras, but no, it's not real. It's a set-up. It's a con. And yet the talentless people who appear on these shows are called stars and are fawned over by the tabloids. And the public breath oxygen into this merry-go-round of artificiality and mediocrity by watching it and reading about it. Your mind is a valuable tool; why soak it in garbage, where it will rot and become indistinguishable from the garbage itself?"

Bianca was watching too, in total disbelief, but there was something about the man on the television that she couldn't quite put her finger on; something familiar, something she couldn't help but like.

"You're being manipulated. TV companies are appealing to your shallow side, enticing you, collecting you, wrapping you up into parcels of ratings and selling you off to businesses and corporations purely so they can reach you with their commercials, most of which are even more brainless than the shows in which they appear. Maybe you should turn over. Or turn off. Maybe you should read a book. Thanks for watching. Nemesis."

Once Jonathon had finished speaking, all the channels suddenly snapped back to their normal schedules and people across the country were left stunned at what had just happened, some of them feeling thoughtful and introspective and some of them angry that they had just been made to sit through an unwelcome lecture. But they all felt that, whoever he was, he had a point.

Jonathon turned off the television, poured himself a large Laphroaig and had a quiet, private celebration to mark the end of his adventures with the media, although he was already planning a bit of fun with some other companies. Later he caught the 11 o'clock news on the radio, where the lead story was what had happened on the television that evening. The media are going to have a field day, he thought, and he couldn't wait to go and get the morning's papers.

As Detective Inspector Foot sat in his armchair, he knew two things, neither of which was very helpful. One was that the man he wanted to catch definitely didn't look like the man he had just witnessed hack into the country's television networks; the other was that he didn't sound like him, either.

Before he went to bed, Jonathon cleared everything back into the kitchen and, just in case, he checked the result of a football match that had taken place in Manchester earlier in the evening.

19 | Yogi the yacht

He was awoken by a text arriving on his black phone. It was from Brian.

'Congratulations. You're quite the TV star now, eh?'

'Does the Pope shit in the woods?' replied Jonathon.

He rang Cecil and congratulated him on a job well done. He also told him there was a briefcase waiting for him at the Dorchester and described to him the other case that he could collect from the lost property office. He gave him the two combination codes, advised him not to be too conspicuous spending the money, wished him well and hung up.

He then prepared a cafetiere and while it was brewing he nipped around the corner to the newsagents to get the Sunday papers, all of which had led on their front pages with news of what he had done the night before. Strictly speaking it wasn't all of the papers, because four of them were still out of production.

Back home he poured coffee and devoured what had been written, which varied between indignant outrage to mild admiration, with each paper offering a range of theories as to who was responsible, why he had done it, and what he hoped to achieve. All of them noted that the man on the television had been more avuncular than dictatorial and had done no evil. One of them spotted that he had avoided using the first person singular, just like he had done in his letter to the papers a few weeks' prior.

Jonathon texted Bianca, 'are you awake yet?'

She replied, 'no.'

'Ok I'll see if you're awake in a hour or so.'

'Shush.'

Jonathon shushed and gave some thought as to what he and Bianca might do that day. He decided in the end to take her to the Natural History Museum, followed by a leisurely late lunch and then back to her apartment to play with the new toys they'd bought in a shop in Soho on Friday night.

He was enjoying some deeply wicked and lascivious thoughts when the white phone interrupted him.

"I didn't see it live but I've seen the stills; I know it was you," said David.

"How?"

"Partly because you told me you were going to be on the TV and partly because you described your disguise, you plonker."

"Ah yes," said Jonathon, "so I did."

"But let's talk about it on the yacht."

"Eh?"

David was too excited to talk about anything other than Yogi, which had recently finished being fitted out in Southampton and which was about to have her final sea trials before being taken to her permanent mooring on the Hamble. He was planning to sail her over to Cherbourg the following weekend and would Jonathon and Bianca like to come? And maybe Nicholas and Jackie?

"We'd love to," said Jonathon.

"Great. Amy's coming of course and she's going to bring her little daughter Charlotte and her brother Spencer."

Jonathon choked on his coffee; he remembered that in Amsterdam Amy had said something about her brother working in IT and having recently started to do rather well.

"Are you alright?"

"I'm fine; some coffee went down the wrong way," he said, "are you sure you're ready to sail this thing?"

David chuckled, "God no, I haven't got a clue yet," he said, "but fear not, I've hired a skipper and two crew to take us over there, plus a steward to look after us all."

"And this skipper, does *he* know what he's doing?"

"And what do you think yourself?"

"And there'll be eight of us; can Yogi sleep eight?"

"Jonathon," said David, "Yogi can sleep ten, plus the crew."

"Shall I shut up?"

"Please do."

Jonathon's mind was whirling. Surely Amy's brother Spencer couldn't be *his* Spencer? Surely there were lots of Spencers working in IT and surely some of these Spencers had recently started to do rather well. No, he thought, you're kidding yourself. He cast his mind back to the day they had met on the steps of the Albert Memorial. He had been wearing his disguise and using his Birmingham accent, so what was he worrying about? But still, he didn't want to wait until Friday to find out whether this man was Amy's brother. But of course, he was going to have to wait; he couldn't very well get in touch with him and ask if he was sailing over to Cherbourg next weekend. But he could maybe tease something out of him.

He picked up the black phone and sent him a text, 'remember I said I might have another job for you?'

Spencer wasted no time in replying, 'yes.'

'Can you make a start next weekend?'

'I'd rather not.'

'Why?'

'I've been invited on a boat.'

'Ok, it can wait. Have fun.'

So that was it. He was going to be stuck on a large yacht with the man to whom he had paid two hundred and fifty thousand pounds to help commit some major crimes. And where did the money come from originally? From the owner of the yacht.

Jonathon burst out laughing at the absurdity of it all.

But he was confident in the effectiveness of the disguise he had used, so he calmed down, ate a small breakfast and texted Bianca once more, 'now are you awake?'

'Not really.'

'Then get awake. I'm picking you up in an hour.'

'Please, an hour and a half.'

'Ok sleepy head.'

A couple of hours later they were wandering around the Natural History Museum, the aura of which always instilled in Jonathon a sense of wonder. Did these creatures really roam the earth tens of millions of years ago, and was their fate really sealed by the impact of a massive meteorite? He had to assume it was so.

They were attracted by different galleries so they agreed to go their separate ways and meet back at the diplodocus in the entrance hall after an hour. Not surprisingly, Bianca made a beeline for the small vertebrates. Meanwhile Jonathon headed up to the mineral collection, which was the most serene room in the building. It staggered him that the planet could be home to so many thousands of completely different substances of varying hues, lustres, densities and chemical compositions, and all of them made from just eight or so different elements. He paused at a selection of hexagonal crystals and considered their beautiful, maximal use of three dimensions.

Next he visited the botanical room, where he stood in silent awe of the genetic codes embedded in nature's seeds. Most were tiny, perhaps only one or two millimetres, yet they could be cast upon the same soil and give rise to such diverse fruits as apples, oranges, lemons, strawberries, blackberries and a myriad others.

If there *was* a God, he thought, he'd done a grand job.

It occurred to him that, while Bianca seemed to be more

interested in living, breathing creatures, he was more interested in the very building blocks of creation, and he wondered what that said about their respective psychologies.

He met up with her in the main hall as agreed and she immediately greeted him with one of her delightful left-field questions.

"Did you know," she said, "there are over five hundred million domestic cats in the world?"

"No sweetheart, I didn't know that."

"That's a lot of cats," she added, pressing home her point.

Jonathon agreed that five hundred million was indeed a great many cats but he was hungry and he turned the conversation to the question of lunch.

"What do you fancy eating?"

"Sushi," she said, quick as a flash, "and tempura."

They walked back to his car and headed to a Japanese restaurant in Marylebone where he often used to take lunch and where he often drank too much sake to be able to return to the office with any chance of hiding the fact.

"I completely forgot to tell you," he said as they ate, "we're sailing over to Cherbourg next weekend on David's new yacht."

"Oh wow."

"Amy is coming, and her daughter Charlotte, and her brother Spencer. And also it's my turn again with Nicholas and Jackie."

"I can't wait to see them again."

"I believe they feel the same darling; you made quite an impression on them."

"How was the match yesterday?" she asked, out of the blue.

"It was good, except it was a draw."

Jonathon knew she was testing him, and he was relieved that he had remembered to check the result of the game.

After a long and very satisfying lunch they went back to her apartment, where one of the Sunday papers was resting on the kitchen table.

She pointed to the headline on the front page. "Did you hear about this?"

"Of course, hasn't everyone?"

"I suppose you were driving back down from Manchester but I actually saw it," she added, "and whoever this man is, I thought he talked a lot of sense."

"I guess so, yes."

"I'd love to meet him; he reminded me a little of you."

Jonathon sidestepped this and suggested they had an early night, to which she readily agreed, and they made long and satisfying use of the collection of naughty knick-knacks they had picked up in Soho.

In the morning, as they ate breakfast, the talk turned to the trip to Cherbourg and what she should pack for the voyage.

"Bring anything you want," he said, "but don't…"

"…bring any dumb-bells?"

"Correct."

"And are you still busy with your 'media studies' this week?"

"No, I've finished with that."

As soon as the words left his lips, he regretted the timing of them in relation to Saturday night. He couldn't put his finger on why, but he felt she was teetering on the edge of suspecting that it was he who the papers were talking about. He badly wanted to open up to her; to tell her the truth. But they had something special between them and he was scared of spoiling it.

He left her to her veterinary studies and went home to chase the progress on the house in Hampshire. It would soon be Christmas and, since Wendy had had the children the previous year, he was keen for them to enjoy the festive season in a spacious, rambling house in the countryside, instead of a grim little flat in Clapham. In his mind's eye, he had already pictured the position of the tree in the large oak-paneled entrance hall; a tree that would be decorated by Bianca, naked on high heels.

It occurred to him that he should put his flat on the market, so he invited a local estate agent to come round and take instructions. Given there was no need to squeeze the maximum out of the asking price, he pitched it very competitively in the hope of making a quick sale.

Meanwhile, in an incident room at Scotland Yard, Detective Inspector foot was holding a meeting with his team.

"Right, so what have we got?"

"Still nothing," said Detective Bill Waters, "fuck all."

"But we do know that there are at least five people involved," said Foot, "the last four presses were bombed simultaneously by four individuals and the websites were hacked at exactly the same time, which suggests at least one more person was in on it."

"Yes," said Waters, "but we've got fuck all on all five of them; we've got no clues."

"And I have a hunch," Foot continued, "that there may be at least six or possibly seven of them."

"How so?" said Waters.

"I strongly suspect," said Foot, "that the person who hacked the TV stations is not the same as the person who hacked the websites or any of the people who planted the bombs, and I also reckon there's another person behind it all, which makes seven."

"So it's not just five people we've got nothing on; it's seven people we've got nothing on."

Detective Inspector Foot banged his fist hard on the desk. "Then *get* something!"

Out in the Solent, David was being unofficially tutored in the art of sailing a large yacht in what had turned out to be a stiff breeze. He was thrilled at how fast Yogi sliced through the water, throwing up spray as her elegant bow came crashing down on the crests of the waves. The real purpose of the trip was to put the yacht through her paces before she could be officially signed-off as seaworthy, but David couldn't resist coming along for the ride. The skipper for the day was a craggy-faced character called Geoff, the same man who would be captain on the trip to Cherbourg. Reassuringly, he was an experienced trans-Atlantic yachtsman and had also won the Round the Island race. Starting and finishing at Cowes on the Isle of Wight, this race was one of the jewels in the world's yacht-racing calendar and David looked forward to competing in it himself one year, when he felt confident enough to do so.

In Clapham, Jonathon caught himself twiddling his thumbs.

The excitement was all over and he now felt he needed a new adventure. He totted up what he had spent on meddling with the media; eight hundred and seventy thousand pounds. Had it been worth it? Shit yes. Had it been fun? It had been the most fun he had ever had in his life.

Out of curiosity, he did an internet search on the circulation figures for the country's national newspapers and was pleased to find that the quality papers had all seen an increase in sales, although he doubted if it would be sustained. The public gets what the public wants, and the public wants what the public gets.

He received a phone call giving him top-line news about the results of the survey on the new house and he was happy with the outcome. There were a few missing roof tiles and evidence of a small area of rising damp at the rear of the property, but there was nothing to stop him pressing to exchange contracts the week after returning from Cherbourg.

The management of Quasar knew that Saturday evening's debacle had to have been an inside job, but there were dozens of technicians who were capable of tampering with the systems and, in the same way that Spencer had hacked the MailOnline, Cecil had organized everything as a Cron job; he hadn't even been in the building at the time of the broadcasts.

The next couple of days dragged by for Detective Inspector Foot, who could see his longed-for promotion slipping from his grasp. The next couple of days also dragged by for Mr. Jonathon Taylor, who needed a new challenge, preferably something legal. But first, he still had one more bit of mischief he wanted to carry out, for which he would once more need Spencer's help, and for which he would be willing to pay him another hundred thousand pounds.

Fortunately it was half-term week so there was no need to take Nicholas and Jackie out of school for the sailing trip and, having briefed them on what to pack, Jonathon and Bianca collected them on Wednesday afternoon. On the doorstep, he couldn't resist asking Wendy if she had any conger eel stew left and the look on her face was priceless.

"I only asked," said Jonathon.

The conversation was easy on the drive down to the Hamble, with Bianca teasing Jonathon mercilessly about his occasional rants at other road users and ticking him off for using the F-word in front of the children. For much of the journey, Jonathon's mind was on how he was going to cope with meeting the man he had met once before, on the steps of the Albert Memorial.

Sure enough, Amy's Spencer turned out to be Jonathon's Spencer and, after stepping aboard Yogi, it was with some trepidation that he shook his hand, studying his face closely for any signs of recognition.

"What do you reckon?" said David, gesturing with pride at his new toy and crouching down to run his hand over the immaculate teak decking.

"She's magnificent dear boy," said Jonathon, in all sincerity, "absolutely bloody magnificent."

David finished making the introductions and was careful to include the skipper Geoff, his two crew, George and Pete, and also the steward, Adrian, for although he was a very wealthy man and these people were essentially his servants, he was determined not to be the kind of rich sod who kept his employees at arm's length, dismissing them as mere lackeys. This was partly because he wasn't used to being wealthy and partly because he was fundamentally a good egg, which is why he and Jonathon had got on with each other so well for so many years.

David went on to run through the sleeping arrangements and had assumed that Nicholas and Jackie would share a cabin, but Jackie had other ideas.

"No, please," she said, looking at Amy, "I want to share with little Charlotte; she's so cute!"

Amy was happy with this and led the two girls to the cabin which she had earlier earmarked for Charlotte and her uncle Spencer.

"Let's play I-Spy," Jackie suggested to Charlotte, and soon they were bonding well, with Charlotte showing off the two dolls she had brought along because they had never been on a boat before and, well, it didn't seem fair to leave them at home. The truth was, she took them with her everywhere, including to the loo.

Up on deck, Jonathon couldn't help glancing at Spencer whenever he thought he could do so subtly and, detecting nothing to worry about, he eventually allowed himself to fully relax and look forward to the next couple of days.

Geoff and David outlined the itinerary, such as it was, as it basically involved departing after an early dinner on deck and sailing through the night to Cherbourg, where they would moor up for a couple of days before returning overnight on Saturday and docking back at the Hamble early on Sunday morning.

"How long will it take?" asked Bianca.

"Depends on the wind," said Geoff, "but probably around twelve hours or so each way."

"Golly," said Bianca, "will you be able to stay awake that long?"

"There are three of us," Geoff replied, indicating George and Pete, "we'll be taking it in turns to sleep."

"Oh good," said Bianca, "we don't want to go bumping into any of those huge tanker thingies."

Jonathon smiled and turned to David. "And what are the weather conditions like?"

"They're good, probably between force 3 and 5 all the way with maybe a bit of gentle drizzle, 'for a time'; sorry, I've become addicted to the shipping forecast."

Jonathon was sorely tempted to get David on his own and tell him what a naughty brother his girlfriend Amy had, but he thought it unwise; it could wait for another time, if ever.

Adrian did them proud at dinner, serving platters of fine cuts of meat and slices of smoked salmon and gravadlax together with salad vegetables and also some fried treats geared more towards Nicholas, Jackie and little Charlotte, who throughout her meal never once let go of either of her two dolls.

Jonathon heard a faint sound behind him and turned to find David pouring a bottle of La Lagune '82 into a ship's decanter. "I hear you're rather partial to this one, sir?"

After dinner, as Yogi glided majestically downriver towards the Solent, and after more than his fair share of wine, Jonathon chose to sail close to the wind. "Spencer, Amy mentioned that you work in IT; do you enjoy it?"

"Well, you know," said Spencer, "it has its ups and downs like in any job, I guess."

233

"And who do you work for?"

"For the Daily Mail."

"Ouch," said Jonathon, "were you affected by what happened?"

"Actually," said Spencer, "it led to me getting promoted to the head of IT there."

"Crikey, how so?"

"I stitched up my boss on the back of it."

"Hah! Good for you," said Jonathon, "so there's no chance of a repeat, now that you're in charge?"

"No way," said Spencer.

"It's a funny old thing though, I reckon," said Jonathon, "first the Mail; then those other four get it, too."

David was amused at Jonathon's audacity, and he would have been even more amused had he known the truth about Spencer's involvement. Bianca, meanwhile, was looking calmly at Jonathon and wondering. She was wondering why Jonathon hadn't yet mentioned that one of the four stolen vans had been his. David was wondering the same thing, as were Amy and Nicholas.

"Dad," he said, "aren't you forgetting something?"

"What?"

"Your van!"

Jonathon had been so caught up by one dimension of his conversation with Spencer he had completely forgotten that the others knew about his visit from Detective Inspector Foot, and the reason why. Of course, it would be extremely odd not to mention it.

"And guess what Spencer," he said, "one of the four vans that were stolen belonged to *me*!"

"You're joking."

"Nope."

"Bloody hell," said Spencer, "how weird is that?"

Bianca hadn't taken her eyes off Jonathon, and she was again wondering why he had referred to his van being stolen as a 'coincidence'.

One by one, with the exception of Jonathon and David, they all drifted off to their cabins to sleep, with Yogi now under full sail after using her engine for the trip down the Hamble. Geoff was taking the first watch and after three hours he would be relieved by George and Pete, then vice versa until they neared Cherbourg, when it would be all hands on deck.

"I've got to say," said Jonathon, clutching a large Bowmore, "this is beyond fabulous David; I love it."

"That was very naughty of you, you rogue," said David, "but bloody funny, too."

"I was just making conversation; how the hell was I supposed to know he worked for the Mail?"

"Fair enough; good point."

Crossing the English Channel was a piece of cake for Geoff and his crew, whose only active involvement was to take Yogi off automatic pilot to negotiate two large container ships, and by the time they had to retract the sails ready to slowly enter Cherbourg harbour, dawn had broken, casting a pale milky light onto the old sandstone buildings.

Adrian was up and busying himself in the galley, having taken note of everyone's breakfast preferences the evening before, and was carefully slicing a black pudding when Jackie burst in, breathless with urgency, as if Yogi was about to be boarded by pirates.

"Adrian, Adrian" she exclaimed, "Charlotte's mummy is still asleep and she needs her orange juice!"

"Well, goodness me," said Adrian, taking a plastic tumbler and opening the fridge, "I think I can do something about that."

"And Adrian?"

"Mmm?"

"May I have some too?"

Yogi's passengers gradually assembled around the large indoor dining table, for it was still a bit chilly to gather outside on deck, especially in their sleepwear. The first to arrive was David, who remembered that Nicholas had expressed an interest in casting a line overboard, and he prepared for him a simple small fishing rod and tackled it up for him.

By the time Geoff had steered to the berth he had reserved, and George and Pete had made secure fore and aft, breakfast was prepared and was being kept warm on the heated sideboard ready for people to help themselves.

Bianca appeared, bleary eyed, and she blinked in the early morning sunshine that was now streaming into the saloon. "Oh David, this is all so lovely."

"Did you sleep alright?"

"I was snug as a bug in a rug."

The last to surface was Jonathon, who was a little hung-over, having had one Bowmore too many before turning in. Jackie rushed up to him and wrapped her arms around his waist. "Daddy, guess what, I wasn't sick *all* night!"

"That's lovely darling; keep it up. I mean, keep it down."

Nicholas grunted. "You mean keep up keeping it down."

"Yes Nicholas, thank you," said Jonathon, "can't you see that your poor father is feeling a little delicate?"

Amy prepared a plate of scrambled egg and chopped up a sausage into little pieces for Charlotte, who was busy talking to her dolls. "We're in French," she told them.

"France, darling," said Amy, "we're in *France*."

Breakfast taken, the conversation turned to what people felt like doing that day, and Spencer announced that he was more than happy just to tag along and go with the flow.

David had done his homework and put forward to his guests a number of options for them to consider, none of which seemed very appealing to Nicholas, who preferred to stay aboard Yogi and fish and maybe to wander around the quayside by himself. Jonathon thought this was fair enough; he was nearly fifteen and provided he didn't stray into any back streets he would be fine.

Sensing that the two couples would probably prefer to explore as a foursome, Spencer said he would be happy to chaperone Jackie and Charlotte and let them take the lead as they explored the harbour.

The seven of them disembarked, leaving Nicholas with his feet dangling over the stern, rod in hand, trying to tempt fish with the small bits of bacon he had saved from breakfast. Sadly, the fish weren't biting and after an hour he gave up and went for a wander round the port, stopping at a small café for a strawberry milkshake, a picture of which he could see on the tables' laminated menus.

His French hadn't improved much since the trip to Calais, but even if he were now fluent, he would still have been reduced to a gibbering idiot by the staggering beauty of the young brunette waitress who came to take his order. She couldn't have been more than 16 years-old and Nicholas was instantly captivated by the way her neat bob haircut framed her exquisite face. She wore no make-up, for she didn't need to; her skin was porcelain, and it was flawless.

"Um, a shake au lait," he said, "avec, er, strawberries."

The stunning vision laughed. Luckily for him, her English was streets ahead of his French. "You would like a strawberry milkshake, yes?"

"Yes," said Nicholas, "er, oui, merci."

His eyes didn't leave her for a second as she turned on her heel and reentered the café, where her father was standing, arms folded, staring out of the window. He didn't like the look of Nicholas; at least, he didn't like the look of what Nicholas was thinking.

A few minutes later she returned and, bending at the knees in the manner of a bunny dip, she placed his drink on the table. "Voila!" she said.

"Je m'appelle Nicholas," he said, taking himself by surprise.

"Je m'appelle Michelle," she said, but instead of entering into a conversation, she teased him by once more turning on her heel and sashaying back into the café.

"Je m'appelle Michelle," he said to himself softly, captured by the rhythm of her simply announcing her name, "je m'appelle Michelle."

He realised he was now hopelessly in love and there was absolutely nothing he, nor anyone else, could do about it. Of course, he would leave school as soon as he could and come to live in Cherbourg. Yes, that's what he would do; he would find work on one of the fishing boats, or be a waiter somewhere, just to be near his new love. And he would immediately start to study hard at his French.

It took him a full hour to finish his milkshake, all the while praying for another glimpse of the beautiful, sweet Michelle, but she never reappeared. Instead, her father approached and summarily placed the bill on the table. Nicholas laid a twenty euro note on top and watched as the father of the sweet angel, his sweet angel, went back into the café. After a couple of minutes he heard some shouting coming from within and Michelle appeared, walking quickly towards him. But she didn't speak; she just put his bill and his change on the table and turned to go. But first she gave him the sweetest smile and she winked at him.

'She winked at me', he thought; 'bloody hell, she *winked* at me!' He picked up some of his change and was about to get up to leave when he noticed some ink showing through from the other side of the bill. He picked it up, turned it over, and read her handwriting; 'tomorrow, 11 am, the fortress, M x.'

Meanwhile, on the other side of the harbour, Spencer, Jackie and Charlotte were each licking ice-creams, watching the boats come and go, and the other four were settling down to a light lunch at a restaurant that Geoff had recommended.

Nicholas felt light-headed as he got up from the table and, although he tried not to, he turned his head to see if he might get one last glimpse of Michelle. He was disappointed not to see her, but never mind; he would see her again tomorrow at eleven in the morning at the fortress, wherever that was.

He walked back to Yogi and went straight to his cabin, where he lay down and daydreamed about Michelle and about the wonderful life they would have together. The sound of the water lapping against the hull slowly sent him off to sleep, in which he had a real dream, a deep dream, about the beautiful girl who had just taken his breath away.

He was woken by squeals of laughter coming from Jackie and Charlotte, and by Spencer stomping his feet and roaring loudly as he chased them around the boat, threatening to tickle them to within an inch of their lives when he caught them and pinned them down.

David and Amy and Bianca and Jonathon weren't far behind, and everyone gathered on the aft deck and talked about their day.

"Dad," said Nicholas, "have you got a French phrasebook?"

"No, sorry, why?"

"I just thought I might try to improve my use of the language, that's all."

"Are you alright Nicholas?" asked Jonathon.

Nicholas gave a grunt; the one that he used to suggest that he was fine, thank you very much.

Geoff overheard and disappeared off to his cabin. Earlier, when he had been taking a stroll ashore, he had caught sight of Nicholas and had seen him speaking with the beautiful young waitress. Soon he reappeared on deck and handed Nicholas his well-worn English-French phrasebook. "Here you go son," and then he whispered to him, "learn page 128."

Adrian had been given the evening off and dinner was taken at one of Cherbourg's better restaurants, where Nicholas was mostly silent and only picked at his food, his mind and his heart elsewhere.

In the morning, Geoff announced that there was forecast a brief period of a force 6, which would abate by early afternoon and which would offer some exhilarating sailing if anyone was interested. Amy and Bianca declined and said they would take Charlotte and Amy ashore and entertain them, while David, Jonathon and Spencer were keen to experience Yogi being put through her paces in strong winds.

"What about you, Nicholas?" asked Jonathon.

"No thanks Dad," he said, "I thought I might go and explore the fortress; I've read that it played an important part in World War Two."

Jonathon was baffled; first French, now history; what had happened to the boy? "Ok but make sure you're back on board by five o'clock; we need to eat and then set sail for home."

By ten past eleven, Yogi was hurtling along and heeling over at an angle that David found both exciting and alarming; the two women and the two girls were playing on the swings and roundabouts at the children's playground, and Nicholas and Michelle were locking lips and passionately exploring each other as they lay in the undergrowth at the rear of the Cherbourg fortress.

Five o'clock came and went, as did five thirty, and Jonathon was starting to worry. Everyone else was back on board but there was still no sign of Nicholas. He was about to go off and search for him when he spotted him in the distance, walking along the jetty with a distinct spring in his step.

"How was the fortress?" he asked, as his son clambered aboard.

"Oh it was terrific dad," said Nicholas, "I learned all sorts of things."

Geoff looked at him and smiled. "Was that phrase book any use?"

Nicholas handed it back to him. "Yes thanks, and you were right about page 128."

Adrian served up one of his specialities; a hearty chili con carne that everyone tucked into except Charlotte, who ate just her baked potato with butter and some baked beans.

As Geoff, George and Pete readied Yogi for departure, Nicholas took his father to one side and had a quiet word with him. Despite him being divorced from his mother, or perhaps because of it, their relationship had always been very open and honest and they could talk to each other about anything.

"Dad, you know you told me to always carry a condom, just in case?"

"Er, ye-es."

"You were right!"

David started up the engine and steered Yogi out of the harbour under the watchful eye of Geoff, who stood at his shoulder and took over the wheel once they were out in open water, where George and Pete raised the sails. Leaving Cherbourg was a bitter-sweet moment for Nicholas, who took out his mobile phone and gazed longingly at the photographs he had taken of Michelle, who in many of the poses was naked. He was eternally grateful that it had been a mild day.

His father, meanwhile, had a grin on his face. His son had beaten him by almost a year.

Again the crossing was uneventful and again Jackie didn't throw up, and they docked on the Hamble at around eight the next morning. After another fine breakfast cooked by Adrian, the eight of them thanked Geoff and his crew, piled into their cars and headed for London, where Jonathon dropped off the children before heading over to Bianca's apartment.

Later, she felled him with the question that been on her mind for a long time. "Jonathon, why did you say that your van being stolen was a coincidence? A coincidence *why*, exactly?"

"I see what you mean," he said, "I don't really know; I guess I just used the wrong word, that's all."

And with that she had to be satisfied, at least for the time being.

In the morning, he left her to study the canine world and he returned home to chase up the house purchase, the sale of his flat, and to speak to Spencer, which was a conversation he was looking forward to with relish.

First he dealt with the estate agents and the solicitors and then he texted the man with whom he'd just shared a boat trip to France and back.

'Can you talk?'

'Yes,' replied Spencer, who was as keen to speak to James as Jonathon was to speak to Spencer.

Jonathon dialed his number and slipped into his Birmingham accent. "Hi, how was the trip?"

"James, you will not *believe* what happened."

"You capsized?"

"No nothing like that; get this: you know your gang stole four vans?"

"Of course."

"Well, on the boat, I met the owner of one of the vans that was *stolen*!"

"You're kidding me."

"No, straight up, his name was Jonathon; a friend of the owner of the boat!"

"Bloody hell, I hope you were careful."

"Don't worry, I handled it very well."

Jonathon smiled, for he thought he had handled it pretty well himself, too. "Listen, can I brief you on this other job I'd like you to do for me? It's worth another hundred grand."

"Go ahead."

Spencer listened carefully as James identified the companies he wanted to attack and in what way. He also stipulated that, just like the last four tabloids had been dealt with, everything would have to be done simultaneously. Spencer observed that the companies' firewalls would be a devil to break down but James assured him there was no rush; no rush at all.

"Do you want some money upfront?" Jonathon asked finally.

"No thanks James, I don't need it; I'd rather get it all in one go when the job's done."

20 | Foot takes steps

Six months later, as he was casting a fly on his own personal stretch of one of the most beautiful chalk streams in Hampshire, Jonathon reflected that his life was about as perfect as any man could wish for. He had managed to complete the purchase on the house two weeks before Christmas, and he, Bianca, Nicholas and Jackie had entertained themselves royally, tucking into a fine rib of beef after all the presents had been opened and enjoying the contents of a Fortnum and Mason hamper that David had sent over. In the evenings they had lazed by the large open fire, which was fuelled by logs that Nicholas had chopped in the outhouse and then stacked either side of the inglenook. Jonathon thought there was no point in having a son if you didn't make him prepare the firewood, and Nicholas was pleased to be trusted with the axe.

From time to time, Jonathon checked the circulation figures of the national newspapers, and was pleased to see that the five tabloids were down and the quality papers were up by a corresponding amount. It wasn't much, but it was in the tens of thousands, and he wondered what the opposite was of dumbing-down. Brightening up?

In April, there had been a short spell of warm weather that allowed the pool to be put to good use for the first time and the children had each brought a friend down for the weekend to take advantage and frolic around in the water. David, Amy and Charlotte had come down too, and Charlotte had finally learned to swim. She encouraged her dolls to do likewise and it was left to Jackie to dive down and rescue them from the bottom of the pool.

It was now May, and Bianca had been dividing her time between Hampshire and her apartment near the college, where in January she had finally been able to officially start her veterinary course. With almost two months of textbook study under her belt, she had got off to a flying start and her tutors were impressed by her progress. She and Jonathon had grown ever closer and he had postponed his plans to buy an apartment in London, preferring to wait until the lease was up on her flat, for they were unlikely to ever want to sleep apart when they were both in London.

Meanwhile, he had donated large sums of money to various charities, mostly to do with children, animals, and victims of gross political injustice. He had also relented and given a sizeable chunk to Wendy, partly for old times' sake and partly because he knew that Nicholas and Jackie would benefit indirectly.

He had also found a new purpose in life; he had enrolled in the Open University and had started working towards a degree in criminology. There was a certain symmetry to this, he thought, given that he had masterminded some crimes which were both famous and which had remained unsolved. If he could achieve that, he reasoned, then maybe he could become an effective private detective, not that he needed the money. But it might be interesting.

David needed money even less than Jonathon and in fact he struggled to know what to do with the fortune he still had available. He was now a fully licenced and accomplished helicopter pilot, and had also obtained the qualifications necessary to skipper both Yogi and Boo-Boo, although he sometimes hired another skipper when he spent time on either of them, so that he could be free to be irresponsible. Boo-Boo had a berth at Antibes and he had named her tender Baby Boo-Boo, much to Jonathon's amusement, for the name belied the fact that it was powered by twin Evinrude outboard engines which could each develop 200 bhp. The water-skiing was exhilarating, as was the para-gliding.

The more time David spent on the water, on either vessel, the more he felt at home being afloat and he organised several short trips over to different ports on the north coast of France, including another to Cherbourg, to which Nicholas was lucky enough to be invited again, although very little had been seen of him all weekend.

Spencer, who now had a small flat of his own, had given James regular updates on the progress in the task he had been set, a task which had proved to be every bit as tricky as he had suspected. He had managed to hack into the mainframes of four of the five companies that James wanted to play around with, but he had yet to conquer the fifth. Nonetheless, he assured Jonathon it was only a matter of time.

Detective Inspector Foot had been passed over for promotion, much to his dismay, and he had been taken off the investigation into the attacks on the media and replaced by one of his peers, who also failed, much to Foot's relief. In the meantime he had been put in charge of solving an armed bank robbery on a jewellery shop in Hatton Garden. Happily for Scotland Yard, this crime had been solved. Unhappily for Foot, he had not been responsible for the breakthrough which had led to catching the culprits. The same was true of two further investigations with which he had been entrusted, and it soon became clear that his superiors were starting to lose faith in him.

It was then that he decided that he would show them what he was made of, and were it not for an extraordinary example of blind faith, which he would later put down as brilliant detective work, he would probably have forgotten all about tracking down whoever had been responsible for the attacks on the media.

He reopened the files and time and time again he pored over what little there was to go on, and time and time again he gave up, frustrated, just like he had done before he was removed from the case. But he was still niggled by the conversation he had on Mr. Jonathon Taylor's doorstep, the morning after the quadruple bombings. True, he had a cast-iron double alibi, with both Miss Bianca Bennett and the concierge in her apartment block confirming that he had been there all night, but nevertheless, there had been something unnatural about his demeanour when he told him about his van being involved in one of the bombings. He had no evidence but his instinct told him that Mr. Taylor had somehow been involved. And what about that expensive car in which he had arrived? He had said it was a present from a friend, but what if he had bought it himself, with his own money, and what if he had had lots more money, the sort of money he could have used to pay people to do his bidding?

He decided to use one of his underworld contacts to help him investigate Jonathon's bank account. It was illegal, but needs must. What he discovered made his eyes water. There had been a deposit of ten million pounds just under two weeks before the attack on the Daily Mail, prior to which there were only small and irregular deposits that didn't amount to very much. Subsequently he had spent fairly large sums on hotels and restaurants in Calais, Venice, Amsterdam and Cherbourg and there was a large payment to an estate management company, which he later established was the firm that looked after Miss Bianca Bennett's apartment block. There was also a substantial payment to a classic car showroom in Chelsea. It seemed he had lied about the Bristol, and if he had lied about the Bristol, what else had he lied about? The biggest payment was to an estate agent in Hampshire, which had gone through in early December.

The problem for Detective Inspector Foot was that there was nothing remotely illegal suggested by any of Mr. Taylor's transactions, and there were certainly no cash withdrawals of the size one might reasonably expect would have been needed to pay people to go around setting off bombs and hacking into websites.

Apart from the lie about the car, he was back to square one.

And also, *was* it actually a lie? If someone had given Mr. Taylor a present of ten million pounds and he had chosen to go and buy himself a car, then the car was, at least indirectly, a present.

Detective Inspector Foot didn't like being back at square one, but he did like the thought of proving his superiors wrong, of proving that he really was a fine detective, and he decided to assume that Jonathon was definitely guilty. All he had to do was get some proof. Police work usually involved gathering evidence that would eventually point the finger of blame at someone, but this was the reverse. He *had* his man, he was sure of it, he just didn't have a shred of evidence.

He would have to find some, and in the absence of a better idea he decided to visit Jonathon's flat in Clapham. This he would do without telling any of his colleagues, for he had started to have ideas that were unconnected with the normal aims of police work.

Carrying a 30 megapixel camera, he arrived at 8.30 one morning, rang the bell and was greeted by a young woman with a baby on her hip.

"Sorry to trouble you madam," said Foot, "I'm looking for a Mr. Jonathon Taylor."

"You're a bit late mate," she said.

"Oh, has he left for work?"

"No you're about five months late; he doesn't live here anymore."

"Ah, well, would you mind if I came in?" asked Foot, holding out his ID card.

"Police?" said the woman. "What do you want to come in here for?"

"I just wanted to take a quick look around, that's all."

"What's the bloody point?" she said. "He doesn't bloody live here anymore!"

He eventually convinced her that with his finely honed skills as a detective, he might unearth something that nobody else could.

"Tell me, Mrs..."

"Miss Thompson," she said.

"...when you first came to look at the property, do you remember Mr. Taylor having a computer somewhere, or maybe a laptop?"

"He had a laptop, yeah, said the woman."

"And whereabouts was it?"

She led him through to a small room full of boxes that still hadn't been unpacked. "There was a desk, well just a table actually, against that wall, where my table is now."

"And have you redecorated this room since you moved in?"

She laughed. "I haven't redecorated anywhere yet."

Detective Inspector Foot pulled out the table so that he could get behind it and he positioned himself between it and the wall. Crouching down, he asked Miss Thompson to help him establish, as near as was possible, roughly where the top of the lid of Mr. Taylor's laptop would have been, when it was open. He then held his camera in the position in which he thought it would most likely replicate the position of a laptop's built-in camera and took several photographs of the wall opposite, using a variety of different exposures.

"Thank you Miss Thompson; you've been very helpful."

"What's he done, this Mr. Taylor?"

Foot extricated himself from between the table and the wall and pushed the table back into position. "Let's just say I have reason to believe that he was responsible for one of the most extraordinary series of crimes in recent history."

"Oh," she said, "and he seemed such a nice man, too."

"That I don't doubt, Miss Thompson," said Foot, "but he's still a very naughty boy."

In fact, Detective Inspector Foot believed both of these things; that Jonathon Taylor probably was a nice man but that he was also a highly mischievous individual. After all, the five bombs had gone off only when the buildings had been evacuated, which proved he had respect for human life. But nonetheless, he had caused tens of millions of pounds worth of damage and had erased computer data that had taken several years to accumulate.

Back at Scotland Yard, and out of sight of his colleagues, he loaded his camera's files onto his computer and deleted all those that didn't provide a clear, sharp image of the wall behind where Jonathon would have been sitting at his laptop. He then found a still image of the TV broadcast that had interrupted everyone's viewing, in which a man with long dark curly hair had belittled some of the output of various TV channels.

At the time Jonathon had made his recording, he had removed the pictures on the wall behind him and had even removed the picture hooks on which they were hanging, but there still remained three tiny holes, no greater than 2mm in diameter, which to the human eye were very difficult to see, but which a 30 megapixel camera could record with great clarity.

He enhanced the still image as best he could and then superimposed it over one of the pictures he had taken that morning. In the still, the holes in the wall were nowhere near as clear as in the other image, but they were nevertheless discernible, and after adjusting the relative sizes of the two images, he could bring two of the three tiny holes almost together, the third being hidden behind Jonathon's head. In the upper right-hand corner of the frame, there was also a tiny crack in the paintwork, and that too corresponded. The disparity between the positions of the two holes and the crack in the paint were identical in distance and direction from each other, which simply meant that his camera lens had been in a slightly different position from the lens in Jonathon's laptop.

"Got you," said Detective Inspector Foot, "now all I have to do is find you."

Twenty minutes later, he arrived at Bianca's apartment block, rang the bell and tapped his foot as he waited for the concierge to let him in.

"Afternoon, I…"

"…good afternoon sir" said the concierge.

"…I need to speak to Miss Bianca Bennett," said Foot, holding out his ID card.

"Again sir?" said the concierge, who remembered him from all those months ago.

"Yes, again, and I don't have time to chat."

"Very well sir, I'll see if she's in", and he tapped in the number 27 on the internal intercom.

Bianca was in bed with Jonathon and reluctantly she rolled over and picked up the receiver. "Hello?" she said, still half asleep.

"There's a gentlemen down here to see you madam."

"Who is it?"

"Detective Inspector Foot madam."

"Detective Inspector Foot?" she said, purely for Jonathon's benefit, and she elbowed him in the ribs.

"Yes Madam," said the concierge.

"Well I suppose you'd better send him up," and she replaced the handset.

"Honey, it's not you that he wants," said Jonathon, "it's me."

"I know that," she said, "get in the cupboard and leave this to me."

While Bianca grabbed a towel and wrapped it round her, Jonathon did as he was told and went to hide, with the words 'I know that' bouncing around in his head. What did she know, exactly?

Detective Inspector Foot knocked on the door and Bianca answered, clutching the towel around her and pretending to be more drowsy than she really was.

"Ye-es?"

"I'm sorry to disturb you madam, but I'd like to have a word with your boyfriend."

"Boyfriend?" she said, and she now pretended to cry. "I haven't got a boyfriend; I wish I did have a boyfriend," she sobbed.

"Jonathon? Mr. Jonathon Taylor?"

Bianca now surpassed herself and she started to wail. "I don't know what went wrong, I thought we were getting on so well; I thought he loved me but we split up; he left me, the complete and utter lying bastard!" With that, she buried her face in her hands, sobbing uncontrollably.

Like a lot of otherwise strong and capable men, Detective Inspector Foot wasn't much good at dealing with a woman who was crying, let alone one who was on the verge of hysteria. There was something about them that was beyond reach, and beyond reason.

"I'm sorry madam," he offered.

"YOU'RE sorry?!" Bianca screamed, now really getting into her stride. "YOU'RE bloody sorry?!" She dabbed her eyes with a corner of the towel. "I loved him, don't you understand?" she blubbed. "I really, really LOVED him."

In his cupboard, Jonathon was seriously impressed by this performance and it was all he could do to stop himself from giggling.

"Er, well," said Foot, "do you know where I can find him?"

"He lives in Clapham, unless he's gone to HELL by now!"

"Well, um, thank you, I won't take up any more of your time."

"Promise me something," she said, reverting back to whimpering little sobs, "I don't know what he's supposed to have done, but for God's sake just you make sure you catch him and then bang him up for a very long time."

'Steady on,' thought Jonathon.

"I'll do my best," said Detective Inspector Foot, although his intentions were rather different to what she had suggested.

Bianca closed the door behind her and went to open the cupboard to release the still naked Jonathon.

"Have you ever been on the stage?" he asked.

"I did a bit at school, yes," she said, "and a bit of am-dram later."

"It shows; you were wonderful," he said, "for a minute there I thought you genuinely wanted me behind bars."

"I know it was you," she said, evenly.

"What was me?"

"All those attacks on the tabloids, and the television thing."

Jonathon needed to give himself time to think. He reached for his dressing gown and sat down on the chair in the bedroom, idly flicking bits of imaginary fluff from his sleeve. But who was he kidding? She knew, and that's all there was to it.

"How do you know?" he asked.

"You remember the weekend when Jackie brought her dressing-up box down to Hampshire, and you went off to buy some fishing tackle?"

"Yes, I remember."

"Well, she wanted to play some dressing-up games and guess what I found in her box?"

Jonathon didn't have to guess, and he kicked himself for being so stupid. Knowing how Jackie loved to play different costume games with her friends, he had given her his long dark curly wig, the stick-on moustache and the glasses he had used as his disguise.

"It wasn't difficult darling," she continued, "I just took a black pen and scribbled over a picture of you – one of the pictures we printed out after that fishing trip."

"And there I was, the man on the television?"

"Yes, but there were other clues, too."

"Such as?"

"Your van being one of the four that were stolen, and you calling it a 'coincidence'," she continued, "you're too careful with words for that not to have meant anything significant."

"Anything else?" asked Jonathon.

"Yes," she said, "I know you, and I know how you think. And who the hell uses *two* phones unless they're up to something?"

"And you don't mind?"

She flung her arms around him and planted on him more kisses than he could cope with, until eventually he had to defend himself with his forearms. "Of course not, idiot. I think it's fun, and also I agree with your point of view," she said, adding "media studies; hah!"

In that instant he knew for a fact that Miss Bianca Bennett was going to become the next Mrs. Jonathon Taylor, but this was not the time to propose. The police were onto him, God knows how, and it was only a matter of time before they discovered his address in Hampshire.

"I think I should leave the country for a few days; give me time to think this through."

"I agree," she said.

He crossed to where his jacket was slung on a chair and took out his white phone. "I think I'll use this one," he said with a wink, and he dialed his best friend.

"David? It's Jonathon. I need to get out of the country; can you help?"

"Now what have you done?" asked David.

Jonathon explained where he was and what had happened and David thought about it for a while. "Listen, you mustn't leave your car there or it might compromise Bianca. Pack a bag, put it in the boot and leave the key in the ignition. Then take a cab to Piccadilly Circus. You might be being followed so get out, then walk through Leicester Square and jump in another cab to the heliport in Battersea. By the time you get there I'll have arranged for you to be flown in my helicopter to Virginia Water. You'll probably get there before me but just wait, ok?"

Jonathon trusted him. "Okay," he said, "anything else?"

"Yes, relax," said David, "and pack swimming shorts."

Jonathon packed a small bag and kissed Bianca goodbye. "Don't worry," he said, "they've got nothing on me; it's not possible."

While Jonathon was in a cab en route to Battersea heliport, David was in a cab en route to the underground car park at Bianca's apartment block, where he jumped in the Bristol and drove back to Virginia Water. By the time he arrived, his garden landing pad had already seen the arrival and departure of the helicopter carrying Jonathon, who was now sat patiently waiting for him.

They transferred Jonathon's bag from the Bristol to the Bentley and then hid the Bristol in the garage, before David grabbed a few things from his house.

"Where are we going?" asked Jonathon.

"Antibes," said David, "we'll spend a little time on Boo-Boo."

"But I don't have my passport!"

"Maybe not, but this thing has a very big boot," said David, "you'll be comfortable enough; and anyway, it won't be for very long."

On the M20, they stopped at the last service station before Folkestone and bought a litre of water and a few nibbles to sustain Jonathon, who visited the loo to make himself comfortable before returning to the car park and climbing into the boot of the Bentley.

A few minutes after they were back on the motorway, Jonathon's black phone rang, and for the first time in his life he found himself speaking in a Birmingham accent while being carried at 80 mph in the boot of a car.

"Spencer," he said, "how nice to hear from you."

"I've cracked the fifth one James," said Spencer, "we can do it as soon as you're ready."

"That's great news, but it's a little difficult to talk at the moment."

"Oh dear, why?" said Spencer.

"Because I'm speaking to you from inside the boot of a fast-moving motor vehicle and the signal isn't very good."

"I see," said Spencer, who didn't see at all, "well, call me when you can, yes?"

"In a few days, yes."

Spencer hung up and wondered, not for the first time, if James had been in any way affected by the cloak and dagger existence of an habitual saboteur.

Jonathon managed to nod off for a while, using as a pillow a plastic bag containing fifty thousand pounds. Two hours later, David pulled over onto the hard shoulder of the A26 towards Reims and Dijon and pressed the button to unlock the lid of the boot, which sprang open to disgorge his friend.

"Actually, that wasn't too bad," Jonathon said, as he climbed into the passenger seat, "we should do it more often."

"Shall we drive down in one hit," asked David, "or would you prefer to stop off somewhere?"

Jonathon looked at his watch. "It's too late to get a decent meal anywhere; let's take it in turns and drive through the night."

Meanwhile, after leaving Bianca in tears at her apartment, DI Foot had returned to his desk to do some digging. The police had all manner of tools at their disposal; the Driver and Vehicle Licensing Agency, the Passport Office, the Land and Property Registers; the Births, Marriages and Deaths Registers, the UK Ship Register, and all the mobile phone companies, who were obliged to help when asked to disclose information. And what the police couldn't find out from the usual channels, they could often discover by enlisting the help of various contacts in the criminal underworld, on the understanding of 'you scratch my back and I'll scratch yours', which was how he had discovered the large deposit Mr. Jonathon Taylor had made.

By examining his mobile phone records and establishing which numbers he had dialed most often, and received calls from most often, he identified a Mr. David Strange, who less than a week before Jonathon's windfall had banked over £83m. He also noticed a great many phone calls to and from a Miss Bianca Bennett.

What a good little actress, he thought, but he was more interested to note that the last time Jonathon Taylor had called David Strange was just a few minutes after he had questioned Miss Bennett at the door of her apartment. He also spotted that there was no phone call from Miss Bennett to Mr. Taylor at around the same time. 'Damn', he thought, he had been right there in her apartment all the time she was faking her histrionics.

DI Foot decided there was no point in visiting Jonathon's

house in Hampshire; he wouldn't be foolish enough to go there. Instead, on a hunch that he might choose to leave the country, he put out two passport alerts and two vehicle licence plate alerts to all the border controls in southern England.

He then jumped in his car and visited David's penthouse in Chelsea, followed by his house in Virginia Water. It didn't surprise him to find nobody in residence at either and, by now exhausted, he went home to bed, pleased with his work and convinced that it was only a matter of time before he got his man.

He was unaware that, had he known of the existence of Jonathon's black phone, he would also have been able to track down Brian, Spencer and Cecil; three of the six members of his gang.

21 | Antibes and Paris

At around the time that David and Jonathon arrived in Antibes, DI Foot was woken by a phone call from the border control office at Folkestone, informing him that a Bentley registered to a Mr. David Strange had left the country about an hour before he had issued the alert.

"Thank you, and how many people in the car?"

"One."

He then called the Eurostar office, gave the special code that obliged them to share information with the police and discovered that Mr. Strange had made his booking only about four minutes after Jonathon had called him.

They were obviously in cahoots and he assumed there were just two possibilities; one that David had smuggled Jonathon out of the country in his car and the other that Jonathon had panicked and had left on the first flight he could get, having arranged with David to meet him overseas.

The question was, where overseas?

He followed his hunch and booked himself a flight to Nice, from where he would take a taxi to Antibes, for he correctly assumed they were heading for David's yacht.

David parked up in the space that was permanently reserved for him and, before boarding Boo-Boo, he and Jonathon stopped at a small supermarket and bought a basketful of fresh produce. There was always plenty of food in the boat's freezer, but milk, eggs and other perishables had to be obtained before each trip.

David would usually call ahead and have this arranged for him, but he didn't want any of his standby crew to know he was coming.

It was only the second time Jonathon had stepped aboard Boo-Boo and again he marveled at the sheer size of her, and the sleek beauty of her lines. So many diesel-guzzling large yachts were ugly, but there was a simple grace to Boo-Boo and he had to admire David's taste. With a range of 400 nautical miles she could cover the entire length of the southern coast of France, and with a cruising speed of 33 knots she could quickly get to wherever you wanted to go.

They decided to travel west to Cannes, drop anchor offshore, take the tender into the harbour and have lunch somewhere. Had David not forgotten to turn off Boo-Boo's marine GPS system, Detective Inspector Foot would probably never have caught up with them.

As they approached a jetty in Cannes harbour, Jonathon couldn't contain himself any longer. "David," he said, "Boo-Boo is bad enough but why the hell did you have to call this thing *Baby* Boo-Boo?"

Meanwhile, DI Foot was at 35,000 feet and his flight was about to begin its descent into Nice airport.

Over lunch, David and Jonathon had a virtual repeat of the conversation they had had in the car as they drove down through France.

"So you're absolutely sure this detective bloke has nothing on you."

"I'm positive; I was so careful; I didn't leave a trace."

"Then how come he's after you for Christ sake? He must have something."

Again, they went over the conversation Jonathon had had with DI Foot the morning after the four bombings. It was hardly verbatim but, again, neither of them could see how anything could have had led to Foot suspecting him.

In the taxi from Nice to Antibes, Detective Inspector Foot spoke on the phone to both the harbour police and the coastguard and was told yes, a police launch could be made available to him and yes, the location of the yacht belonging to Mr. Strange had been pinpointed.

Later, back on board Boo-Boo, David and Jonathon were enjoying a coffee on the aft deck when David happened to glance up and see in the distance a vessel bearing down on them, at speed. He grabbed the binoculars. "Jesus," he said, "it's the French police."

"Shit," said Jonathon, "game's up."

"No it's not," said David, "remember, you can dive."

Jonathon instantly knew it was his only option and David indicated the large storage locker on the port side. "The gear's in there."

While Jonathon stripped off, David picked up one of the coffee mugs and hurried to the galley to wash it up. He then took Jonathon's bag to the master cabin, stowed it away and returned to fetch Jonathon's clothes, which were in a heap on deck. He picked them up, took them to his cabin and mixed them into a pile of his own clothes on the armchair.

Meanwhile, dressed in just his swimming shorts, Jonathon had decided he had no time to struggle into a wetsuit and instead he just opened the valve on the air tank and strapped himself into the buoyancy control device, which was already attached to the tank. Had he stopped to think for a second, he might have wondered *why* it was already attached to the tank. He slipped on a pair of fins, donned a weight-belt, a mask and, as an afterthought, he grabbed hold of a spear gun. Then he put the regulator in his mouth, briefly tested it, noted the position of the sun and did a backward roll into the water, on the blind side from the direction the police launch was coming from.

He had deliberately chosen a weight-belt that was heavier

than he would usually use and, immediately expelling air from his BCD, he descended rapidly to about 60 feet, where he released some air back into the BCD, leveled off and finned in the direction of the sun. His hope was that the sunlight glinting off the water would effectively camouflage his exhaled air as the bubbles reached the surface. Rolling over, and looking upwards and backwards, he could see the hull of the police launch drawing up alongside Boo-Boo. All he had to do was swim against the current to maintain his position relative to the vessels above, to keep his air bubbles breaking the surface between them and the sun.

He looked at his air gauge and was horrified at what he saw. With a full tank, he could hover at 60 feet under for roughly an hour, but the tank was only half-full, and the tension of the situation was causing him to breathe far more deeply and rapidly than normal. He estimated he could stay down for maybe another twenty minutes, a little more if he ascended to 40 feet.

Meanwhile, Detective Inspector Foot and two French police officers had boarded Boo-Boo and Foot was asking questions.

"Are you by yourself sir?"

"I'm the only one aboard, yes," he said, in all honesty.

"And do you mind if these two take a look around?" said Foot, indicating the two French officers.

"Not at all, be my guest," said David, confident that he had disguised any evidence of Jonathon's presence.

"Do you know a Mr. Jonathon Taylor sir?" asked Foot, who knew damn well that he did.

"God yes, he's one of my closest friends."

"And did he telephone you yesterday evening sir?" again knowing damn well that he did.

"Yes," said David.

"And did he say anything about going away?"

"Actually yes, he did," said David, "anyway what's all this…?"

"…and did he say where to sir?"

"No, he didn't."

Again, this was the truth, for it was he, David, who had said where they were going to go.

At 60 feet below the surface of the Mediterranean Sea, Jonathon was still breathing too heavily and he regularly glanced at his air gauge, cursing whoever was responsible for refilling the scuba tanks.

He then saw something that took his mind off his immediate predicament; a small shoal of Atlantic Bluefin tuna. So as not to spook them, it was very slowly and very smoothly that he reached for the spear gun, released it from its holding-clip, armed it, and took careful aim. He would have one chance and one chance only, for the fish would disappear like lightning when their sensitive lateral lines detected the shockwave of the weapon being fired.

What happened was ugly, but effective. Instead of the spear piercing the body of his target, it went straight through one eye and out the other, killing it instantly. He pulled on the line connecting the spear to the gun and drew the fish towards him, its blood oozing inky green into the water.

The first time he had seen blood at a depth of sixty feet it had been his own. He was swimming through the wreck of a vessel off the Queensland coast and had failed to notice that the walls were lined with a forest of razor clams, one of which sliced straight through his dive glove and also through the tip of his middle finger. It was painful, but what alarmed him most was the sight of his blood flowing out, as green as an avocado. He knew why; that the colours of the spectrum were absorbed one by one the deeper you dived, but he had still reached for his torch and shone light onto his finger to reassure himself that he was still red-blooded.

He looked at his gauge again; maybe five minutes left. He looked up to find that the hull of the police launch was still there and he decided he had no choice but to ascend a little to prolong his air supply. His other worry was his body temperature; without a wetsuit, he had become progressively colder, and he was now starting to shiver. A shortage of air and encroaching hypothermia was a dangerous combination, but he could still see the hull of the launch and he didn't dare do anything but stay where he was.

Meanwhile the two French police officers had finished searching Boo-Boo and they returned and confirmed to Foot that there was nobody aboard the vessel but David.

As Foot prepared to step back on board the launch, he turned to David and gave him a parting shot. "Will you do me a favour, Mr. Strange?"

"Certainly," said David.

"The next time you see your friend, tell him that I have proof of his involvement and that it would be in his best interest to call me," said Foot, handing him his card, "my private number is on here."

"I'll do that," said David, "but exactly when I see him next is anybody's guess."

As the police launch motored back in the direction of Antibes, David hoped to God that Jonathon wouldn't surface immediately, for Foot was very likely to be watching through binoculars for any signs of activity.

But David needn't have feared that Jonathon would suddenly appear and climb aboard, for at that moment he was still 30 feet under and was slipping into unconsciousness. He had had no way of knowing that his air gauge had been misreading, and in the wrong direction.

It gradually dawned on him what was happening as he floated, suspended in the water, the current now taking him further and further away from the yacht, for he had lost the presence of mind to keep moving his legs. He was about to pass out when he thought of the children, and of Bianca, and with a supreme act of will, the kind that people are capable of only when they are facing death, he groped for the buckle on his weight belt with one hand, and the air inlet for his BCD with the other. He released the belt, which plummeted to the sea bed, took one last deep breath of whatever thin air might still be available and manually breathed it into his BCD, which expanded, but only slightly. He didn't care if the police launch was still there or not; he was now ascending, and he would soon be able to breath air once more; beautiful, sweet, life-giving air. It was what he wanted more than anything else in the world and he was encouraged by the increasing brightness of the sunlight as he slowly neared the water's surface.

Satisfied that the police launch was now far enough away to remain cause for concern, David scanned the sea for any signs of air bubbles popping up, but he found none. It was a hopeless task, for he had no idea in which direction to look and he had to constantly rotate his search through 360 degrees.

He was looking in the opposite direction when Jonathon finally bobbed to the surface, gasping for air, eternally grateful that he hadn't died that day, and mouthing the kind of prayer that even an atheist is capable of uttering. By the time David located him, he had filled and refilled his lungs deeply and repeatedly and if anything he was now close to hyperventilating.

Had David had any idea of what his friend had just been through, he would have kicked off his shoes, dived in and retrieved him, but as it was he simply shouted to him. "Jonathon, are you okay?"

Jonathon gave him the universal dive signal of a circle formed by the thumb and the index finger and started to swim towards Boo-Boo, his skin already starting to slowly warm up

265

from the higher temperature of the water at the surface, but his body was still chilled to the core.

Eventually he reached the low swim platform, removed his fins and mask and handed them to David. He then held aloft the tuna, which was still impaled on the spear. "Fancy some sashimi old chap?"

"Idiot."

Once on board, and despite the heat from the sun, Jonathon was quick to wrap himself in a toweling robe before sitting on the aft deck and describing to David what had happened to him. David had thought to pour him a balloon of brandy, which Jonathon cupped in both hands and slowly swilled around as he sipped it and told his tale.

David was furious to learn that the tank had been only half full of air and that the gauge had been over-reading and, despite being a forgiving man and a considerate employer, he immediately made up his mind to fire the crew member responsible.

He handed over Detective Inspector Foot's card and kept the promise he had made to him. "He says he has proof that you were involved and that it would be in your best interests to contact him."

"Bullshit."

"I don't think so," said David, "he seemed adamant enough."

"I need to think about this," said Jonathon, "let's enjoy ourselves for a couple of days."

The tuna had been in the freezer for only twenty minutes but it was long enough to chill it down sufficiently for eating, so while David prepared a salad and dug out the sake, Jonathon head and tailed the fish, gutted it, skinned it, and sliced two neat fillets from either side of the backbone. Half of one fillet would be plenty for both of them, so he bagged up the rest and put it back in the freezer.

After dinner, as they sat and looked at the stars in a sky that was deep black from the lack of ambient light pollution, a thought occurred to Jonathon. "What I'd like to know," he said, "is how the hell he traced us to this exact spot."

"Beats me," said David, but then he remembered about the GPS system and, feeling rather silly, and without telling Jonathon, he went to the bridge to turn it off.

After they had each downed a couple of nightcaps, Jonathon went to bed and lay for a while with his eyes open, eternally grateful that he had clung to his life and that he would see Bianca and the children again. He was also looking forward to finally briefing Spencer and setting the day and the time for the attacks on five of the largest companies in the UK.

They both slept soundly and after breakfast the following morning, David weighed anchor and set an eastbound course for the nearest bay to St-Paul-de-Vence, which was about 5 kilometres inland and which was home to La Colombe D'Or, one of the finest restaurants in the south of France and where David had been able to get a table due only to them having had a last minute cancellation. He still felt guilty about a couple of things; forgetting to turn off the GPS and also the dangerous state of the scuba gear, and he had decided to treat Jonathon to a lunch he would remember for the rest of his life. He also wanted to gently encourage him to think carefully about what he had done, and to persuade him to get in touch with Detective Inspector Foot when they got back to England, for he knew Jonathon couldn't avoid the inevitable for much longer, and he wanted his friend to face up to what he had done and to make things as easy as possible for himself.

Their route took them back past Antibes, whereupon they headed due north, dropped anchor just off the coast and took Baby Boo-Boo for a wild ride around the bay. Jonathon was less practiced at handling such power and when he took the helm and started taking sharp turns at the wrong time, they were lucky not to have ended up overboard. After a few crazy minutes, David took over and throttled right back before they headed for shore, moored up and took a taxi to the restaurant, where they did go overboard.

It was fully five hours later that they fell into another taxi to take them back, and through the haze generated by some of the finest wines and cognacs ever made, it was only with grim determination that David managed to get them safely back to the yacht, where he almost forgot to tether Baby Boo-Boo to Boo-Boo.

He had, however, persuaded Jonathon to get in touch with DI Foot and they agreed that the following evening they would drive back to Calais overnight and return on the Eurostar, again with Jonathon in the boot of the car, for it was the only way to get him back into the country undetected.

They both passed out on deck, with unfinished whiskies on the table, and Jonathon was the first to wake up, at two in the morning. He shook David back into consciousness and they wandered off to their cabins, from which neither of them emerged until gone ten o'clock.

"That was a hell of a lunch David, thank you."

"Oh, we had lunch did we?"

"And I appreciate the lecture; you're right."

Jonathon disappeared off to the galley to peel some oranges and he was less than keen on the piercing noise made by the juicer as he forced the pieces through. Meanwhile David stoically winched Baby Boo-Boo out of the water and secured her onto the davits at the stern.

Neither felt like eating so after a breakfast of just orange juice and coffee, they headed back to Antibes, docked and transferred their stuff to David's car, where he made a couple of phone calls before they set off. One was to brief someone to come and return Boo-Boo to her usual immaculate state and the other was to fire the man to whom he paid good money to maintain the equipment on board.

They drove back up through France and, early the next morning, shortly before getting to Calais, Jonathon once more took up residence in the boot of David's Bentley. Again he used as a pillow the plastic bag containing fifty thousand pounds, but this time, when he was released from his temporary home when back on English soil, he packed it away in his bag, for he would need it, and another fifty from his house, to pay Spencer.

It was now Thursday morning and the coming weekend was his turn with Nicholas and Jackie. Although he had promised David he would contact Detective Inspector Foot, he wanted to first spend some time with Bianca and the children before finding out what fate had in store for him, and he had decided to delay making the call until Monday. But until then, he had to be careful. He assumed the house in Hampshire would be under surveillance and he didn't dare retrieve his car from David's house, nor stay with him either there or at his place in Chelsea. He also couldn't risk going to Bianca's apartment, so he asked David to drop him in central London, where he would find the kind of B&B which didn't ask questions when being paid in cash.

He had thought through what was likely to happen to him once he had given himself up and had made a wild guess that, with good behavior, he would likely be released from prison after maybe five or six years, during which time Bianca would become qualified as a veterinary practitioner and they could marry and live together happily in Hampshire. Or perhaps they could marry before he was locked up, provided she didn't mind having a husband in the clink.

Meanwhile, he wanted their last weekend together to be special, and he wanted it to be special for Nicholas and Jackie, too.

He found a B&B, gave a false name and address, paid in cash and went up to his room to lie down and think. He knew that Bianca had been to Paris before but he also knew that the children hadn't and, despite having just returned from France, he made the decision and acted upon it immediately, even though it meant he would have to cross the channel again, twice, in the boot of a car. It amused him as to how he would explain this to the children, but he was sure they would find it exciting that their father had to smuggle himself out of the country.

He was nervous of using his white phone and he was also reluctant to use the black one, so he went out into the street to a phone box and called Nicholas, telling him that he and Jackie should pack their passports and that it would be Bianca who would be collecting them at 6 o'clock the next day. He then rang her, but she refused to talk on the phone and demanded that he tell her the address of his B&B.

Thirty minutes later she was with him, hearing about his adventures with David, about how DI Foot had tracked them down and about how he had nearly lost his life underwater. This time, her tears were real, and he spent a long time stroking her head and neck and telling her everything was going to be ok.

"So, you're going to give yourself up?"

"It seems I have no choice, and anyway, if I turn myself in, it's bound to reduce the sentence I get."

"I'll wait for you," she said, "and I'll do my best to keep in touch with the children; maybe take them out sometimes, if Wendy will let me."

They agreed that she would book the train crossing, hire a car, collect the children and meet Jonathon at Putney underground station before they drove down to Folkestone.

The next day, once they were all together in the hire-car,

which Jonathon thought alarmingly small considering he was again going to have to hide away in the boot, Jackie was curious. "Where's Boris?" she asked.

"He had to go in for a service and he's not ready yet," said Jonathon.

"Where are we going?" asked Nicholas. "Bianca said it was a secret."

"Paris," said Jonathon.

"Yay," said Nicholas, "that's near Cherbourg."

"No it isn't; I'm afraid you won't be seeing Michelle this trip."

"Who's Michelle?" asked Jackie.

"She's my girlfriend – my girlfriend in France," clarified Nicholas, who by now had another couple of interests in London.

Jonathon had already worked out how he was going to explain to them the reason for his unusual travel arrangements and, as they pulled off the motorway at the same service station he and David had visited just a few days before, he announced to them that he had lost his passport and would be crossing the channel in the boot.

"Are you kidding?" asked Nicholas.

"Isn't that a bit naughty Daddy?" asked Jackie.

"No I'm not kidding, Nicholas, and yes it is a bit naughty, Jackie, but only a tiny little bit," said Jonathon, who considered it nothing more than a minor misdemeanor compared with some of the other things he had been up to.

"Will it be safe?" asked Jackie.

To create more room in the boot he transferred a couple of bags to the back seat and got in, making himself as comfortable as was possible. Bianca had already supplied a bottle of water and a sandwich and, despite being able to rest his head on Jackie's squishy travel bag, he decided that if he was ever going to have to do this again, it would be in a Bentley, or not at all.

Meanwhile Spencer, who still hadn't heard from James, was keen to earn his next hundred thousand pounds and he couldn't resist calling.

"James," he said, "when do you want…"

"…Spencer," said Jonathon, "you're not going to believe this but again you find yourself speaking to me while I'm in the boot of a moving motor vehicle."

"Yes, of course," said Spencer.

"I'll call you on Monday, ok?"

"Yeah, sure, er, have a nice trip."

Once on the road from Calais to Paris, Jonathon was freed and after stretching his legs for a while at the side of the road, he took over the driving. Bianca had booked three rooms at a reasonable hotel in Montmartre, and given there would be little traffic that late in the evening, they would arrive in just a little over three hours.

"How was the boot?" asked Bianca.

"I've had better," said Jonathon.

"Will we go to the top of the awful tower?" asked Nicholas.

"Eiffel," said Jonathon, "*Eiffel* tower."

"Just kiddin' dad."

Naturally the children had fallen asleep by the time they reached the hotel and after shaking Nicholas awake, Jonathon had to carry Jackie through reception and up to her room. Bianca asked that each room receive an alarm call at eight, for they wouldn't have much time in Paris and she wanted to make the most of it with Jonathon and the children, for this was going to be their last weekend together for a very long time.

They managed to hide it well from the children, who thoroughly enjoyed all the sights they visited in the one and a half days they spent in the city, but both Jonathon and

Bianca's enjoyment was dulled by an ever-present undertone of melancholy, which only increased as they made the journey back towards Calais, back towards London, back towards Jonathon's impending showdown with the police.

Jonathon was tempted to get out of the car around the corner from Wendy's house, but he thought to hell with it; if any officers were lying in wait for him then at least it would cut short the agony of waiting. He and Bianca gave the children goodbye hugs that lasted longer than usual and Jackie could sense something. "Are you alright daddy?"

"Of course darling," said Jonathon, "see you in a couple of weeks," although he feared that the next time he saw her it would be through a sheet of toughened glass.

He then took Nicholas to one side. "I need to tell you something."

"What?"

"I don't know for sure, but I may have to go away for a few years."

"Why? Where to?"

"To prison."

"Bloody hell dad; what have you done?"

"I've done something naughty; not wicked, but naughty."

Nicholas didn't know what to say; all he could do was hug his father, and his eyes moistened and welled up.

"It'll all be okay," said Jonathon, "but I want you to tell Jackie for me; I can't face it."

"Dad, what did you do?"

"Remember a few months ago, when your paper round became a bit easier for a few weeks? Well, it was me who brought down those missing papers."

"You're kidding me."

"No, I'm not."

"But dad…"

"…remember what I told you about goodbyes; keep them short but sweet."

"I love you father."

"I love you too; now go and see mum, and look after Jackie."

Jonathon watched as Nicholas walked up the path to the front door, and there were tears in their eyes as they waved goodbye to each other.

"So," said Bianca, as he sat back in the car, "where to?"

"I suppose we'd better give this thing back," he said, tapping the dashboard, "then find another B&B somewhere."

"I've got a better idea," she said, "if anyone's waiting at my place, they'll be looking for your car, not this one, so we can use it to smuggle you in."

She explained that if he were to hide in the boot again, she could reverse the car right up to the lift door in the underground car park, under the pretence of getting her bags out of the back as close to it as possible, and he could sneak out and take the lift up to her flat.

"Bloody hell," he said, "not the bloody boot again," but he relished the idea of spending one more night in the comfort of her flat, and in the comfort of her arms, "okay, let's do it."

They needn't have worried, for nobody was watching Bianca's flat, nor Wendy's house, nor Jonathon's house, nor David's house, nor David's penthouse, because Foot was acting alone. None of his colleagues had any idea of what he was up to, and that's the way he liked it, for he wanted the satisfaction of confronting Jonathon alone, and following his own course of action.

Jonathon and Bianca were soon settled in apartment number 27, where they ordered a Chinese meal and opened a bottle of wine, one of three they were to get through that evening, for Bianca drank more than usual in an effort to forget about the dark cloud that was shortly to descend upon Jonathon, engulf him and take him away from her. Again she told him that she would wait for him, that he meant more to her than anything, but their verbal interaction was otherwise awkward and strained. However physically they were closer than ever and after enjoying each other at length they collapsed, sated, and while shrouded in sadness at what the next day might bring, their heartbeats slowed down and they drifted off to sleep, their limbs entwined.

22 | You lose some, you win some

It didn't matter that Bianca had skipped college on the Friday afternoon, but she had two important lectures on Monday morning and it was with an apologetic tone that she told Jonathon she really should attend.

"Yes, of course you should," he said, "it's not as though you can do anything about this Foot fellow."

"You don't mind?"

"No, really," he assured her, "besides, I have something important to sort out before I make contact with him; something I've been planning for a long time, and I need to make a phone call."

"Using which phone?"

"The black one."

Bianca sighed, fearing he was about to get himself into yet more trouble, but she had learned not to interfere. "Just don't make things even worse, you promise?"

"Don't worry, this is completely unconnected; there can be no comeback."

She kissed him goodbye and tried to put on a brave face. "I'll see you when I see you," she said, but as soon as she closed the door behind her, she burst into tears and was still crying when she reached the ground floor, where the concierge voiced his concern.

"Are you alright, miss?"

"Yes, yes, it's nothing, really."

As she made her way to college, Jonathon picked up the black phone and dialed Spencer.

"James," he said, "can I assume you're not in the boot of a car again?"

"Yes, you can, so tell me the latest."

Spencer explained that he now had complete access to the computer control centres of all five of the companies that were to be attacked and that, best of all, he could interfere with every aspect of their operations, including their most remote branches.

"I don't want to do anything fancy," said Jonathon, "just shut them all down simultaneously, put up the words I gave you, then prevent any further access."

"When?"

"Let's do it on Saturday morning, when they'll all be really busy."

"Cool," said Spencer, "and James, can I ask you something?"

"Is it about the money?"

"No, I trust you to look after me," he said, "what have these people done to upset you?"

"They just piss me off, that's all, let's leave it at that."

Jonathon hung up and remembered that he needed to retrieve the briefcase containing fifty thousand pounds that was hidden at his house, concealed behind some loose bricks to the right of the main fireplace. It was important to him to make sure that Spencer was looked after before he handed himself over to Detective Inspector Foot, and he gave thought as to how he could retrieve the money unseen, assuming the house was being watched.

It irritated him that the best he could come up with would involve him having to spend yet more time in the boot of a car.

But first he had to leave Bianca's flat undetected, again on the assumption that it might be being watched. From the kitchen, there was a door that led out onto a fire escape which doubled as the means whereby the rubbish was collected, and he was in luck, for it was a Monday and the garbage truck signaled its arrival with a hiss of its air-brakes followed by the footsteps of the men spreading out to collect the bins. Quickly, he turned up his collar, shoved his bag into Bianca's bin and, hefting it onto his shoulder, descended the steps.

At ground level, he retrieved his bag, walked quickly to the end of the alley and went in search of a mini-cab company; the kind whose cars bore no markings whatsoever.

"You want me to do what?" asked the driver, incredulous.

"Just go to this address, let yourself in and retrieve a briefcase that's hidden in the fireplace."

Jonathon went on to describe exactly where in the fireplace he would find the case, and gave instructions for what he wanted the driver to do next.

"And you'll be in the boot of my car, yes?"

"That's right."

"And then you want to go to Heathrow airport?"

"Yes."

"And then to Richmond Library?"

"Yes."

"It all sounds a bit dodgy to me."

"I'm doing it for a bet," said Jonathon, "what do you think the fare will be?"

"Probably about two hundred quid."

"I'll give you five hundred."

"Hop in," said the driver.

Glad to have reached an agreement, Jonathon threw his bag onto the rear seat and sat in the front next to the driver.

"I thought you wanted to be in the boot?"

"Well, not yet," said Jonathon, "I'll get in when we're about five minutes away; I've spent too long in the boots of cars recently."

The driver thought it best not to ask.

On the way to Hampshire, Jonathon told him what to say if anyone approached him at the house; that he worked for the owner of the property and that every fortnight he came to check the swimming pool's heating system and clear out the filter, and that the keys to the pool house were kept in the main house.

"For five hundred pounds," said the driver, "I'd be happy to say I've come to catch all the naughty little elves in the garden."

On the approach to the village, Jonathon handed over the front door key and transferred himself to the boot, where he was assaulted by the smell of spilt engine oil and something else vile and acrid that he couldn't quite identify.

He felt the car come to a halt and waited, keen to be released as soon as possible from the most unpleasant car boot he had ever experienced. Thankfully, his wait was over after just a couple of minutes and they soon hit the road again. Before long he was sitting back in the passenger seat and the driver handed him the briefcase containing the other half of Spencer's fee.

"What's in there?" asked the driver, "if you don't mind me asking."

"It's twenty-five thousand pounds."

"What?!"

"I'm only pulling your leg," said Jonathon, "it's fifty," whereupon he reached over to the back seat, took out the plastic bag from his luggage and added it to the briefcase.

"And now it's a hundred."

Again, the driver decided not to ask.

After first visiting Heathrow, they pulled up outside Richmond Library and Jonathon gave the driver five hundred pounds from his inside pocket.

"Are you sure I can't take you anywhere else?"

"At your prices?" said Jonathon. "No thank you."

After slipping in and out of the library, he went in search of a pub, where he ate a pie and fortified himself with two large whiskies before dialing the number on Detective Inspector Foot's card.

"Hello Mr. Taylor."

"How do you know it's me?"

"Because I have your number and I put it into my phone," said Foot, "in fact I know a great deal about you, possibly more than you know yourself."

"I'm sure you do," said Jonathon.

"I think it's time we had a little talk," said Foot, "don't you?"

"We're having a little talk now."

"You know what I mean; face to face."

"You want me to come to Scotland Yard?"

"No, there's no need for that, I'm sure we can think of somewhere else."

"I'm happy to speak on the phone."

"But Mr. Taylor," said Foot, "I have something you need to see; something very important; something that proves it was you."

"Proves *what* was me?"

"Please, Mr. Taylor, don't insult my intelligence and I won't insult yours."

"What do you want to show me?" asked Jonathon, who was now as intrigued as he was worried.

"I would like to show you two images; one is a photograph that I took last week, and the other is a still image taken from some footage that unexpectedly appeared on the television a few months ago."

Jonathon's mind went into overdrive. He knew that the still image would be of him, but what the hell was the other one, and why had it been taken so recently? "Okay, I suppose I'd better meet you somewhere."

"When?"

"It might as well be this afternoon; 4 o'clock."

"Where?"

"Room eight at the National Gallery, in front of Michelangelo's 'The Entombment'," said Jonathon, who thought the symbolism appropriate to his fate.

"Where are you now?" asked Foot.

"Why is that relevant?"

"I'm just making conversation."

"I don't want any conversation," said Jonathon, irritated, "be there at four."

"I'll be there," said Foot, "prepare yourself for a surprise."

It wasn't a surprise he needed to prepare for, thought Jonathon, but a nasty shock, and he had another large whisky before walking to the bus stop and heading to Trafalgar Square. It was a warm summer's day and he managed to take some comfort from the view he had, looking down from the top deck.

The National Gallery was an easy ten minute stroll for DI Foot, and as he made his way up Whitehall, with his laptop in a bag over his shoulder, he reflected on his career in the police force. He hadn't done too badly, starting as a copper on the beat not long after he had left school, and his rise through the ranks had been steady enough. But he felt that he had plateaued, and he needed to solve a case like this to propel him to the next level. Now in his mid-fifties, he had a nice enough little house and a nice enough little car and he and his wife were able to take two holidays a year, which was nice enough.

But none of it was *really* nice enough. He wanted more, and by solving this case, although he would enjoy all the congratulations and the back-slapping, any promotion would better his lot by only a small amount. He felt he deserved more than a small amount and he was confident he was shortly going to get it.

Jonathon was the first to arrive at their rendezvous point and as he waited for Foot, he sat and drank in the calm that was rare to find in places other than museums and art galleries. He liked the way that people generally spoke in hushed tones, and how they walked softly out of respect for others.

He felt Foot's presence even before he sat down beside him, and he looked up to see an outstretched hand. Jonathon declined, and he felt a tinge of guilt at doing so; after all, Foot was only doing his job.

"Have it your way, Mr. Taylor," said Foot, and he withdrew his arm and sat down.

Jonathon had no desire to spend any longer than necessary with Foot, who he assumed had planted a few plain-clothes officers in the gallery lest he make a run for it, but gazing around, nobody was looking in their direction.

"Let's get on it with shall we?" he said. "You wanted to show me something?"

It was with a palpable air of smugness that Foot reached into his bag and removed his computer, which he placed upon his knees. "I admire you in a way," he said, "you could so easily have got away with it."

"I neither want nor need your admiration," said Jonathon, "just show me."

Foot opened his computer and double-clicked on a picture file. It opened and Jonathon was nonplussed. "There's nothing there," he said, "it's just whiteness."

"Oh, but there is something there," said Foot, who was enjoying himself. He clicked on another file, which was identical save for four red circles positioned apparently randomly on the image.

"Very nice," said Jonathon, "and what do they signify?"

"I'll show you," said Foot, and he blew up the image and dragged it around the screen, stopping in turn at each of the four red circles. In three of them, there was a tiny pin-prick of black, and in the fourth, a small crack in what Jonathon now realised was white paintwork.

"I'd now like to show you another image," said Foot, clicking on another file.

It sprang open to reveal Jonathon, wearing his wig, moustache and glasses, and with his mouth open, mid speech.

"And I suppose you think that's me?" said Jonathon.

"Come now," said Foot, "I thought we had an agreement about not insulting each other's intelligence."

"Are there any more?"

"There's only one more; let me show you."

Foot opened another file which again was identical save for three small red circles in the same position as three of the four circles in the first image. The fourth would have been behind Jonathon's head.

"I get it," said Jonathon, "you don't need to go any further."

"Oh but I insist," said Foot, "this is my favourite part," and he made translucent the image that contained Jonathon before superimposing it on the other. Sure enough, the red circles coincided, apart from the slight distance between them caused by the parallax resulting from the relative positions of Foot's lens and the camera in Jonathon's laptop.

"It's a funny thing, isn't it Mr. Taylor?" said Foot. "If the woman you sold your flat to had redecorated, this evidence wouldn't exist."

"How long do you think I'll get?"

"You mean in prison?"

"Yes."

"I should think around ten years, or perhaps none at all," said Foot, smiling.

"Please stop speaking in riddles," said Jonathon.

"I'm sure we can reach some kind of compromise."

Jonathon realised he was being blackmailed. "How much?"

"Four million."

"Four MILLION?!"

"Mr. Taylor, you have way more than that in your bank account; you're lucky I'm not demanding all of it."

"And if I refuse?"

"Then you're looking at around ten years, and I'm looking at having to keep working until my retirement."

In that instant, Jonathon knew he would pay, and he also knew that he would get half of it back. "Ok, write down your bank details and I'll make a transfer in the morning."

"I already have," said Foot, handing him another card, "they're on the back."

"Blackmail is an ugly business," said Jonathon.

"It's just tit for tat," said Foot, "nothing more; it's nothing personal."

"Tell me," said Jonathon, "how did you manage to find my friend's boat a few days ago?"

"Simple," he said, "the GPS system was turned on."

'Bloody hell David', thought Jonathon, 'you total plonker'.

"And what I'd like to know," Foot continued, "is whether you were on board."

"No, I wasn't."

"Then where were you?"

Jonathon got up to leave. "I was scuba diving," he said, and he walked off out of the gallery and went to sit on the steps by the fountain in the middle of Trafalgar Square.

His first instinct was to call David and tell him that he was a dickhead, but instead he called Bianca.

"What's happened?" she said, before he could even say hello.

"He has proof it was me," said Jonathon.

"Oh my God!"

He described to her the two images that Foot had shown him, and how they had married up perfectly.

"Oh Jonathon," she sniffed, "so when can I see you again? Where can I visit you?"

"Are you doing anything this evening?"

"What?"

"Get down to Hampshire, okay? I'll explain later."

"What?!"

He hung up, called David, told him about Foot and also told him that he was a dickhead.

"Yes, sorry about that bit," David said, "but this is great news; we should celebrate."

"Saturday night?" said Jonathon. "There'll be even more to celebrate by then."

"Eh? What?"

"Bye."

Finally he called Nicholas, and they both shed tears of joy.

"Dad?" said Nicholas.

"What?"

"Promise to behave yourself now, ok?"

Jonathon was keen to be reunited with his car, so he made his way to David's house, retrieved the keys from their hiding place and drove down to Hampshire, where Bianca was already waiting for him, a glass of wine in hand.

"So why aren't you banged up?" she asked.

"It's nice to see you too, sweetie," he said, and he explained everything.

"You really do have the luck of the devil," she said, "only you could go and get yourself found out by a bent copper."

They drove into the village for dinner at the local pub and in the morning, after he had dropped her off at the station, he returned home and transferred four million pounds to Detective Inspector Foot, after which he texted him 'done, please confirm safe receipt,' before he went to do a few lengths in the pool ahead of breakfast.

He was busy sorting through his fly collection before spending some time on the river when his white phone buzzed with news of an incoming text, 'thank you, have a nice life.' Jonathon wondered how long he would give Foot before breaking the news, and he decided to wait until late afternoon, when he would call him and give him something unpleasant to ponder over.

A couple of hours later he returned from the river with two nice brown trout, each around a pound and a quarter, which he cleaned before putting one in the fridge and cooking the other in plenty of butter and several turns of the pepper mill.

After a nap, he picked up the white phone and dialed Detective Inspector Foot.

"Mr. Taylor? I received the money; our business is done."

"Not quite inspector," said Jonathon, "I want half of it back."

"But…"

"…don't argue," said Jonathon, "just do it."

"And if I don't?"

"Imagine the headlines," said Jonathon, "Scotland Yard detective found guilty of blackmail; bent cop demands four million pounds; policeman lets villain go free in exchange for money."

"You bastard."

"I fear you'd get called worse than that in prison, inspector, and from what I understand, policeman have a particularly nasty time of it behind bars, surrounded as they are by lots of vicious men who are not renowned for their forgiveness towards representatives of the law. Who knows, you could even meet one or two men who you were responsible for putting in jail."

"You total bastard."

"On the other hand, of course, you might find that some of them would be very nice to you, and that they might want to make you their 'special' friend."

He couldn't be completely sure, but Jonathon had reckoned that money was Foot's achilles heel, and that he would rather settle for just two million than to call his bluff.

"You complete and utter bastard."

"There again," said Jonathon, "you could always use the time to work on your vocabulary."

There was a silence.

"You're bluffing," said Foot.

"Far from it," said Jonathon, "I'd already reconciled myself to spending time at Her Majesty's Pleasure, and I'd rather go down than let you get away with keeping 4 million. And if I go down, I'm taking you with me. Besides, my reception in jail would be far more accommodating than yours."

There was another silence.

"Ok, I'll do it."

"I'll give you twenty-four hours," said Jonathon, "after which I'll be getting in touch with Scotland Yard."

"Blackmail is an ugly business," said Foot.

"It's just tit for tat," said Jonathon, "nothing more; it's nothing personal."

The following day, he received two million pounds back from Foot, which reduced his outgoings to the same sum. He considered it a fair price to pay for his freedom, which would be permanent.

Meanwhile, Spencer had been busy.

On Saturday morning, at exactly 10.30 am, in all the supermarkets across the country, every single automatic checkout machine ceased to function and their screens displayed the message 'sorry, unexpected virus in the blatant desire to increase profits area'.

Released from having to monitor the confusion that was regularly caused by the machines, thousands of supermarket staff were instead able to go and man the conventional checkouts, where they could properly interact with the customers and make important small talk about anything and everything.

At home, Jonathon waited to hear confirmation on the news channels, whereupon he texted to Spencer the title of a book in which he would probably be interested.

———————

Appendices

Appendix I

These are the results of a keyword search, made on July 15th 2015, which indicate the total number of *articles* containing the relevant word.*

	Mail	Express**	Mirror**	Star	Sun***
Pert	2,165	307	510	59	?
Derriere	2,965	246	337	77	?
Abs	4,772	1,038	67,510!	0	?
Taut	2,557	251	280	11	?
Cleavage	9,276	1,010	3,562	617	?
Curves	13,036	2,860	4,613	637	?
Toned	24,017	5,792	8,833	235	?
Pins	9,560	5,140	44,015!	202	?
Flaunts	2,319	1,457	4,437	320	?
Busty	1,484	189	1,468	285	?
Stuns/wows/ dazzles	5,091	24,813!	49,510!	499	?
Sexy	28,208	4,073	18,571	6,067	?
Tummy	6,734	864	2,344	100	?
Photoshoot	4,758	643	3,290	394	?
Bikini	18,858	1,702	7,873	1,345	?
Showcases	2,614	2,468	3,376!	61	?
Kardashian****	13,615	957	7,652	1,516	?
Jenner	7,520*****	307	3,556	387	?
Caitlyn******	455	29	266	44	?

Readers are urged not to jump to unfavourable conclusions, although the eagle-eyed may have noticed that with classics like 'derriere', 'cleavage', 'curves' and 'Kardashian', the Daily Mail's tally exceeds all the others put together.

*   These results are not mutually exclusive. It is not beyond the wit of a tabloid to construct something like 'so-and-so flaunts her ample cleavage, toned pins, taut abs and pert derriere in a sexy bikini photoshoot just WEEKS after losing her baby-bump!'. Furthermore, a piece about a member of the Kardashian clan is highly likely to mention a member of the Jenner clan, and vice versa. It should also be noted that two-word terms such as 'baby bump', 'wardrobe malfunction', 'thigh-gap' and 'side-boob' had to be excluded.

**   A peculiarity of the Express and Mirror search functions is that they return words found within other words. 'Abs' for example, is returned within crabs, absolve, absolutely, etc. Also, they return article headlines that happen to appear as links in other, unrelated articles, so some of these figures should be taken with a pinch of salt, especially those marked '!'.

***   The Sun's search facility does not give a running total.

****   It should be noted that, especially in the Mail, even an article about public transport can somehow find a way to reference Kim Kardashian.

*****   To be fair, 9 of these were referencing the cricketer, Terry Jenner.

******   Most of these appeared from June 1st 2015 onwards, when a certain 1976 Olympic gold-medal winner announced a successful 'transition', and when he/she appeared on the cover of Vanity Fair. That really got the ball rolling, as you may well imagine.

Appendix II

Here are a few links which you might find amusing and/or edifying. Of course, typing them all out would be a pain, so for a list you can simply click on, just send an email to: laurence@laurencesimpson.com and put 'ATTDM links please' as the subject. If cyberspace is behaving itself, you should receive the list by return. If it's not behaving itself, please be patient.

http://www.dailyshame.co.uk/2012/11/satire/police-swoop-to-arrest-daily-mail-the-paedophiles-friend/

http://tabloid-watch.blogspot.co.uk/2012/09/mailonline-publishes-creepshots.html

https://action.sumofus.org/a/daily-mail-newspaper-ad/

http://www.theguardian.com/commentisfree/2007/aug/20/mydailyhell

http://mailwatch.co.uk/forum/

https://dmreporter.wordpress.com

https://www.youtube.com/watch?v=_c7-nHHZ86o&t=150

http://www.theguardian.com/science/brain-flapping/2014/oct/07/addictive-carcinogenic-daily-mail-spoof

https://www.youtube.com/watch?v=5eBT6OSr1TI&feature=youtu.be

http://blogs.independent.co.uk/2012/05/21/how-the-mail-online-turned-us-into-misogyny-addicts/

http://www.themediablog.co.uk/the-media-blog/2013/01/daily-mail-turns-the-creepiness-up-a-notch.html

http://www.anorak.co.uk/338558/news/why-the-daily-mail-is-evil-starring-sexy-toddler-suri-cruise.html/

http://www.anorak.co.uk/338391/celebrities/daily-mail-pervs-at-14-year-old-elle-fanning.html/

http://jezebel.com/i-read-the-daily-mail-every-single-day-because-im-a-mo-513278977

http://www.qwghlm.co.uk/toys/dailymail/

http://www.thedailymash.co.uk/news/society/the-heartbreaking-moment-mail-online-journalist-realised-his-soul-had-died-2014032585040

http://newsthump.com/2014/06/05/daily-mail-to-become-top-shelf-publication-to-protect-children-from-extremism/

http://tktk.gawker.com/my-year-ripping-off-the-web-with-the-daily-mail-online-1689453286

http://www.cmcstir.org/jou9x2/tabloid-sensationalism-the-daily-mail-and-immigration/

Appendix III

...and here are some links from MailOnline and the Express. Likewise, typing them all out would be a pain so, again, for a list you can simply click on, send an email to: laurence@laurencesimpson.com and put 'ATTDM articles please' as the subject. Again, if cyberspace is behaving itself, you should receive the list by return. If it's not behaving itself, please be patient.

http://www.dailymail.co.uk/tvshowbiz/article-2856405/
Elaine-Lordan-pictured-swigging-bottle-wine-walking-street.
html#comments

http://www.dailymail.co.uk/news/article-2661323/Angel-Jade-Smith-
3-dies-house-fire-year-baby-brother-died-suddenly.html

http://www.dailymail.co.uk/news/article-1284505/Baby-twins-
Isabella-Lola-Koupparis-seriously-injured-fox-attack.html

http://www.dailymail.co.uk/news/article-3142048/British-coach-
carrying-30-children-crashed-Belgium-killing-driving-leaving-
scores-injured.html

http://www.dailymail.co.uk/femail/article-2188193/Emily-Lloyd-
Wish-You-Were-Here-star-looks-scruffy-unkempt-20-years-on.html

http://www.dailymail.co.uk/news/article-3117982/Harley-Street-
dentist-clear-wife-s-death-saved-life-gave-birth-child-family-s-
Volvo.html

http://www.dailymail.co.uk/news/article-2984445/Home-Just-four-months-admitting-killing-three-terminally-ill-children-1-2m-family-house-seen-surviving-child-picture-banker-s-wife-centre-tragedy.html

http://www.dailymail.co.uk/tvshowbiz/article-3085247/Troubled-star-Jonathan-Rhys-Meyers-looks-worse-wear-disorientated-s-pictured-drinking-bottle-vodka-London-street.html

http://www.dailymail.co.uk/news/article-2963906/McLaren-supercar-worth-250-000-destroyed-head-crash-convertible-one-London-s-expensive-streets.html

http://www.dailymail.co.uk/news/article-2262695/Shipping-tycoons-daughter-Alexandra-Hoegh-2-hanged-window-blind-cord-neck.html

http://www.dailymail.co.uk/news/article-2976866/Has-Gazza-fallen-wagon-Former-England-great-pictured-bottle-gin-carrier-bag-just-days-insisting-healthy.html

And from the Express:

http://www.express.co.uk/news/uk/288605/Britain-faces-killer-arctic-blast-and-130-mph-gales

http://www.express.co.uk/news/uk/571751/British-countryside-EXPLODE-WILDFIRE-hot-weather-temperatures

http://www.express.co.uk/life-style/health/543755/Red-wine-beat-cancer

http://www.express.co.uk/life-style/health/475571/Previously-hailed-health-boosting-properties-of-Red-Wine-disproved